Jack appea[...]
was wearing just a t-shirt and shorts, and I became aware of how little clothing we were both wearing. I wore light cotton pajama pants and a tank top. We had seen each other in bathing suits, but somehow this seemed more intimate.

We moved toward opposite sides of the bed. I raised the duvet and slid in, and Jack did the same. We hugged the edges of the bed, careful not to let any parts of our bodies brush.

Jack clicked off the lamp and the room plunged into darkness. There was just the sound of his breathing and the smell of his shaving cream. I wondered what he was thinking.

I must have fallen asleep because I started awake just after dawn. I was facing the window and I could see the night haze fading into daylight. As the fog of sleep cleared, I realized that Jack's body was pressed against mine, his arm thrown over my side. I thought about moving away, not wanting him to wake up and be embarrassed or regretful. But I didn't move. Instead, I memorized the feel of his chest against my back, the feel of our thighs touching, the feel of his breath on the back of my neck.

LOOKING FOR LILY

AFRICA FINE

Genesis Press, Inc.

INDIGO

An imprint of Genesis Press, Inc.
Publishing Company

Genesis Press, Inc.
P.O. Box 101
Columbus, MS 39703

All characters in this book have no existence outside the imagination of the author and have no relation whatsoever to anyone bearing the same name or names. They are not even distantly inspired by any individual known or unknown to the author and all incidents are pure invention.

Copyright © 2008 by Africa Fine

ISBN: 13 DIGIT : 978-1-58571-319-6
ISBN: 10 DIGIT : 1-58571-319-8
Manufactured in the United States of America

First Edition

Visit us at www.genesis-press.com
or call at 1-888-Indigo-1-4-0

DEDICATION

For Parker Abraham

ACKNOWLEDGMENTS

I would like to thank my mother, Gwendolyn Spencer, and my great-aunt, the late Eunice Hopkins (1913–2006) for the inspiration for this story. Although the characters and situations in the novel are fictional, my mother and Eunice's experiences helped me explore my characters' emotions. The Alzheimer's Foundation of America was extremely valuable in my search for accurate information on the disease. Deborah Schumaker and Doris Innis provided many essential suggestions that helped me shape this novel. Jeff, Owen, and Parker are the loves of my life—they support me and believe in me, no matter what.

CHAPTER 1

"Cleveland is home, Ernestine."

The first thing I noticed when I walked into the tall, narrow house was the smell. It was the scent of the discarded past: yellowed photographs, thirty-year-old furniture, and White Shoulders perfume, which no one born this side of 1960 wears. Aunt Gillian has lived here forever, my entire life and longer. My childhood and adolescence were spent in this echoing house in East Cleveland, with its ancient hard candies set in rust-colored ceramic bowls on the coffee table and its cream-colored furniture that was not meant to be sat upon. I set down the boxes I carried and waited for my friend Jack to bring in the rest. We were packing up Aunt Gillian's things and saying good-bye to an era.

Aunt Gillian raised me after my parents died when I was just six months old. She never thought twice about adopting her sister's child, but I have to say that neither of us was ever quite what the other wanted. While the mothers of my classmates all had jobs or were going to night school to get their degrees, Aunt Gillian worked nights and took care of me during the day. She believed it would take her undivided attention to mold me into her image.

"Ernestine, you have to stop climbing trees and playing ball with those boys. A lady doesn't do those things," she would say.

At eight years old, I already knew two things for sure: I hated my name, and I didn't want to be a lady.

"Call me Tina."

My aunt put her hands on her hips and shook her head.

"Your mother named you Ernestine, and that is what I will call you."

Even then, I realized that I could never win a verbal argument with her. Subversion was the only way to get my way. So I agreed to wear the frilly dresses to school. Once I arrived, I went straight to the bathroom to change into the jeans and t-shirt I smuggled in my backpack. I spent all of recess playing kickball with the boys. And I demanded that all my teachers and friends call me Tina.

I remember coming home from elementary school to find my aunt engrossed in the details of cooking something I would refuse to eat. I may have been the youngest vegetarian in the history of Cleveland. A PBS documentary on slaughterhouses, watched with secret relish, made me pity the poor pigs whose carcasses populated our dinner plates. Around that same time, I noticed the hives and throat-swelling that visited me whenever I ate fish. I told my fifth-grade teacher, who thought I might be allergic to seafood. She suggested I see a doctor, but Aunt Gillian scoffed at this notion.

"All that allergy business is just a way for you to get out of eating the perfectly good food I cook for you."

The next night, she berated me until I gave in and ate a piece of cod. I don't remember whether she apologized after I swelled up with hives the size of golf balls, but I think she felt bad for me afterwards. She didn't think she was *wrong*, of course. She contends to this day that there is no such thing as a food allergy. She had been a nurse before I was born, so you'd think she would have believed the physical evidence of my allergies. Even science couldn't disabuse Aunt Gillian of her convictions.

Throughout my childhood, she cooked elaborate, gourmet-quality meals that were flawless in both presentation and nutritional value. Her meals always had names that made them sound appealing. It was never just pasta; instead, we had linguine with shrimp and lemon oil. Instead of baked chicken, we ate chicken vesuvio. Once, I looked in one of her cookbooks and requested home-baked macaroni and cheese, with almond blueberry popovers for dessert. She said it was too fattening and instead set a plate of iceberg with summer tomatoes in front of me.

I refused to eat what she cooked because I was a vegetarian, because I was allergic, because I was spiteful. It depended on the day.

"You spend more time pushing your food around than eating," she said one night. "You'd think you'd be as thin as a stick."

I shrugged my chubby shoulders. I was already in the early stages of what would become a lifelong struggle with obesity. I might have starved to death if it wasn't for the Twinkies and Moon Pies I shoveled into my mouth just before falling asleep each night. Not to mention the taco boats and Starburst candy I bought in the school cafeteria after I'd sold my lunch to a girl named Gretchen, who liked turkey on whole wheat, hold the cheese, hold the mayo.

Aunt Gillian had no firsthand knowledge of Gretchen, taco boats, and Moon Pies, but she knew something was up. At the dinner table, we were in silent agreement: I was in no danger of starvation.

But her days of cooking were long gone. When Aunt Gillian turned sixty, she announced that she was old enough to let other people do the cooking, although I had not asked about this particular topic. Now she was almost seventy, and I hadn't lived in Cleveland since I left for college. I was settled in South Florida, far enough away so my aunt couldn't run my life, but also too far for me to help her. The older she got, the more guilt I felt, but she wouldn't let me arrange for household help. Instead, she paid local girls to run to the store for her to buy toiletries and pick up her takeout dinners. She told me that I was not to worry about her, that she had taken care of herself all her life and she didn't intend to stop any time soon. When I came from West Palm Beach to visit her two or three times a year, I took her out to dinner but I never stayed in my old room. I couldn't face the reminders of childhood, and my aunt didn't seem to mind me staying at hotels. When I visited her at home, she would rush me out of the house before I could take in the peeling paint on the walls and the cobwebs in the corners.

This year, I had rescheduled my spring visit to Cleveland to attend a conference. As an associate professor of English at Mizner University, I was obligated to present papers at conferences, and this was not one I could skip. So I came to see Aunt Gillian after the spring semester, at the end of May.

My aunt was expecting me, but I wasn't expecting what I saw when I got there. I was going to use my key, but the front door was already unlocked and ajar. I found her sitting on the living room floor, dazed and disoriented, surrounded by four or five people I had never seen before. Although the air-conditioning was going full blast, the air in the house was moist and still. Summer had come early to Ohio, and by late May there had already been several ninety-degree days. The day I found Aunt Gillian on the floor—the last day, as it turned out, that she spent on her own—was another scorcher. The air was hazy with impending rain showers, and it was only eleven o'clock in the morning.

I had expected a relaxed day spent catching up with my aunt. Although we had never seen eye to eye on what was most important to us both, I was looking forward to seeing her. I was single, often alone, with my career and Jack as mild comforts. I wondered if I'd ever have a husband and children of my own, and I wanted to feel a family connection, even if it was with Aunt Gillian.

But when I arrived at her house, the ambulance had already been called, and my day—my life—was about to change.

The people standing around, who identified themselves as neighbors, told me that Aunt Gillian had blacked out and fallen. Later, I wished I had asked more questions—questions like who they were and why they were all just standing around her instead of helping. I rushed over to her and said a small prayer, thanking God or fate or whatever it was that sent me to her house on this day.

I found out later at Holy Cross Hospital that it wasn't the first time she had fallen. My aunt was, at best, taciturn. At worst, she was completely withholding. She didn't like to talk about herself or the past. It wasn't just that she didn't like it. She refused to do it, no matter how many questions I asked, no matter how much I claimed it was my right to know. She insisted on looking forward, not backward, and she never seemed to consider the damage that her secrecy could do.

So it wasn't a surprise to me that I didn't know about her falls. She was the most independent, self-sufficient person I had ever known. If she had boyfriends, I never knew about them. Her women friends were acquaintances rather than confidantes, which made sense, since Aunt Gillian confided nothing. She didn't seem to need anyone. Not even me, and we were each other's only family.

But at the hospital, painkillers loosened her tongue. She admitted that she had been blacking out and falling often, and by the tired tone of her voice I could tell that she had come to terms with the fact that she could no longer maintain her total independence. It was a bitter admission from a woman who'd prided herself on self-sufficiency for so many years. But she was also smart, and she knew that the next fall might result in something way worse than a bruised shoulder and a damaged ego.

"I know I can't live on my own anymore," she said in a small voice. She had been sleeping since we arrived at the hospital and I was sitting next to her bed, watching and waiting, preparing myself for a fight that never happened. I never thought she would agree to leave her home, the house she had lived in since she was little more than a teenager. I never thought she would welcome my interference in her life because she never had before. After years of pushing away my concerns, she now looked happy to see me. Thank God for Percocet.

"Where do you want to go, Aunt Gillian? What do you want to do?"

She turned and looked out the window, where I could see Lake Erie far to the west. The hospital was the best in the city, offering everything a patient could want except the guarantee of health. The walls were painted in pastels and every corner was clean, but the smell of bleach and Lysol were constant reminders of illness. Aunt Gillian was quite well-off, having lived many years on her salary as a nurse. After retiring from nursing, she made savvy investments using money whose source was always a mystery to me. That and Social Security made her economically comfortable.

"I don't want to be any trouble," she said. "I'm sure I can hire someone to come to the house once in a while."

I pictured those neighbors who'd been in her house when I arrived. Who would check up on her? I lived hundreds of miles away. What if she fell again, or worse? I knew it was my responsibility to figure out a solution. The only one that seemed viable was also the one that was the most difficult.

"You'll come live with me," I said, my voice firm even though I hadn't even thought the whole thing through in any rational way.

"In Florida?"

She looked at me, doubtful. She had only been to Florida once, last Christmas, and she had complained most of the time. She'd lived in Cleveland since 1956, and I'd never once heard her talk of moving. To me, Cleveland was the worst of what America had to offer: de facto segregation, a bad economy, racial strife, and a staid Midwestern attitude. No Rock and Roll Hall of Fame, sports arena, or lake cruise was going to make me see Cleveland as a great place to be.

There was a generational disconnect as well. For Aunt Gillian, home was created by circumstance, by responsibility, by convenience. You didn't worry about whether home made you happy. She scoffed at such ideas.

"Home just is. You don't choose it," she always said.

I knew other older people who seemed to think the same way. They lived their lives in places they didn't love, just because. They never considered moving to try to find someplace better. People my age seemed to believe that home was indeed a choice, and one that needed to be made without consideration of obligation. I would never live somewhere just because I had ended up there by accident. When I told this to Aunt Gillian, she frowned.

"When you have a family to care for, you can't think only of yourself."

When I was a teenager, it seemed to me that thinking of herself is how Aunt Gillian had always operated, but I knew better than to ever say that her.

To Aunt Gillian, who'd followed her ex-husband here from Howard University, Cleveland was more home than her native Baltimore. She'd spent most of her life here. I had spent most of my life trying to get away.

"Maybe you could move back home."

There was a long pause after she said this. We both took time to digest how difficult it was for her to ask this of me. Aunt Gillian had never asked me anything in her life. She demanded, cajoled, threatened. To now be in a position to *ask* showed me just how serious the situation was.

I shook my head. "I have a good position teaching at the university, and faculty positions are not easy to come by, not in this economy." And I hate Cleveland, I wanted to add but didn't.

"Cleveland is home, Ernestine."

Aunt Gillian had never been one to give up on an argument, especially not one as important as this. She was still the only person who ever called me Ernestine.

But she was weak, and her voice shook when she spoke.

It hit me then. Aunt Gillian was getting old.

Our discussion continued for a few days, during which my arguments grew stronger and hers weakened. I realized that she wanted to come to Florida, but it was impossible for her to say so. Her pride, while wounded, wouldn't allow it.

On her third day in the hospital, she was due to be released. Her doctor was the one who gave us the means to make the final decision.

"Mrs. Jones, your head is fine and you were lucky not to break anything. But I don't want you living alone anymore. It's not safe."

I was sitting in a chair by the window as he spoke, looking out at the gray skies, watching the heat make waves in the air above the pavement, wishing I were back in Florida. I looked over at my aunt. Her shoulders slumped.

She didn't answer the doctor, just nodded. He looked at me for a moment, and then smiled as he turned to leave.

"I'm sure your niece will take excellent care of you, Mrs. Jones. You're very lucky."

I almost laughed. This was the first time Aunt Gillian had ever been told she was lucky to have me.

"What about my house?" she asked after the doctor left.

"We'll close it up for now and decide what to do about it later."

"I don't want to be any trouble," she said, still proud. "I can take care of myself, no matter what that doctor says."

I shook my head. "Of course it's no trouble. We're family."

Here I was a week later, standing in Aunt Gillian's house, ready to clear out her things in preparation for her move to Florida. In my more forgiving moments I looked up to my aunt, who, all on her own, had supported herself—and then me—after her ex-husband, Jeremiah, left her years before I was born. When I was feeling loving, I saw toughness in her, instead of a mean spirit. And I could sometimes see humor in the biting jokes about my weight and my hair. I tended to take things too personally. On nights when sleep was elusive, I saw fragility in my aunt's insistence on independence. Now that she needed me, I couldn't walk away.

Jack, who volunteered to fly to Cleveland to help us pack up, did not think moving Aunt Gillian into my house was a good idea.

"You don't want to put her in an assisted living facility?" he had asked when I called him to tell him that my aunt was moving to Florida. I'd just relayed all that had happened, and he asked patient questions.

"A nursing home." I said this as if the idea had never occurred to me, although it had over the past few days. I tried, but I couldn't picture myself taking Aunt Gillian to a *facility*.

"It'll work out," I told him.

There was long pause.

"You could convert the downstairs office into a bedroom for her so she doesn't have to climb the stairs," he said. I could hear the smile in his voice, and I knew what that smile meant. It meant that he would help me even though he was sure I was doing the wrong thing.

"As long as you do the converting."

But I already knew that he would help, even do most of the work. Jack and I had known each other for five years, and I had grown to depend on him. The role fit him—he was a caretaker, a problem-solver. Although my life seemed pretty together on the outside, I had a lot of problems that needed to be solved. Struggles with weight, concerns about my teaching career, worries that I would never have a family of my own, a man of my own to take care of me the way Jack did. When we first met, I thought Jack might be that person. I hoped he would be that person. But things never worked out between us, whether it was because of my own insecurities or his lack of interest. I only admitted to myself, on nights when I was feeling especially lonely, that I still had feelings for Jack. But I was convinced that he saw me as just a friend, so I pretended to feel the same.

On nights when I was feeling cynical and bitter, I thought that I was just another project for Jack. Engineers live to fix things, to build things up, to make them better. Why wouldn't the same apply to people? Maybe I was broken.

CHAPTER 2
"Lily Jones"

Jack came up Aunt Gillian's stairs, already sweating and complaining that he didn't like parking his car in this neighborhood. I sighed, trying not to be annoyed. "This neighborhood" was a series of tree-lined streets in East Cleveland that had seen better days. The houses were tall and built just a bit too close together by city planners in the last century. If you looked down the street and squinted, you could imagine that they had once been considered grand residences by their original owners. Now they were more neglected than imposing. Although I'd grown up in this house, I didn't know much about the history of the area. That was what things were like when I was a child. Always look forward, my aunt said. Never dwell on what can't be changed. I could see her point, but I believed this was an excuse telling me next to nothing about my parents, our family, her ex-husband, or anything else that had happened before I was born.

The neighborhood itself predated Aunt Gillian's arrival in Cleveland, but whatever stood here before had been razed, replaced by a series of colonial revival homes. Her house was two stories high and sat up on a hill. I remember as a child feeling that it was the biggest, loneliest house in the world. The house was made of bricks that used to be vibrant and clean but had faded over the years to a dull reddish brown. Aunt Gillian kept the shutters on the symmetrical windows painted a pale yellow, the same color as her kitchen walls.

I always liked the outside of the house, with its tulips planted in the narrow side yard and rose bushes that brightened either side of the ornate wooden door. But once inside, I always felt out of place in the foyer, where my aunt had precise places for hats, coats, shoes, and umbrellas. God help you if you put something in the wrong place. The formal living and dining rooms were filled with dark, heavy furniture that Aunt Gillian polished to a high shine. These pieces too often revealed the prints of my small fingers, and on the weekends I was required to wipe away smudges and even the thinnest layers of dust. I wasn't allowed to sit on the white living room sofas, and Aunt Gillian maintained the room's white carpeting in pristine condition.

The kitchen was the only place on the first floor where I could lower my guard even a bit. Even so, being there meant doing dishes, sweeping the floor, and listening to lectures on nutrition and diet. She believed that children should be of use from an early age. I always wished she believed less in work and more in play.

My bedroom was the place in Aunt Gillian's house that I could call my own. Abdicating control of at least one area of my life, my aunt had given me free rein to decorate it for my twelfth birthday. She took me to Dillard's one Saturday afternoon, hoping I would choose peach-colored linens and photos of flowers for the walls. Peach, she had told me many times, was a demure and appropriate color for any young girl, especially someone with my skin tone. This was one of many sore points between us: where she was fair-skinned with long, straight hair, I was dark-skinned with nappy hair that just wouldn't grow. She always seemed annoyed by this, which I never understood, as even in the few black-and-white photos I had of my parents, my father had my skin tone and hair.

I didn't choose peach. I picked deep golds, hunter greens, and dark reds. I could tell by the look on my aunt's face that she hated my choices, but she paid for sheets, a comforter, curtains, and all the accessories (which included a poster of Michael Jackson I knew she found tacky) without a word. I loved my room. On that birthday, she had given me the greatest gifts: freedom and silence.

My aunt's house was much the same as it had always been, but the neighborhood was changed for the worse. Cleveland always had its black neighborhoods and white neighborhoods, but black didn't necessarily mean poor when my aunt first moved here. Back then, this neighborhood was a haven for the black middle class—those teachers, doctors, and business owners who had formed their own insulated community. Before blacks and whites were mandated by law to share the city, there existed two Clevelands. From the little my aunt had told me, they coexisted in relative peace for years. Then came civil-rights marches, and later, angrier, desperate protests in the form of riots. My aunt's East Cleveland neighbors began to change. Those blacks who could afford to move, did. Those who stayed were not teachers, doctors, and business owners. They worked for a living but, according to my aunt, were of a lower class. They held service jobs and had no appreciation for what it meant to be a member of the black bourgeoisie. Aunt Gillian always seemed shocked that many of her neighbors not only didn't understand what it meant to have middle-class values, but they didn't aspire to better themselves at all.

My aunt never wanted to leave her house, even as the neighborhood deteriorated. This was her dream home, and no one would take that from her. So she stayed, and disapproved. And each year, she had her shutters painted pale yellow.

The rest of the block had not fared so well. Jack turned up his nose at the dilapidated houses with peeling paint and overgrown yards that surrounded my aunt's home. The neighborhood was more dangerous now, with drugs changing the character of the young people who lived here with their aging parents. They took advantage of cheap rents and advancing senility to sell weed and crack from one house to another.

It was ten o'clock in the morning. There were pockets of young men standing at the corner in front of what used to be Jones Liquor but what was now a Quik Stop convenience store. Their faces serious, they held bottles in paper bags, preparing for another long, hot day without jobs or hope.

I was no happier than Jack to be back here, but I still managed to be offended. I accused him of worrying too much about material things.

"No matter where we go, you make it your business never to set foot anywhere where the median household income dips below $100,000," I teased him.

He shrugged. "Look, I've been poor. I know what it feels like, and I never want to feel that again. And when I'm around poverty, it brings all those feelings back."

I scoffed, and he said it was because I had always been pampered.

"You call living with my aunt being 'pampered'?"

"Economically, yes." He smiled at me. It was an argument we had had before, and we were long past the point where either of us got mad about it. His middle-class elitism reminded me of Aunt Gillian. I called him materialistic. He called me idealistic.

"The rental car will be fine. You set the alarm, didn't you?"

Just then a car alarm—not ours—went off. He rolled his eyes. "It better be," he muttered, wiping his forehead. He stalked into Aunt Gillian's bedroom to begin packing.

A moment later, he called to me. I went into the bedroom and was almost knocked backward by the smell, a mix of urine and dust. It looked as if the room hadn't been cleaned in years, and it smelled as if Aunt Gillian hadn't changed her sheets or washed her clothing in about as long.

"She told me she had a girl come in to clean every week," I said, my voice weak. There was a thick layer of gray dust over every flat surface, and unidentifiable stains dotted the threadbare carpet. The bathroom door was ajar, and I wondered what horrors lay behind it. Tears came to my eyes, and Jack walked over and put his arm around my shoulder.

"You couldn't have known it was like this, Tina. She wouldn't *let* you know."

I knew he was right, but the guilt remained. My tears wet the front of his shirt, but he kept holding me, patting my back, until I could stand on my own.

"Maybe you should let me do this part. You can go down and pack up the kitchen or something," Jack said, squinting at my tear-stained face.

I knew that the last thing he wanted was to clean an old lady's house. He was a good man, dependable and strong when I felt weak and unsure.

I shook my head. "I'm okay. Let's just do it and get out of here." He nodded and handed me a box.

A list of the items found in Aunt Gillian's house:
- A large bottle of cheap brandy hidden at the back of the closet
- Several cartons of cigarettes
- A flattened, dead mouse
- $3,753 stashed in various pockets, purses, and old coffee cans

- A gun
- A birth certificate for a child I never knew Aunt Gillian had

⌒⌇⁓

I was surprised to learn that my aunt smoked. I'd never seen her do it, nor had I ever smelled any evidence of the habit. It was strange that she had kept this secret from me. I shouldn't have been so shocked. I have since learned that Aunt Gillian was a woman who kept many secrets.

As for the other items, I wondered why a grown woman living alone felt the need to hide her liquor in a closet. It seemed bizarre to hide so much cash around the house when I knew she had bank accounts. It's hard to say which was more alarming, the birth certificate, the dead mouse, or the gun. There was no telling how long the mouse had been lying underneath her bed, or how it had been flattened. I wondered whether that was a part of the house's odor. I wondered what fate its brethren had met, since one mouse meant others were nearby. Mice are not known as a species of loners. I shuddered at the thought of Aunt Gillian living among them, sharing space, food, air. It hit me just how old, maybe senile, she must be not to have noticed this, or to have tolerated it. Jack grabbed the mouse using half a roll of paper towels. He looked at it for a moment, and I wondered what he was thinking. But he didn't say a word, just placed it in a plastic garbage bag and went on.

The gun was something different altogether. It was in Aunt Gillian's underwear drawer between the long slips and the girdles. I let out a sharp yelp when my fingers touched the cool metal barrel.

"What? What now?" Jack rushed over, maybe expecting another mouse or worse. I pointed to the gun, not wanting to touch it again. He made no move to pick it up. We just stood there, peering into the drawer.

"What kind is it?" I asked Jack. Guns were something I assumed all men knew about.

"How should I know? I've never even seen an actual gun."

He had a point. He may have grown up in the less desirable neighborhoods of St. Louis, but he wasn't exactly the kind to know about guns.

I cleared my throat. "I guess we should do something with it."

"Something like what?"

"I don't know. Take it to the police?"

I had no enthusiasm for this idea even though I knew it was probably the right thing to do. Like many black people, I'd known enough people who had been in trouble with the police to have formed an instinctive aversion toward those who protect and serve. I knew that all cops weren't bad. That didn't mean I wanted to saunter into a police station with a gun that could have come from anywhere and could have been involved in anything before it found a home between Aunt Gillian's lacy unmentionables.

"On *Law and Order,* they always suspect the person who touched the gun last," Jack said. We looked at each other and giggled. We weren't the kind of people who thought television had anything to do with real life. But he had a point.

"Why don't we just put it in a box along with her papers and files and figure it out later."

Jack nodded and wrapped the gun in a beige half-slip before picking it up and carrying it over to a box. He looked at me and gave me a crooked smile.

"No fingerprints."

After the shock of the mouse and the gun faded a bit, it was the birth certificate that intrigued me. Lily Jones. A girl with no middle name, weighing eight pounds nine ounces, born at Milwaukee County Hospital on February 28, 1960. Father unknown. Mother: Gillian Jones. How was it that I never knew Aunt Gillian had a child? Where was she?

This wasn't the first time I realized how little I knew about Aunt Gillian's life. I grew up with her, but she was a mystery to me. It wasn't just that she kept secrets about her past, but she also kept herself distant from me. I had no memories of us laughing together, of times when she ever seemed like a mother to me, although she was the only mother I had ever known.

The little I knew about our family made me feel as if I didn't quite know myself. I had assumed that things would always be this way. With nothing to go on, how could I discover my past when Aunt Gillian was there to block me at every turn?

But the birth certificate gave me some hope. Maybe it was a way into my family's past, a way to finally find out what Aunt Gillian always insisted was better left behind.

I had no intention of asking Aunt Gillian about the mouse (on the chance she didn't know), the gun (I believed I was better off not knowing), the money, the cigarettes, or the brandy. But I knew I had to talk to her about this Lily that I had not known existed, my cousin. I took a long look back at the house before I closed and locked the door.

CHAPTER 3

"I was fat, and I wasn't cool"

For most of my life, I was fat. And I don't mean fat as in a little chubby around the middle, or needs to lose ten pounds. I was, in a technical, official, life-threatening sense, obese. I'm five foot five, and I weighed more than 200 pounds. I can't be more exact than that, because once the scales tipped over 200, I stopped weighing myself.

As a child, I was just plump. And plumper. And then plumper, until Aunt Gillian took it upon herself to remake me. She still served meat, but there was only baked or boiled chicken available instead of the steak she favored.

"You must watch your weight, Ernestine. You don't want it to get out of control," she warned me one evening when I was thirteen years old. It was clear that she already thought things were well out of control, but she was being polite. We were sitting at the dinner table, where I had already devoured my salad and a small helping of plain rice, no butter. I was staring down at the table, pushing the chicken around my plate and dreaming of a large plate of spaghetti covered with parmesan cheese.

"I'm still hungry," I muttered.

"What? Speak up, Ernestine. You must enunciate if you want people to pay attention to you."

That, I realized, was a fundamental difference between us. I didn't want anyone paying attention to me. I'd already suffered enough under her scrutiny. I wanted to be left to my reading and the stories I wrote in secret when Aunt Gillian thought I was asleep.

I knew better than to repeat myself, but my aunt sat stern and still, waiting for me to demonstrate improved diction.

"I'm still hungry."

I didn't even have to look up from my plate to feel her frown.

"Nonsense. Now, if all you're going to do is play with that chicken, then get up and come help me clear the dishes."

I could feel my stomach grumbling for more food as I carried the plates to the kitchen sink.

I'm not sure that was the true turning point for me, although I remember it as such. It seems to me that after that night, I ballooned from a chubby girl into full-fledged fat, and no amount of disapproval, cajoling, or demanding by my aunt could turn me back.

By the time I was fifteen, I was faced with the 80s culture of cool juxtaposed with my own extreme uncoolness. I didn't see what all the fuss was about LL Cool J. I didn't know the words to any Run DMC song. My hair was of the tightest nap, so tight it wouldn't take a relaxer or a curl, so I wore it in a tiny, unfashionable afro. I wore shapeless sweatshirts over jeans, hoping they would make me look less fat.

Sometimes, I tried to fit in. I tried to hide the fact that I had a boy's name, but at the start of each school year, my teachers would remind everyone by calling out my full name. People looked at me as if I spoke Portuguese whenever I said something was "fresh." It was 1986. I was fat, and I wasn't cool. So I became smart.

Being the smart girl was my defense against my schoolmates, who laughed when I talked, saying I sounded like someone's mother trying to be fly. On Friday nights, while my peers drank peach schnapps they had stolen from their parents' cabinets and groped each other in darkened corners, being the smart kid kept me company. Being the smart girl got me into Georgetown, geographic and emotional worlds away from home. Being the smart girl meant graduating with honors, going to graduate school to study African-American literature, becoming Dr. Jones to a generation of college students who knew nothing about my struggle to be cool.

There was a time when both my aunt and I hoped I would somehow turn out to be one of the popular kids. When I was a plump twelve-year-old, Aunt Gillian, former belle of Howard University, current envy of every woman she passed in the street, decided it was time to pass on a few of her beauty secrets. I sat down at the kitchen table, my aunt's makeup and hair-styling products at the ready, latex gloves on her hands as if I were going into surgery.

"Maybe if we tried a different kind of relaxer, one of these new ones they have on the market," my aunt said, a tight, critical look on her face as she picked at my uncooperative kinks.

I nodded, hopeful. Two hours later, I heard her gasp as I washed out the chemicals and my hair pulled back into itself like a turtle, and the small, unfashionable afro reasserted its dominance.

"A little eyeliner, some lipstick, and you'll look just like Janet Jackson," Aunt Gillian promised. An hour later, I still looked like me.

"How about some new clothes?"

I stood in the Dillard's dressing room, patient and dutiful, trying on outfits that were at least a size too small for my chubby frame, clothes that stretched tight around my waist and sagged around the breasts I didn't have. Each time my aunt went to find another outfit, I stood in my underwear, looking at my reflection. Round and brown and plain. I didn't think I was ugly, because I had dimples in my plump cheeks and long eyelashes. But glancing at my aunt's long hair and hourglass figure, I knew I wasn't pretty.

At some point, Aunt Gillian had to concede defeat. "It must be your father's genes," she sighed, fluffing her hair in the mirror before turning toward the exit.

The first time I tried to lose weight was four and a half years ago, when I met Jack. It was December, I was turning thirty that month, and I decided enough was enough. But I had no idea how to start. I'd spent my life finding comfort in the taste, textures, and aromas of food. Health had been the least of my concerns.

I was too embarrassed to go to Weight Watchers or Jenny Craig or anywhere else where I'd be with other fat people. The gym was out of the question. I'd joined Ultima Fitness on Clematis, right near the university and not far from my house. The place was filled with recent graduates and young professionals who, as it turned out, were almost all taut and toned. I'd braved the sea of Lycra a few times, wheezing on the treadmill as I glared at couples wearing coordinated gym outfits (his, black V-neck t-shirt trimmed in blue; hers, blue V-neck sports bra trimmed in black, bearing expensive logos and made out of something much more hip than cotton). They recorded their every move in elaborate leather-bound exercise diaries as they listened to the newest music on their iPods (blue, to match the outfits). There's nothing like the sight of navel rings and bulging biceps to conquer an already shaky motivation. Of course, I quit going. I continued to pay the dues in penance.

Next, I took matters into my own hands. The English Department offices were not far from the Mizner University Medical Center, so I asked a couple of doctors I knew about best diets and exercise programs for someone my size. I first asked Dr. Krespe, a resident in pediatrics, because I figured anyone who loved kids would be sensitive and nice about the whole thing. He suggested gastric bypass surgery in a kind way. But I had seen the gory details of surgery on the Discovery Channel, and I was unwilling to volunteer to be opened up, prodded, poked, and sewed.

And I needed to prove to myself that I had the willpower and discipline to change. I knew I wasn't fat because of genetics, or because of some kind of metabolic disorder. I ate too much—it was that simple. Surgery seemed like cheating, and I knew that if I didn't change my lifestyle, surgery might make me thin, but it wouldn't keep me that way.

I decided that what I needed was more practical advice, so I called my best friend from college, Monica Coleman. We had gone to Georgetown together, then to the University of Maryland. Even though she worked at a law firm in Atlanta, we had remained friends. She, too, had struggled with her weight all her life, but while we were in graduate school at Maryland, she had gotten thin. Her thinness had made me jealous and, ironically, hungrier than ever, which put a strain on our relationship. We dealt with the strain by never talking about how she lost the weight. Now, I was ready to know.

I managed to catch her in between meetings. She practiced corporate law and loved it, which I found mysterious and fascinating.

"Monica, I need to lose weight."

"Really?" Her voice dripped with good-natured irony.

I laughed. Monica's dry sense of humor always got to me, even when I wasn't in a laughing mood. She was always kind, even while she watched me down a dozen doughnuts in a sitting. But she was also always honest, which is one of the things I loved about her.

"No, seriously, Mon. I'm going to lose all the weight. I just don't know the best way to do it. What did you do?"

I could hear the smile in her voice. "It only took you fifteen years to ask."

"I don't like to rush these things."

She laughed and thought for a moment, then told me to eat less and swim often. So I went to the YMCA every day before work and at least once each weekend and I swam. My rhythm was slow and disjointed at first, and then, as the pounds began to drop off, with greater speed and confidence.

I felt comfortable wearing a bathing suit because there was almost no one else using the YMCA pool. It was an older facility that had become run-down and shabby after it was eclipsed by fancy health clubs, community pools, and apathy. It suited me fine, since I preferred not to reveal my cellulite-ridden thighs and oversized belly to the world.

In fact, the only other person I saw at the pool on a regular basis was Jack, and he seemed just as averse to social contact as I was. Focused on our own personal demons, we ignored each other. Or, I ignored him and focused on mine until about nine months into my regimen.

"You need a new bathing suit."

I had been standing near the steps to the diving board, considering whether I could remember anything from the swimming lessons I took as a child, wondering whether I would maim myself if I attempted a dive. I hadn't noticed Jack standing near me until he spoke.

I looked at him. "Excuse me?"

I used my frostiest tone in an attempt to conceal my embarrassment. I resisted the urge to look down at my suit. What was wrong with it? It was a simple navy blue one-piece that I'd bought at the beginning of my training regimen. I'd considered other suits, ones with frilled skirts that claim to hide fat and flab, but I'd decided that there was no use pretending that three inches of ruffles made any difference whatsoever.

He cleared his throat and pointed. "Your suit. It's too big."

I took a deep breath and looked down. He was right; the leg holes gaped where they used to cling, and there were folds of fabric around my middle. Still, he didn't know me—what gave him the right?

I looked up to ask him this, but he was gone. The next time I saw him, neither of us said a word to each other, and it was as if the whole thing had never happened, except that I stopped ignoring him and instead watched him swim when he wasn't looking. He had perfect form, his strokes precise and metered, as if he had been born in the water. He approached the pool with a businesslike intensity, never stopping to catch his breath or daydream as I often did. His workouts took forty-seven minutes.

Over the next few weeks, I found myself wondering about him. What kind of man tells a stranger that her bathing suit is too big? Was he looking at me because I was fat? I wondered where he worked and how he managed to time his workouts to the minute without ever seeming to glance at the clock. And I noticed that, even wearing goggles, he was handsome. His skin gleamed deep brown in the fluorescent lights, and he had a perfect swimmer's body—broad shoulders, lean muscles, long legs.

Another month passed before he spoke to me again. We both happened to be leaving the pool at the same time and our eyes met.

"I'm Jack. Want to have dinner sometime?"

His voice was formal and deep, and he smiled at me. I smiled back.

"I'm Tina."

CHAPTER 4

"We were a perfect match"

There was nothing conventional about my brief courtship with Jack Kennedy Kingston. We were, I learned, as different as two people could be and still be attracted to each other. He was an engineer and had started his own (successful) firm, then had left his partner to run the business while he taught at Mizner University. The fact that I had never met him, although we shared an employer, spoke volumes about how different our professions were. Teaching English and teaching engineering are like living in different countries on opposite ends of the planet.

He was methodical, logical, rational. I don't believe that a person's occupation reflects his true self, but Jack was as typical an engineer as one could imagine. He was, in fact, everything I was not, and I invented an "opposites attract" fantasy to explain why we were perfect for each other. I was a collection of contradictions, and I felt as if I'd spent most of my life opposing my aunt instead of doing what I wanted to do. I spent entire days talking to students and my colleagues, yet I was shy and avoided socializing whenever possible. I was contradictory and unpredictable in my moods, and I hated that my personal life didn't have much direction. When I met Jack, he was what I thought I needed.

Some of what I knew about Jack he told me right away, but most of what I know about him I learned later, after we became friends. Jack Kennedy Kingston understood me from the moment we met. He had pretended he didn't have a middle name since he learned about the other Jack Kennedy in fourth-grade civics class. It wasn't that he had anything against JFK, but even at age ten he knew what a cliché was.

So he got how much I hated being named Ernestine, and even though he had been skinny all his life, he got how much I hated being fat and why, until I was almost thirty years old, I'd never even tried to be thin.

Jack hadn't seen his mother since he was a teenager, although as far as he knew, she was still living in St. Louis where he grew up. His father had moved out and took Jack with him after coming home from work to find eight-year-old Jack sitting in front of the television and eating potato chips while his mother was sprawled on the sofa, passed out next to an empty bottle of Absolut.

"Pop liked to joke that what hurt most was that she had passed out on the most expensive liquor in the house." Jack laughed at this, but I didn't.

So neither of us had a mother growing up. He had a father who made cruel jokes, and I had an aunt to whom I was a perpetual disappointment.

We both grew up in the Midwest, we had both escaped the first chance we got, and we both ended up in

South Florida, teaching at Mizner University. As far as I was concerned, we were a perfect match.

The afternoon of our first date, I started getting ready three hours before. I needed the time to try on every possible outfit I could wear, and maybe run out to CityPlace to buy something new if nothing in my closet worked. Plus, I had to wade through piles of fat clothes that I was scared to throw away. I had been fat for so long that I didn't feel at home in my new thin skin. Being overweight isn't just about the body, it's about the mind. I wasn't sure I could ever think of myself as thin, or believe that I would stay that way. I hadn't eaten a chocolate-chip cookie in months, but sometimes I dreamed about eating an entire batch, soft and gooey right out of the oven. I didn't think this was the dream of a woman who was meant to stay thin.

This was one of those times I wished Monica was here. She knew how it felt to be a fat girl, knew how it felt to change. She had stayed thin, and I knew she would understand my fear. My closet was still full of conservative clothes, no V-necks or tank tops. I could wear them now, but I wouldn't dare. It would be like throwing my weight loss in the face of fate, which might then make my chocolate-chip dreams a reality.

I tried on eight outfits before I grabbed my keys and headed out. I called Monica on my cell phone.

"Mon, I have a date."

"You do?"

"Try not to sound so shocked."

She laughed. "Tina, when was the last time you had a boyfriend? Or went on a date? You're not much of a dater."

I sniffed. "Guys don't like fat girls."

I could almost see her eyes rolling. "You're not fat anymore. And even when you were, that didn't mean you couldn't date."

"Okay, cut the lecture. What I need to know is the best place to find a good date outfit."

"Where are you going?"

For the date, Jack took the initiative and planned everything. He wanted to e-mail me the details, but I told him I'd rather be surprised. I told her that I assumed we would go out to dinner at one of West Palm Beach's many steak joints; he seemed like a steak-and-potatoes kind of guy who exercised enough to stay lean without trying. I'd begun to look forward to dinner because I hadn't eaten a steak in months. I'd stopped being a vegetarian once I moved away from my aunt, but steaks were not a part of my new thin-person diet.

Monica cut me off. "You always do this."

"Do what?"

"Assume too much. Worrying. Looking too much ahead instead of just living in the moment."

I sighed. "Now you sound like Aunt Gillian. Can we get back to my clothes?"

I was just pulling into a parking spot. I put the car into park and waited. Monica came through.

"Something simple but elegant. A dress is too much for a first date—makes it seem like too big a deal.

Tailored pants, something neutral, white shirt with an open neck and closed-toe heels. Add some color with a bag, maybe red. Don't forget lipstick. Go to Ann Taylor, then hit the Clinique counter at Macy's."

I smiled. "Thanks, Mon."

"Who is this guy, anyway?"

"He's a swimmer. I'll tell you all about it later."

I told Jack about my guess about the steaks when he picked me up, but he smiled and shook his head.

"I'm not a big steak guy."

"So where are we going?" I eyed his casual fisherman's sweater and jeans. It was early December and West Palm Beach was in the midst of a cool winter, which meant fifty-degree temperatures during the days. Elsewhere, this constituted a winter heat wave; in South Florida, people were wrapped in parkas and hats. I wore the outfit Monica prescribed, with an expensive pair of boots I'd bought when I lost the last five pounds.

"Am I overdressed?"

He shook his head. "You're perfect."

I knew what he meant, that I was dressed fine for whatever he had planned. But it had been so long since a man had made me feel special that I blushed and decided to take the compliment, intended or not.

We left my house then and Jack opened the car door for me, which I included in my mental list of why Jack was the man for me.

Jack drove us to a small airfield that I didn't know existed. There was a field filled with small airplanes that shone in the bright lights of the narrow runway. It was quiet and the night was clear, but there didn't seem to be anyone else interested in flying that night besides us. As we walked toward a small, square building, I could smell motor oil and the scent of the melaleuca trees off in the distance.

"Are we going somewhere?"

He smiled. "I wanted you to meet someone special. I don't introduce her to just anyone."

I frowned, worried that I had misinterpreted the evening, that this wasn't a date at all. Had Jack brought me all the way out here to meet his girlfriend? And what was she doing at an airfield?

We stopped in front of a tiny plane, which I later found out was a single-engine Tinassna Skyhawk. It had propellers, which I thought were obsolete in air travel, and was decorated with brown and black designs that reminded me of Chinese characters. There was a large identification number near the back, and the wings were narrow.

Jack smiled broadly as I looked around. Did he want me to meet the pilot?

"This is Eleanor." He pointed to the plane and I smiled. I was afraid of flying in small airplanes and I hated the name Eleanor, but I didn't say a word as he led me onto the plane and strapped me in. The leather seats smelled like a new car, and I tried to remember one of those more-people-get-killed-in-car-accidents-than-in-

37

plane-crashes statistics while Jack told me about the plane. It was his company's plane, and they used it to impress clients and visit building sites. But he had always loved flying and had decided to become a pilot himself when he realized his engineering firm needed a small plane.

It wasn't until after a smooth takeoff (it felt smooth; my eyes were closed and I was trying to remember how to say a rosary) that I relaxed and sat back in my seat. And then I threw up, all over the tiny cockpit.

Later, I couldn't meet Jack's eyes as he dropped me off, and I imagined myself crumpling up my Jack Is My Soulmate list and burning it.

I thought I'd never talk to him again. I planned to avoid him if I ever saw him on campus, and I considered avoiding the pool, but it was my only way to exercise. I hoped he would have the decency to swim elsewhere, or else take up weight lifting or something. But the next week at the pool, he said hi. After a few fumbling starts, we talked. Neither of us mentioned the date, and I assumed that he wanted nothing more than friendship from a woman who defiled Eleanor and ruined what could have been a nice evening. Jack was the kind of man who said what was on his mind and didn't think much about social graces and tact. It's not that he didn't care about other people's feelings; it was just that telling little white lies didn't make much sense to him. So when I started to gain the weight back, and my bathing suit began to get tighter, he noticed. He didn't say anything, but I caught him looking one day while he thought I wasn't paying attention.

"I've gained some weight." I tried not to sound defensive. I failed.

He just looked at me.

"I'm not meant to be thin. Not everyone has to be thin, you know. People come in all shapes and sizes."

We both knew that Jack wasn't the one I was trying to convince. I couldn't read the expression in his eyes, but I was relieved it wasn't pity. I didn't think I could endure his pity. It was a long time before he spoke.

"Low expectations are a lot easier to meet," he said.

I told him to shut up and opened a fresh bag of Oreos. He never brought it up again, even after I gained back every pound I'd lost.

CHAPTER 5
"Is this a date?"

When I met Jack, I was just a junior faculty member in English, and I was very concerned about appearances. I thought that playing politics would get me ahead and ensure a successful tenure bid. So when the dean of Arts and Sciences held his annual cookout in the fall, I felt I had to go. But I didn't want to go alone, so I called Jack.

By then, we were friends, somewhere between acquaintances and confidantes. We had lunch sometimes, we exchanged books we liked, and we never talked about the date. I spent a lot of time trying to convince myself that Jack and I weren't right for each other. The problem was that I couldn't stop thinking of him as the perfect man. I knew better than to believe in Cinderella and her prince, but sometimes fantasy is more compelling than reality.

"Want to go to a boring faculty party with me?"

Jack cleared his throat. "You make it sound so attractive."

"I'm an English professor. I have a way with words."

He laughed. "Tonight? I'm supposed to be going to my own boring faculty party, but with engineers, so it's bound to be at least three times as dull."

"But *you* don't have to go." Jack was a wunderkind who had been the object of a bidding war when he decided to teach. He already had tenure even though he was a couple of years younger than I was. Only people trying to get tenure felt obligated to go to these things.

"Well, I hear I'm up for department chair when Wong leaves." His voice was both nonchalant and serious.

"Do you even want to be department chair?"

He paused for effect. "Nope. So what time should I pick you up?"

Dean Sid Goldman was the kind of man who didn't think it was funny that he was an imposing, dark-skinned black man who was raised as a Muslim, but who had the name of a Jewish accountant. He had no sense of irony whatsoever, so talking to him was always a minefield of inevitable disaster. English teachers only survive through sarcasm and irony.

The party was at his house, so my strategy was to speak to him briefly, then hide for the rest of the night. Jack made the perfect buffer—he was tall and studious, the kind of man who only drew attention when he was speaking about his passions, or swimming in a YMCA pool.

To call the Goldman home a house would be to do it a disservice. Although Dean Goldman's parents were Muslims, he embraced capitalism as a religion. For many years he ran a company that conducted those touchy-feely seminars at companies during the 90s: diversity training, sexual harassment workshops, job-advancement training. The company offered off-site workshops as well, retreats and team-building trips. He made a fortune. He came to Mizner University when the administration decided it needed someone with more of a business sense to run the arts and sciences division. That translates into, "How can we make more money and produce graduates who make money and provide free publicity for the university?"

Most faculty members hated him. There was a definite sense of us (the faculty) and them (administration) at the university, and that feeling was exacerbated by someone like Goldman, because he was not only not one of us (faculty), but he didn't even have a solid academic background. He was a businessman, and many people saw his business as dubious at best. Anyone who had ever been to one of those teamwork retreats or attended a training session on diversity knew they were a waste of time. You couldn't teach people to work together better by making them complete ropes courses. You can't create trust by asking people to close their eyes and fall back onto their coworkers' outstretched hands. And there was no way to "teach" diversity—the only way people learned to accept each other was by forcing them to work together in normal circumstances.

But administration types loved these kinds of exercises. It made them feel as if they were doing something, and so opportunists like Goldman made millions peddling these seminars and retreats. He had made a name for himself, not only in the local community but also on the national scene, and his name alone made him valuable to Mizner University. They stuck him in arts and sciences because he had a master's degree in English, and they figured that was where he could do the least amount of academic damage.

None of the black professors knew him very well. He made it clear that he did not believe in affirmative action; thus, to show how fair-minded he was, he had to pretend he didn't even see black faculty. I wondered what his Black Muslim mother thought about that.

The Goldman home was located on the river in Fort Lauderdale in a gated community, where several former football and basketball stars were rumored to own homes. The mansion, one in a block of mansions, dwarfed the homes next to it and featured absurd gothic spires everywhere. The message was clear: Goldman was not upwardly mobile. He was at the top. I was like a serf visiting the king. I was out of my element, and I knew it.

As Jack and I pulled up to the driveway, I had a flash of panic. Is this a date? I looked at him. He was dressed in dark jeans, a crisp white dress shirt, and a black linen blazer. Date clothes? Did he think I was asking him out when I called about this party? Or was he just a colleague helping out a friend? I felt like an idiot for not considering all of this before I called him.

My weight was up again, and I began to feel compressed in my simple black pants and V-neck sweater. It was a bit warm for the sweater but it was the only top I could find that didn't make me look like a grilled bratwurst. When I was fat, I could always hear my aunt's voice in my head as I looked in the mirror, criticizing, wondering why I couldn't just control myself and eat less. Her sharp eye noticed every roll of fat, every bulge, and it made me feel like staying home and eating a quart of Breyer's vanilla with chocolate chips sprinkled on top.

The knot in my stomach kept me from talking as we walked to the door. Two other couples arrived at the same time as we did, so when Goldman opened the door with a false hearty welcome, I was able to quickly greet him and drag Jack away before we got stuck in one of those casual/work conversations that never seem to go anywhere or end. We crossed the marble floor of the foyer, and I pulled Jack toward a large entertainment room where there were the sounds of voices and music, and, I hoped, the food.

"You're hurting my hand," he informed me when we got to the bar. I decided that a drink was more important than food to help me get through the night. Between being at the dean's manse and the possibility of being on my second date with Jack, I felt nauseated.

"Toughen up. This is no place for wimps."

He snorted and ordered a glass of red wine. I rolled my eyes and got a vodka sour.

We found an empty spot on a love seat across from a giant-screen television. It was displayed on the wall like expensive art. We were forced to sit close, and I was so conscious of his shoulder against mine that I caught only isolated snapshots of my surroundings. Two Spanish professors were already on their way to getting drunk and were standing closer than they should, considering they were both married to other people. A communications graduate student spilled wine on the Persian rug, looked around to make sure no one was watching, and then rubbed it in with her foot. The walls were painted a deep chocolate, and its decoration was one immense water-color, probably done by someone famous. We sat there long enough for the panic to rise again.

"It's okay, Tina."

"What is?"

"Being here. With me. It's all okay."

I took a gulp of my drink and realized the glass was empty. I wasn't sure what he meant by okay.

Jack glanced at my glass. "I'll go get you another."

When he came back, the entire side of his body brushed against mine.

"Is this a date?" I blurted.

Jack looked at me and smiled. "Do you want it to be?"

"Do you?"

Before he could answer, Dean Goldman appeared in front of the love seat. We both rose. He and Jack shook hands and exchanged greetings, then he turned to me.

"Tina, I was hoping to introduce you to some faculty members I don't believe you know. It's important to mingle." He gave a laugh that was meant to be congenial but sounded diabolical. This was the most he had ever spoken to me.

"Of course." I glanced over at Jack and let the dean take my arm. I stifled a giggle when Jack mouthed "mingle" and wiggled his fingers at me.

Dean Goldman alternated between introducing me to people I already knew or didn't care to know and showing off his home. He pointed out the art on the walls, letting the artists' names slide off his tongue as if he not only bought their wares but was close friends with each of them. His hand remained on my arm the entire time, and if I hadn't been so distracted, I might have wondered if he was flirting with me. But even though there wasn't a Mrs. Goldman, the rumors were that he only dated skinny white women, so I was safe.

We passed by the bar again and I longed for another drink. During pauses in the dean's narrative tour, I tried to find Jack in the crowd. I passed him once and he wiggled his eyebrows at me. I mouthed "help," but he just shrugged and took a sip from his drink.

It was thirty minutes before I escaped from Dean Goldman's introductions and made my way back to Jack. He was standing in a corner facing the room while the grad student who spilled the wine was pushing her cleavage at him. She also tossed her blonde hair and threw her head back when she laughed. When I approached, she looked me up and down before returning her attention to Jack.

I was used to being ignored by girls like her—fat girls always were. If I were sixteen, I would have slunk away, embarrassed and ashamed that I wasn't thin enough or pretty enough to compete with women like this. But I was thirty and an English professor. She was twenty-three and studying communications. Age offered some advantages over youth, including the realization that she wasn't nearly smart enough for someone like Jack. And I was old enough to pretend her looks didn't intimidate me. I waited for Jack to finish his fascinating story, a tight smile on my face.

But when he saw me, he stopped in midsentence.

"Tina. How did it go?"

I shrugged and looked over at the girl. "It went."

The girl flipped her hair a couple more times before flouncing off, offended that Jack had the nerve to choose me over her. Score one for the fat girl.

My smile widened and I relaxed. "Actually, Goldman seems to like me."

Jack nodded. 'Of course he likes you. You're great."

We looked at each other for a long moment before looking away. I remembered the question that had gone unanswered. Was this a date?

The blonde girl strolled by and I saw Jack's eyes flicker toward her. It was a small movement, and maybe only someone who felt as out of place and unattractive as I did would have noticed it. But I did. This wasn't a date. I was fat again. Why would he want to date me?

"I'm tired. Let's just go."

Jack looked surprised but nodded and followed me to the door.

That night I went over the night in my head. I wished I had spent less time with Goldman and more time with Jack. I wished he had answered my question. Was it a date? In one way, I wished it was, because I wanted a second chance with Jack. In another way, I hoped it wasn't because if it was a date, it had to be worse than the first. Changing into my pajamas, I examined the familiar fat around my waist, the double chin that had returned like an old friend. I hated what I saw, so I moved away from the mirror, went into the kitchen and grabbed an unopened package of Oreos. I ignored the voice in my head telling me not to rip open the plastic, not to pour a tall glass of milk, not to set it all on the tray and sit on the living room couch. I turned on the television, sat in the dark and pressed the remote until I found the History Channel. They were showing something on the British royal family lineage. It was a comforting escape from my life.

CHAPTER 6

"Fat girls aren't supposed to be happy"

After the party at Dean Goldman's house, I went on a binge. A moderate day included the following:

- Breakfast: Sesame bagel with a thick layer of cream cheese; grande mocha Frappucino from Starbucks; cranberry-orange scone, also from Starbucks; orange juice
- Morning snack: Fritos from the vending machine outside my morning composition classroom
- Lunch: Quarter-pound hamburger with cheese, supersized fries, apple pie, cookies, all from the McDonald's drive-through
- Afternoon snack: More Fritos, two vend packs of Oreos, Coke
- Dinner: Microwave popcorn and diet soda
- After-dinner snack: Frozen French-bread pizza, chocolate-chunk ice cream, peanut butter cookie (large)

I hated myself with every bite. But I didn't stop eating until Jack spoke up.

"I'm worried about you."

"Being fat is not that big a deal." I wondered how I could tell the lie with a straight face. We were sitting at lunch near the end of a spring semester. We were cele-brating our impending freedom from classes. I wanted to eat at a steak joint, but Jack said steak was too heavy for lunch. He suggested a health-food restaurant across the street from campus. I only agreed because I had plenty of change to load up at the vending machine later in the afternoon.

"I don't care about your weight. I care that you seem so unhappy."

I dug into my sandwich, which had bean sprouts but also massive amounts of cheese. Even in a healthy place I could find something that would satisfy my cravings.

"Fat girls aren't supposed to be happy." I snickered and took a large bite.

I had gained twenty-five pounds in the last two months. It was a personal record.

Jack just shook his head.

"Why are you doing this to yourself?"

I shrugged. I didn't want to think about why. I just knew that the food tasted good, and it made me feel good, at least for a while. And when I stopped feeling good, I just ate more. I hadn't found anything else that gave me the high food did. The fat was the price I had to pay for that feeling.

I finished chewing and took a sip of my extra-large piña colada smoothie. Jack watched me, his eyes squinted and sad.

"I want to help you. What can I do to help?"

I swallowed. The wad of food settled in my stomach with a thud. I felt full. I felt sick. Love me, I thought. Love me and I'll never eat again.

"You can't help, Jack."

He did not give up. Jack never talked to me about food, just suggested outings that always involved some kind of physical exertion. There was an unspoken ultimatum: If I wanted to see Jack that summer, I had to sweat for it.

First, he tried to get me to keep swimming with him, but I wasn't interested. I didn't have the same drive I'd had before, and I was much more self-conscious about being in a swimsuit in front of Jack. It was different before we knew each other, when he was just a nameless stranger. Now that we had dated, however briefly, now that we were friends, I couldn't bear for him to see me nearly naked in all my roly-poly glory.

"But you love swimming," he cajoled.

"Love is such a strong word. I love pound cake. I love Pringles. I love cheesecake, French fries, doughnuts . . ."

"Okay, I get it."

But he didn't stop trying. When I suggested we go out to brunch, he suggested we go for a run beforehand.

"I don't have the right shoes."

When I suggested we have a cookout, he suggested we go bike riding instead.

"My bike is in storage."

He tried to take me to the gym with him and I suggested we bake cookies instead.

"I hate gyms. Everyone's too skinny." I told him my story about the people in matching outfits, with matching iPods. He laughed but was undeterred from his mission.

We argued, but since most of my excuses were lies (I did hate the gym), Jack won in the end. One Sunday morning, he invited me to his country club, where I thought we would lounge around eating made-to-order omelets and drinking mimosas. I met him at his house, as we planned to go to the club in his car. He met me at the door with a large box. It was wrapped in silver paper and a perfect white satin bow.

"A gift."

The girth of the box was so intriguing I didn't recognize the trap. Inside the box there was a brand-new tennis racket, a t-shirt, and tennis shorts. He had also included sneakers and a sun visor.

"There's sunscreen in there too," he said, watching my face and smiling.

I had to laugh. "You've thought of everything, haven't you?"

He nodded. "So? How about a match?"

I sighed. I hadn't played tennis since I was a kid and Aunt Gillian made me take lessons.

"If I agree to tennis will you get off my case?"

"Only if you agree to play with me twice a week this summer."

I raised my eyebrows. "Do you want me to sign a contract?"

He pretended to consider this. "No, I think I can trust you."

I punched him in the arm. "You're on."

Riding to the country club, Jack put in a mix CD.

"I just made this last night," he said.

The music kicked in and I recognized the song right away. *Jack and Diane*, circa 1982.

I looked at Jack.

"John Mellencamp?"

"John *Cougar*. He was still John Cougar back then."

I smirked at him. "Are you sure you're black?"

Jack waved a hand at me. "You know you love this song."

He started to sing, changing the words, inserting my name for Diane's and adding extra emphasis: "Jack and TINA." His voice was too loud and way off-key. I looked around to make sure there were no cars driving near us. If there were, I would have been obliged to roll down the window and apologize.

I shook my head. Jack kept singing, looking over at me, urging me to join in. It was like Stockholm syndrome—I started to sympathize with my captor. We sang the chorus together, our voices wavering. We collapsed into giggles, and anyone pulling up beside us would have thought we were two teenagers. Just like Jack and Diane.

The first hour of tennis with Jack was a disaster. I was fairly coordinated, but I was handicapped by the fact that I hadn't held a racquet in twenty years. After hitting the ball and practicing shots (Jack practiced his backhand; I just tried not to miss the ball completely), we played a match. I expected Jack to let me win a few games to encourage me to keep playing. He didn't. Instead, he blasted the ball past me to the corners when I hugged the center baseline. His returns mocked my soft serves, rarely even giving me a chance to play the ball.

After the first set, we stopped for water. It was late May and South Florida was already in the grips of a typical heat wave. Although it was morning, it must have been ninety degrees. My clothes felt wet against my skin, and Jack took off his shirt.

"You don't mind, do you?"

I tried not to watch the way his muscles rippled as he stuffed the shirt inside his duffel bag. His shoulders were broad and tight. I took another drink of water.

"Don't they have rules here? No shoes no shirt no service, that kind of thing?"

"It's not a convenience store. Plus no one comes here in the summer—they need my money."

"Well, if you want to run around like some kind of male bimbo, that's your call," I sniffed. I was hoping to deflect attention from the fact that I couldn't stop staring.

"Just don't expect me to take off my shirt."

He laughed. "Ready for more?"

I raised an eyebrow. "You're taking off something else?"

"*Tennis,* Tina."

I picked up my racket. "Ready as I'll ever be."

The trouncing continued in the second set. When I came to the net in a pitiful attempt to serve and volley, he either hit the ball right at me (caused me to duck and scream like a ten-year-old girl), or he lobbed the ball to spots where even if I reached it in time and hit it back, the ball came crashing back at me too fast for me to respond. There was no time to talk or chat, and at one point all I could hear was the sound of my raspy breath and grunting.

The final score: 6-0, 6-0. I declined to play a third set, claiming my legs were about to disintegrate. This felt like the truth. Jack nearly bounced off the court, and I felt like stabbing him between his perfect shoulder blades.

After the match, we showered and Jack treated me to brunch. I hardly enjoyed my omelet with feta and Greek olives on a bed of endive. I hated to lose.

Once I arrived home, I threw down my tennis racquet and called the local public tennis club. I signed up for weekly lessons. As soon as I hung up, the phone rang. It was Jack.

"So, when are your lessons?"

My mouth hung open and I looked around the room as if he had me under surveillance. I didn't even bother to feign innocence.

"How did you know?"

Jack laughed. "Because it's exactly what I would have done. Just let me know when you're ready for a rematch, loser."

After we hung up, I called the tennis center back and asked if I could have lessons twice a week instead.

By the end of that summer, Jack and I were playing tennis five times a week. I stopped worrying about how fat I looked in my tennis shorts, and I even got a tennis skirt to wear. The more we played, the less tired I felt, and I didn't have much time to think about all the cookies and cake I wasn't eating.

When the school year arrived, I realized I had lost eighteen pounds, and I felt happier than I had in a long while. I wasn't sure if it was because of the weight or because of Jack.

CHAPTER 7
"Jack lost his mother to Thomas"

By last December, I weighed 120 pounds, less than I'd weighed since I was thirteen years old. I realize now that getting thin isn't the hard part; staying thin is. But I've grown to like my size-six body, and the clothes that go with it, so I have no intention of being Fat Tina ever again.

Last Christmas, Jack asked if he could have dinner with me and Aunt Gillian. His own family was also fractured, and I think he saw Christmas with us as an improvement over his own. As we drove to the airport to pick up my aunt, Jack told me a story about his parents, a story that explained why he would rather be with a cantankerous old woman and me than go home to St. Louis.

Jack was the kind of kid who was perfect for adult dinner parties. At five years old, he was the perfect fourth for a game of poker and he rounded out a game of spades nicely. No one in the Kingston family remembered teaching Jack how to play chess, cards, Monopoly, checkers, or Life. He just seemed to have been born with a talent for games.

It was even better when outsiders came to visit the Wilsons' small house in St. Louis, because Jack's little afro, red corduroy pants, dimples, and generic sneakers deceived adults into thinking they would win easily. His sister's friends snickered every time a newcomer began a hand of bid whist overconfident and ended the game angry they had lost to a child.

Jack was never what you would call a graceful winner. As the last moments of a winning game were played, Jack giggled and whooped at the other player's mistakes. On his worst days, he mimicked his father and pasted his final card to the loser's forehead, grinning.

Sonya and James, Jack's parents, warned their daughter about treating the baby of the family like a grown-up.

"Just because he's smart doesn't mean he's mature," James reminded her.

"He's just a baby. A smart baby, but still a baby," Sonya added.

Maggie and her friends would nod and say they understood, but Jack managed to make them forget his age every time he kept a straight face for an entire game of spades, only to surprise the table with a string of trump cards to end the game.

As ungracious a winner as he was, Jack was an even worse loser. That was the one problem with playing cards or board games with him—he would throw a fit if he lost, cry and storm up to his room or outside to sulk, effectively ending the game if he was the crucial fourth. By the time he was eight, his sister and her friends shook their heads and found other things to do when Jack went into his one of his losing fits.

The summer Jack turned nine, things began to change in his house. That year, Maggie was a seventeen-year-old senior in high school, and she spent the winter bringing her friends over to hang out. Jack loved the noisy, raucous afternoons spent listening to the girls' gossip about boys and sex. Maggie had always treated Jack like a peer, not a nuisance, and she let him hang around when it was just the girls. Sometimes they flattered him and asked his opinion as a man, which he provided in serious tones.

Their parents would join the group after work, making tacos or bringing take-out Chinese food, and they'd all watch television before the visiting teens had to go home.

Jack noticed that his sister stayed out of the house more and wasn't as interested in him. He missed her. During the day while his parents were at work and Maggie was out, Jack stayed with Mrs. Cambino next door, read Hardy Boys mysteries, searched for anyone who knew how to play five-card stud, and waited for his parents to come home.

That summer, however, they never wanted to play games with Jack and barely looked at each other. In July, James said he was going away on a business trip for a month, something he had never done. He kissed Jack good-bye and was gone.

So it was just Sonya and Jack one Friday night playing Go Fish and drinking milkshakes. Sonya won and tried to comfort Jack. Then the doorbell rang.

"Hi, Thomas, come on in," Sonya said.

Jack sat with his arms folded against his chest, looking up at the tallest man he had ever seen. The man smiled down at him. Sonya twisted her hands, glanced at Jack, and invited Thomas to sit down.

"Jack, this is my friend Thomas."

Friend? Jack knew all his parents' friends. He watched his mother's face. Her mouth was stretched into a false smile.

"He works at the university, and he just stopped by to chat for a while." Sonya rushed the words out and disappeared into the kitchen to get a beer Thomas had not asked for.

Sonya worked part-time at a bank and was a perpetual part-time student at the St. Louis Community College. She'd been taking classes ever since Jack could remember without getting a degree, and she had brought home school friends before. But never a man friend.

Jack forgot all about Go Fish. He'd never seen this myopic, dark-skinned man, never heard about any friend named Thomas, not even when he sometimes spent the day at the bank with his mother. He didn't like it one bit that Thomas came from nowhere to sit in his living room on a Friday night when his father was away. As the man of the house, Jack felt that he should be doing something about it. But he was only nine.

"So, your mother tells me you like school." He talked in that tone of voice that childless adults use when they're uncomfortable around kids. High, slow, two octaves higher than normal.

Jack shrugged.

He pushed on. "Your mom said that you skipped a grade because your teachers think you're smart," Thomas said. He gave a bright smile, tugging at his short-sleeved sport shirt and brushing his khaki slacks.

"Yep."

He answered only because his mother could probably hear them, and Sonya would not tolerate an impolite child. Children were supposed to answer adults, even when they said dumb things. Jack thought Thomas lacked imagination for saying the same thing every other adult in the world had said to him at one point or another.

"So . . . what else do you like to do?" Thomas tried again, glancing at the kitchen door as if willing Sonya to reappear.

Jack sighed. He also wished her mother would come back so Thomas would stop pretending to be interested in him. Plus, Thomas's cologne made Jack's nose tingle, and not in a good way.

"Umm, I like to play cards and, umm, watch *Love Boat* and, well, I guess I ride my bike a lot." Deciding to risk a bit of rudeness, Jack added, "You know, you have the thickest glasses I've ever seen."

Sonya reentered the room with two bottles of Miller and a fresh chocolate milkshake for Jack. Thomas looked relieved as he accepted his beer. Jack sipped his milkshake in silence. He frowned at his mother, who didn't notice.

Thomas sat upright in a leather recliner. Jack sat on the matching couch across from him. Sonya perched on the arm of Thomas's chair and chattered away about the university. Thomas was, it turned out, one of Sonya's professors. Judging from his mother's nervous talk, Jack could tell they saw each other often at school. He knew the bright stories were for Jack's benefit and were supposed to be funny, but the more his mother talked and the louder Thomas laughed, the more Jack felt like crying.

Jack played with the straw in his empty glass. He asked to be excused during a pause.

"My stomach hurts," he whispered. Sonya jumped up to feel Jack's forehead and lymph nodes.

"Well, you don't have a fever, honey, but maybe you should go lie down."

Jack trudged up the stairs to his room. After a while he dozed off to the sound of giggling and glasses clinking downstairs.

During the month James was gone, Thomas came over every Friday night at seven o'clock as if it were his second job. Some nights Jack tried to wait him out, staying on the couch until his head bobbed. Sonya would tell him to go to bed if he was so sleepy. Thomas always hung around longer than Jack could keep his eyes open.

Other times Jack just avoided Thomas, losing a hand of gin rummy to his mother at 6:55 and running up to his room before Sonya could ask what was wrong. Then he listened at the top of the stairs to the hushed laughing, and later, silence. Most nights there was a long time between when the laughing stopped and when the door slammed behind Thomas.

After Thomas left, Jack would scramble to his bed and pretend to be asleep because he didn't want Maggie to come home and catch him eavesdropping.

One night when Jack heard Maggie tiptoeing to her room, he tried to ask her about Thomas. Even though Maggie wouldn't hang around Jack anymore, she usually told the truth about things. Jack quietly followed his sister into her bedroom. Maggie let out a muted yelp when she turned to find Jack right behind her.

"Damn, Jack, why are you sneaking around behind me?"

Maggie clicked on the small lamp next to the bed and the room filled with shadows.

"Sorry."

Jack shuffled his feet and waited. Maggie took off her jacket, tossed it onto a chair and glanced over at Jack.

"So what do you want, Pee Wee?"

Jack grimaced. Nobody was supposed to call him Pee Wee anymore.

"Don't call me that."

Maggie rolled her eyes. "I'm tired, so what do you want? Aren't you supposed to be in bed?"

Maggie hopped into her bed and pulled the covers up to her chin. She looked closely at Jack's face and patted the bed for Jack to sit.

"I wanted to ask you about Thomas," Jack stammered. He sat back against the headboard and tucked his face into Maggie's quilt.

"Thomas?"

"Yeah, you know, Thomas, Mom's friend."

"What about him?" Maggie's expression was wary.

"Well, why is he always here?"

"Always here? When does he come here?" Maggie turned Jack so they faced each other. Jack looked into his sister's eyes and felt scared.

"Friday nights, when you're out." The words felt as if they were choking him.

"Since when?"

Jack was silent. Maggie looked alarmed.

"Jack, since when?"

"Since Dad went on his business trip." Fat tears slid down her face, and he wished he had never said anything to Maggie.

Maggie hugged him and sighed.

"Don't worry, Pee Wee, everything's going to be okay." She rocked their bodies back and forth. "Don't cry."

They rocked for a while. Then Maggie spoke again.

"Thomas is Mom's friend. Everyone has friends over sometimes, right?"

Maggie patted Jack's back. For once, Jack didn't even mind being called Pee Wee.

"Now go to bed, honey, and stop worrying."

Maggie smiled, holding Jack at arm's length. She shooed him out of the room. Neither of them was fooled by Maggie's performance.

First, Jack lost his mother to Thomas. When he left her for a younger student, one who didn't have hostile children, Jack lost his mother to sadness. When she started drinking, Jack went to live with his father. After the age of nine, he never saw his mother again.

Last Christmas in Florida was better than I expected. Despite the fact that my aunt seemed to think that Jack was my boyfriend, the holiday dinner was altogether a pleasant one. For the first time, she didn't scrutinize my plate with disapproval. For the first time, I stopped eating after one helping. It was the nicest she had been to me in a long time, and I felt sad that all those pounds of fat had been at least one of the things that had kept us from being closer.

Jack also noticed. Aunt Gillian's eyebrows rose when he complimented me on the red cashmere sweater and slim-fitting blue jeans ensemble I'd worn for Christmas. Jack was too blunt for my aunt, who valued tact in others, if not in herself, but he was an improvement over the guys I'd dated in high school and university. Back then, I was carrying too much weight and too little self-confidence, dating guys who believed they were doing me a favor with their attentions. They were fast-talking, leather-jacket-wearing types who figured a fat girl would be easy to control. And for a long time, they were right about me—I gave them whatever they wanted and demanded little in return.

"I like that Jack," Aunt Gillian whispered as we cleared the table and loaded the dishwasher.

I narrowed my eyes. She'd never talked to me about my dates, except to turn up her nose when she found out they weren't from what she considered good families. I was thirty-four; it seemed a bit late for us to become confidantes.

"Me, too."

"He's good-looking and he's smart, even though he says what's on his mind." I knew this last bit wasn't a compliment. Only Aunt Gillian was allowed to say what was on her mind; the rest of us were supposed to go along with whatever program she dictated.

But I wasn't surprised that she liked Jack. He had informed my aunt that her shoulder-length salt-and-pepper hair flattered her face and that he hated when older women dyed their hair trying to look young. I had cringed, thinking she would object to being called an older woman. But she just preened, patting her hair and offering him more lasagna.

"Are you two dating?" She was prim, her cheeks reddening as if the question was somehow improper.

"No." I hadn't told Aunt Gillian about the aborted romance with Jack five years ago, and I had no intention of doing so now.

"I'll bet he doesn't even own a leather jacket."

I laughed. She was referring to a boy I'd gone out with a few times my senior year in high school. He wore a clever little brown leather jacket anytime the temperature dropped below seventy degrees. Aunt Gillian had viewed it as a sign of his inferior character, and I did, too, although I mounted a vigorous defense of his right to wear leather when she made comments about it.

"Maybe *you* should date Jack."

She huffed. "I'm just concerned for you. You don't want to end up old and alone, do you?"

I turned to look at her, but she wouldn't meet my eyes. It was the first time I'd ever heard her allude to any dissatisfaction with her life. Aunt Gillian was the type to soldier on, no matter what happened. Her husband left her—she figured out how to support herself. My parents died—she took me in. Aunt Gillian did whatever had to be done, and she never complained about it. The thought of a vulnerable Aunt Gillian was too much for me.

"I'd better go make sure Jack hasn't eaten all the apple pie."

She nodded, her back still to me. If I didn't know better, I would have sworn she was crying.

That was less than six months ago. I'd ignored the signs that all was not well with my aunt, but they were there. I thought the changes in Aunt Gillian, in my life, had come out of nowhere. Turns out, I just wasn't paying attention.

CHAPTER 8
"You drive like Dale Earnhardt"

Aunt Gillian refused to let us hire movers to transport her things to my house. "I don't want strangers going through my things," she told me.

"Aunt Gillian, they don't go through your stuff. They just move the boxes and put the furniture where you want it." Patience, I had decided, was the key to dealing with Aunt Gillian. I was getting to know her all over again, because we hadn't spent this much time together since I was a teenager, and because her increasing dementia was making her even more difficult than usual.

She rolled her eyes as if I didn't know what I was talking about. Jack could see me getting angry.

"Let's just leave things where they are for now. We'll lock up and hire someone to check on the place," he suggested, looking from me to my aunt. She smiled at him and glared at me.

I shook my head at the memory as we sat on the airplane. Jack left Cleveland a day before we did, and now Aunt Gillian and I were on our way to Florida. She busied herself by straightening the skirt of the dark blue dress she had insisted on wearing on the flight from Cleveland to West Palm Beach. The dress had a long skirt and an elastic waist that Aunt Gillian had pulled up high beneath her girdled breasts. The Peter Pan collar was made of lace and looked itchy. I'd told her she should dress in comfortable clothes, since it was a two-hour flight. I suggested that she might want to take a nap later, so perhaps a pair of slacks might be more appropriate. She'd frowned at me.

"I don't take naps." She then rang the flight attendant button and demanded a drink of water.

During the plane ride, I hoped she would sleep in spite of her protests, but she sat at attention the entire time.

As the wheels of the airplane touched the ground, Aunt Gillian looked at me.

"Am I going to have my own room?"

We had been over this, several times. From what I'd seen over the past ten days, she seemed to have a selective grasp on both reality and her short-term memory. For example, the entire time she was in the hospital and while we packed her belongings, she kept demanding to know if I'd found any of her "personal" things, and if I had, I should hand them over. I assumed she meant the various items I'd found hidden around the house, and I denied having seen anything personal at all. But she couldn't remember that I'd described the living arrangements at my house at least four different times.

"Of course you'll have your own room. I have a nice house, big enough for the both of us. You'll be comfortable there."

She harrumphed and began to make her way off the plane without waiting for me. I sighed and followed, wondering for neither the first nor last time whether this was all a big mistake.

Beyond criticizing my driving, she didn't say much in the car.

"You drive like you're in that NASCAR they show on the television," she grumbled loudly. That was another thing about Aunt Gillian: She was not quiet, although she had spent much of my youth shushing me. Sometimes I attributed this to her refusal to wear both her hearing aids; she believed she only needed one. But in darker moments, I suspected she spoke loudly just to startle me.

The essential problem wasn't that she complained; she had always done that, in one way or another. The problem was, now as always, that I couldn't just let it go. And she knew it.

"I'm going the speed limit, Aunt Gillian." I made my voice singsongy and bright, but I didn't turn to look at her, lest I be accused of not having my eyes on the road at all times.

"The speed limit? You drive like Dale Earnhardt." She clutched her purse tight to her abdomen, as if it could serve as some kind of makeshift airbag when the inevitable crash happened due to my excessive speed.

"How do you know who Dale Earnhardt is?" I knew I shouldn't even bother to ask, but I couldn't help it. In my peripheral vision, I could see a smug smile spread across Aunt Gillian's face.

"You never change. You think I don't know what's going on. But I do. I may be old, but I know what's going on." She was quiet then, satisfied with getting one over

on me. It took every ounce of my self-control not to tell
her that Dale Earnhardt was dead.

I rolled down my windows as I drove toward home,
relieved that my aunt had dozed off in the passenger seat.
Palm Beach International Airport wasn't far from my
home, but I was in no rush to get there and face the
reality of bringing my crotchety aunt into my life. As I
drove along Federal and then over to Flagler, the air
smelled pleasant and ripe, and it struck me how much
greener everything was here than in Cleveland. It was one
of the things I loved about Florida. Even when the
weather was warm in other places, no place was as tropical and lush as Florida was year-round. The palm trees
lined even the most run-down streets, and there were vast
expanses of grass everywhere, thanks to county development policies that demanded green space in return for
strip malls and superstores.

There was no shortage of squat, uninspired buildings
along Federal, housing everything from electronics repair
shops to hair salons. The architecture was unremarkable,
but the buildings were painted pink and peach, and coupled with the relentless sun shining in a cloudless sky,
there was an undeniable cheer in the air. I began to feel
optimistic about the future.

As we neared my neighborhood, conditions
improved. This was the section of West Palm Beach that
had long been gentrified, with smaller tract homes giving
way to Mediterranean-style houses with a sense of
majesty that was perhaps undeserved in neighborhoods
located not far from streets where poor migrant workers

scratched out a living. Flagler Avenue ran alongside the Intracoastal, the thin strip of water that separated the mainland from Palm Beach and other islands up and down the east coast of Florida. The closer to the water a home was, the more expensive and well maintained it was, and as I turned left off Flagler toward our house, I noticed that several of my neighbors were renovating, no doubt raising the values of their homes and maximizing their views of Palm Beach and passing boaters.

Although I had reservations about being the only black person living on the block, I had none about my beautiful house. Built in 1926, it was a Spanish-style two-story, with a coral-colored barrel tile roof set against the muted cream walls of the house. Separated from neighbors on both sides by old Royal palms, the house had a series of arched windows and doorways. Landscapers had nurtured tropical landscaping in the front and back yards. The house was separated from the street by a wide expanse of trimmed lawn. My favorite part of the house had always been the majestic front entrance, two heavy wooden doors inlaid with carved floral designs. Every time I walked up those steps, I felt I was entering a special place, the special place I had earned through hard work and long days.

The house was too big for just me, of course; I didn't need four bedrooms and three baths. But my realtor had insisted that it made good economic sense to buy a bigger house, and back when I was looking at houses, I was still fat and alone but hopeful that I might someday fill the rooms with my own family.

Aunt Gillian jolted awake as I pulled into the driveway.

"Where are we?"

"Home." I smiled, wanting her to feel welcome and at ease.

"I don't live here." She frowned, still clutching her purse and peering out the windshield.

I stifled a sigh.

"Remember, you're going to live here now, Aunt Gillian? With me."

"With I."

My smile faded. "No, actually. It's *me*."

She snorted. "I thought you went to college. You're an English teacher, and even *I* know grammar better than you."

With that, she opened her door and hopped out, spry for a sixty-nine-year-old woman who couldn't remember where she lived. She was slow but regal as she walked up to the front doors, having gotten over her suspicions about the house. She was prepared to take over.

This time I let out a long sigh before I locked the car and followed her up the path to the door.

It was a Tuesday afternoon in late May, and since I wasn't teaching summer classes, I had nothing else to do but help Aunt Gillian get settled. I'd tried to convince Jack to come over to help, but he had a class and couldn't make it. Also, Jack had a thing about old people. He would never admit it, but I had seen him shy away from Aunt Gillian's touch, as if her oldness was catching. He had the same problem with hospitals. In the five years we had known each other, Jack twice refused to get stitches after sports-related injuries. Instead, he bandaged himself and ignored the pain, as well as the possibility of permanent damage. His argument was that in the old days people didn't get stitches and they seemed to heal fine. I pointed out that people also lived to the age of forty, rode in horse-driven carriages, and communicated via pony express. He ignored me.

Two years ago, I'd had some work done on my teeth and needed a ride home from the dentist. I was to meet him out front, but the procedure took longer than expected. He finally gave up waiting and came in to find me. He was polite to the dental office staff, even charming, but I noticed that the right side of his upper lip was curled, and he managed not to touch anything the entire time he was there.

Still, I had to give Jack credit. Once he had returned from helping me in Cleveland, he had gotten right to work, moving furniture and painting the walls. I couldn't ask for more.

It had been a rush, but we had gone to a lot of trouble to convert the downstairs den into a room for my aunt, complete with a large, adjustable bed, a fluffy down comforter, and fresh flowers in a vase on the windowsill—Jack's idea. I knew that she would need a lot of medical care, but I didn't want Aunt Gillian to feel as if she was living in a hospital.

Before I made any changes to Aunt Gillian's room, I asked her what she liked. I suppose I could have used her old house in East Cleveland as my example, but her dark furniture and classic Midwestern style didn't translate well to my old Florida home. I didn't want to try to recreate her life on a smaller scale; I wanted to do better than that for her. It wasn't in my nature to think too far into the future, but in my more honest moments I had to admit to myself that, with failing health and increasing dementia, Aunt Gillian might not have many years left. I wanted her to spend her last time on earth in a pleasant environment with someone who loved her. And as difficult as she could be, I did love her. There were many times when I didn't like her. But I loved her.

Aunt Gillian had marched right up to the front door, but she seemed to falter a bit as we crossed the threshold. She looked around the front parlor, taking in the maple floors and the dark red walls I'd painted myself, and she sighed. I braced myself for more criticism, but after expelling a breath, she remained silent. I looked into her eyes and saw a tired little old woman. I took her arm in mine, and led her through the parlor, down the hallway and into her room.

She made little comment about her bedroom, an unexpected blessing, and she didn't make a peep as I helped her out of her shoes and the stockings she had insisted on wearing. I worried a little about her dress wrinkling, but it seemed like more trouble than it was worth to change her into something else, and she didn't mention it at all. I placed her purse on top of the dresser where she would be sure to see it when she needed it.

"We'll unpack later. Maybe you'd like to rest." I patted the bed, and it must have looked inviting, because she nodded.

"That would be nice."

I helped her into bed and pulled the covers up over her legs. As I passed by the windows, I drew the curtains to keep out the afternoon light, and just as I reached the door, I turned back to say that dinner would be ready around six. But Aunt Gillian was already asleep.

I was peering into the *Joy of Cooking*, keeping one eye on the frying pan and listening for the oven timer, when Jack stuck his head inside. He came over to the stove and sniffed at the pots. Glancing at the cookbook, he asked, "What are you making?"

"Steak, mashed potatoes, green beans, cornbread, and banana pudding for dessert." I ticked off the menu on my fingers. "I had to look it up because I've never made banana pudding."

He raised an eyebrow at me and laughed. "Since when do you eat banana pudding? Or any of the rest of that stuff, for that matter?"

"Aunt Gillian used to cook this way all the time when I was a kid. At least she did until I started to gain weight. It's no wonder I ended up so fat." I smiled, but Jack frowned.

"I hate when you talk like that, putting yourself down."

I threw a pot holder at him. "You must need glasses." He threw the pot holder back at me and began to lecture me about body image and being hard on myself, but I made a face at him and turned back to the stove.

"Never mind. Just make yourself useful and get the milk out of the refrigerator for me. Banana pudding is Aunt Gillian's favorite."

After helping me put the finishing touches on dinner, Jack went into the living room to watch television. Soon after, I heard Aunt Gillian stirring. Jack, ever the engineer, had set up a monitoring and call system so I could help Aunt Gillian when she needed me but give her enough space so that she could retain some of her old independence. Jack had installed a small transmitter in Aunt Gillian's bookcase so I could hear her calling when I was in another part of the house. I carried a beeper-sized receiver clipped to my waist.

I went down the hall to Aunt Gillian's room and knocked. It was important that she not feel as if she were a patient; only in hospitals did people walk in and out of your room without knocking or asking.

"Who is it?" she demanded. I wondered who else she thought it could be.

"It's Tina."

She grunted, which I took as an invitation to come in. To my surprise, she was sitting on the bed, shoes on, purse in hand.

"I'm ready to go home," she snarled.

Her tone was aggressive, but sadness lay beneath her meanness. She was scared and confused, and I didn't know how best to deal with it. She kept forgetting that she now lived with me. I figured my best bet was a less direct approach.

"Okay, but don't you want to stay for dinner? I made all your favorites." As I described everything I'd cooked, she softened a bit.

"You know how to cook?"

I couldn't help smiling. "Sure. You taught me."

I expected more questions, but she just nodded and stood up, a little shaky, but on her own. "I always was a good cook."

Dinner went well. My aunt didn't say much, but she cleaned her plate and asked for more of everything. Jack also tore into his dinner with gusto, although I'd never seen him eat anything fried and fatty. Maybe he wasn't as removed from his St. Louis roots as he liked to believe. These days, with low-carb diets and gym memberships being shoved down our throats, it was tough not to at least think twice before eating mashed potatoes whipped with loads of butter and cream, but when I was growing up, this kind of food was my comfort, my friend. No matter how much weight I lost, I didn't believe those feelings would ever change.

When Aunt Gillian did look up from her plate, it was to watch Jack, who regaled us with funny stories about the employees at his private engineering firm and his students. I'd never heard these stories, and I smiled into my plate, as I suspected he was making up a great many of them. But Aunt Gillian was his true audience, and she rewarded him with an involuntary cackle during dessert.

After dinner, we went into the living room and Jack sat next to Aunt Gillian on the sofa. I sat in a plump leather chair across the room, pretending to look at a magazine and hoping that every night would be as easy as this one. Then Jack began asking Aunt Gillian about her days as a young woman in Cleveland. I looked up from my magazine, worried that I had jinxed us by thinking

about how well everything was going. Aunt Gillian hated
to talk about her past; whenever I'd asked her about her
life before I was born, she either snapped at me or gave
me the silent treatment until I gave up. I feared that Jack
would face the same treatment.

"So how did a woman like you end up in Cleveland,
of all places?"

Perhaps because of his difficult childhood, Jack
viewed the entire middle section of the country with suspicion. My eyes bore into the side of his head, trying to
signal him to back off, but he never glanced in my direction. I braced myself for the inevitable tirade.

Instead, Aunt Gillian laughed. A genuine laugh.
Almost girlish. "Oh, it wasn't my first choice, believe me.
But when I met my ex-husband Jeremiah at Howard, we
fell in love and I moved back to his hometown. Now *that*
was a mistake."

My jaw hung open, but no one else noticed. Jack sat
riveted while Aunt Gillian told him about Howard,
about how her father had been a barber in Baltimore,
about how she had married the first young man who
caught her eye. I knew some of this, but it was strange
hearing the revelations from Aunt Gillian's lips. She'd
made it her life's mission to look forward, not backward,
and she wasn't one to dwell on what was already done
and gone. And then she shocked me with something she
had never mentioned before.

"I wanted to be a singer, you know. Jazz. But my
father said no daughter of his was going to end up like
Billie Holiday. So I went to college instead, and I was

going to be a nurse in D.C. until I met Jeremiah." She sighed, looking off at the wall as if watching a film of her young self play against the paint.

I didn't know what to think of this new Aunt Gillian, one who had, without warning, decided to reveal herself to my best friend.

Shaking my head in wonder, I slipped out of the room, and neither of them even looked up. As I scraped and rinsed the dinner dishes, I thought this was a good sign. Maybe it wouldn't be as hard as I thought to ask my aunt about Lily, the daughter she never mentioned.

CHAPTER 9
"I forgot I was fat"

I fell in love for the first time when I was sixteen years old. He wasn't the most handsome boy in the junior class at St. Gabriel's School. He was tall but didn't play basketball. He was too gangly and uncoordinated to even consider football. He wasn't the smartest guy I knew, either. He never appeared in any of my honors classes, but he maintained a consistent C+ average, of which he was proud.

He was pleasant-looking, neat and clean. He wore the Catholic school uniform of khaki pants and a blue (or white) oxford shirt that all the boys wore, but he gave the impression that he would have chosen those clothes even without the influence of the St. Gabriel's administration. He had a round head with close-cropped hair that sported none of the fancy parts or shaved designs that were the style at the time. He wore wire-rimmed glasses and had a small, neat mustache. And he had a wide smile that showed most of his bright white teeth. That smile transformed his face. Although we seldom spoke to each other during our first two years of high school, I knew he was kind because he gave me that transformative smile whenever we passed each other in the halls. At a time when all but the cruelest of my classmates ignored me, his smile was often the best part of my day.

His name was Will Brandiman. It was a rather important name for a black boy from East Cleveland. When we were freshmen, that was, in fact, what some of the more aggressive white kids told him, except they preferred the term nigger. St. Gabriel's was a small Catholic school located near crumbling downtown Cleveland. It had an identity crisis. The school catered to lower-middle-class white Catholics who would sacrifice any material comfort to make sure their children wouldn't grow up in what had become of Cleveland public-school system. By the 1980s, what had become of the Cleveland Municipal School District was defined by an influx of black kids whose families were growing poorer, coupled with the panicky flight of everyone else.

St. Gabriel's was proud to serve those staunch Catholic kids from solid Cleveland families. The school was less proud of the small but steady population of middle-class black students whose families weren't Catholic but who shared a disdain for the city's public schools. Of course, our families' disdain was based not on race, but on the declining quality of the education Cleveland was obliged to provide for its darker, poorer citizens.

I became one of St. Gabriel's students because Aunt Gillian believed I'd never amount to anything but a teenaged mother on welfare if she sacrificed me to the public schools. I was thirteen years old, and I argued that she was underestimating both me and the Cleveland

Municipal School District. My argument was based on two things: 1) my conviction that no one would want to have sex with me, thereby negating the possibility of pregnancy, and 2) my sincere hatred of St. Gabriel's uniform, which for girls included a garish plaid skirt in red for freshman and sophomores and green for juniors and seniors. The skirt, and my early lack of romantic prospects, would be the least of my problems at St. Gabriel's.

Like me, Will Brandiman was a junior, but he was eighteen years old, having been held back in the second grade for "social reasons." That he was an older man was part of what convinced me that I loved him and that he loved me. I believed that he could have smiled at any number of sixteen-year-old girls, but he chose me.

I was making too much of his choice. There were five hundred students at St. Gabriel's, and only about forty of them were black. In 1986, there was no such thing as interracial dating at the school. So, assuming that twenty black boys had twenty black girls as potential girlfriends, Will Brandiman didn't as much choose me as he ended up with me by default.

Our romance began on a gray, icy day in February 1986. We passed by each other in the parking lot, I on my way to the bus stop, he on his way to his aunt's dirty yellow Chevette. As usual, he smiled. As usual, I averted my eyes while rejoicing inside my head, because by that time, I'd had a full-blown crush on Will for months. Not so usual, at that very moment, I slipped on a patch of ice that had somehow been spared a coating of industrial-strength salt crystals.

Before I could regain my balance, my considerable bulk plunked down onto the sidewalk with a sonic boom. I lay there on my back, crying from mortification more than pain, although I would soon discover that I'd sprained my left ankle and broken the wrist on the same side. When Will's face, concerned and gentle, replaced the gloomy sky in my tear-clouded vision, I cried even harder, horrified that he had witnessed my lack of grace. To make my misery complete, my ankle and wrist began to sizzle and throb.

I don't think it ever occurred to Will that I might be embarrassed. He took my sobbing as an indication of extreme pain and he shouted to a passing classmate to call for an ambulance. Great. Now I wouldn't just be the fat girl; I would be known as the Fat Girl Who Fell and Had to Ride in an Ambulance. I sat up and tried to stand, tried to tell Will that I was fine. In doing so, I put my weight on my left extremities. The pain was astonishing. I blacked out and woke up an hour later in the hospital.

I was out of school for two weeks after the fall. One week was mandated by my doctor, and one week was tacked on because I didn't want to face school. At the end of the first week, I dragged around the house looking pitiful, which was not a difficult task with a cast on my wrist and a serious limp. I managed to look so sad that my aunt agreed to let me stay home the extra week, provided that I kept up with my classwork. This wouldn't be a problem, I assured her. I had Will.

Will had been by my side every moment he could since I'd been taken away in the ambulance. He consulted each of my teachers, then typed the list of assignments during his seventh-period typing class. He brought all of my books home for me, and he even bought a red Sharpie, which he used to sign my cast.

If I'd had a crush on Will before the fall, by the end of my third day of convalescence, I was imagining our future June wedding during my Demerol-induced naps. He wore a white morning suit, top hat included, and I, rendered slim by virtue of my imagination, wore a strapless, beaded white gown with a five-foot train. We were happy and my aunt cried.

Will kept me entertained during the hours between school and dinner. My aunt had never allowed me to have a television in my room. A broken wrist and sprained ankle were deemed insufficient cause to change this policy. So Will and I played hours of gin rummy and Monopoly. He was a cheerful and willing participant and I let him win every fourth game or so. Even so, Will was awful at games.

"You're getting bankrupted by a girl with only two fully functional limbs," I told him one afternoon as I collected rent on one of several hotels I had placed on Boardwalk.

He shrugged. "Owning Baltic is an investment in the future. You'll see."

I decided to commend Will for his sense of humor in the wedding vows I would write myself.

When Will was there, I forgot that I was fat, that the other black kids accused me of trying to be white when I used the proper English my aunt demanded. I forgot that

I hated my name, Ernestine. I forgot that I had no friends, that I sometimes felt a crippling loneliness. I forgot about my aunt's disapproval, about the world's indifference. Will smiled, and his smile made me into someone who deserved it.

I was so happy it scared me.

"You don't have to come see me," I told Will near the end of the first week. I was being weaned off my pain medication and I was feeling cranky and sore. "Just because you saw me fall doesn't mean you're responsible for me."

I imagined that Will felt an obligation to me, some variation on the loyalty television characters feel when they have saved someone's life. I craved his attention, but I couldn't bear pity.

He just shook his head and gazed at me. I recognized the look on his face. It was the same way he looked at me just before he said "I do" in my dreams.

"I just want to be with you, Tina."

It was the first time in my life that I felt wanted.

Aunt Gillian did not like Will. She tolerated him, because he was the first friend I'd brought home in a long while. He was the first boy I'd ever brought home, and I could tell she didn't want to discourage me. But as in all things, she could not hide her disapproval. She was polite to him, thanking him for helping with my schoolwork and commending him for keeping me entertained. One afternoon, she even baked him chocolate-chip cookies to take home in a tin. But I knew that none of that should be taken as approval. The less my aunt liked a person, the more impeccable her manners.

I didn't want to care what my aunt thought, but I did. After Will left one evening toward the end of the second week, I asked her about it as we were sitting down to dinner.

"Why don't you like Will? He's nice. He saved me."

I had succumbed to the romantic idea that Will and I were linked forever because of my fall on the ice. It was destiny, I had decided. Aunt Gillian raised her eyebrow, a tiny movement that conveyed a considerable amount of skepticism at my interpretation of events.

"I never said I didn't like Will."

She believed it was uncouth to express overt disapproval, although this point of etiquette somehow did not apply to her relations with me. She picked up her fork and took a small, delicate bite of broccoli. She knew I hated broccoli, but it was a staple at our dinner table as a part of her unending quest to put me on a diet.

"I know you. You don't like him." I pushed the broccoli aside and bit into the small piece of French bread I was allowed. I would have preferred fries, but that was out of the question.

She sighed and took another bite of broccoli, as if to demonstrate proper eating form and content. She chewed for a long moment before putting down her fork and looking over at me.

"He's not what he seems to be. He will hurt you."

I dropped my fork, furious. "You just don't want me to be happy. You try to ruin everything for me!"

I screamed this in the dramatic way only a sixteen-year-old can. It was the first time I'd ever raised my voice at my aunt, and I expected her to retaliate.

She was calm. "I've known a lot of men in my life, men who seemed nice on the surface but who had other . . . agendas. I just don't want you to make the same mistakes I did."

"What do you know about men?" I sneered. "I've never even seen you with a man. What man would want someone as old and dried-up as you?"

I didn't know where the words came from. I wasn't even conscious of having such thoughts about my aunt. At the time, she did seem both old and old-fashioned to me, but I wasn't prepared for the force of my own hostility toward her. Looking back, she wasn't that old (just fifty-one years old when I was sixteen), and many of her words now seem protective rather than critical. But then, she was the enemy.

I wanted my words to hurt her. But they either had no effect, or she wasn't willing to give me the satisfaction. She frowned, took another tiny bite of her ultrahealthy dinner, and began to speak in a patient tone.

"Ernestine—"

I cut her off, shouting, "Call me Tina!"

I stomped out of the kitchen, ran up the stairs and barricaded myself in my room. Two days later, I lost my virginity to Will while my aunt was out shopping for a new sofa.

I had never been one of those girls who cherished their virginity, who viewed it as a sacred gift to be given the man of their dreams. In fact, I had not considered the practicality of sex. My romanticism focused on ceremonies and style, or words and gestures instead of what went where, and when.

I did, however, think that the moment of my first sexual experience would be more than a collection of jerky movements, pain, and embarrassment. There was no seduction. I told Will I wanted to do it. He agreed without even a token bit of hesitation. There was no effort at romance or tenderness. It began, it hurt, and it was over. While Will buttoned up his clothing, which had been mussed throughout the entire process, I could only think of my wrist, which ached, and the day of the week. It was Thursday.

I was not surprised that Will didn't come by the next day, or Saturday, as was his habit. I wasn't even surprised that he ignored me in the halls at school. What surprised me was how much I missed his smile.

For another type of girl, the Will Situation might have created a certain level of caution when it came to love. For me, it was the beginning of a five-year stretch of poor decisions, extreme loneliness, and intermittent promiscuity. Instead of avoiding boys, and men, I threw myself into relationships that had two things in common: They were short, and they were painful. My sudden sexual popularity in high school was due to Will's gift of gab. Although the experience hadn't seemed to me like much to brag about, it seemed that my willingness to participate made me a hot commodity. This made me popular among boys with sweet smiles and active libidos, and even less popular (if that were possible) among the girls they dated and called girlfriends.

I didn't care. I ignored all the bad things about my encounter with Will and focused on the one bright spot: I'd felt wanted. All I required of the boys was a week or two of superficial attentiveness, and I was theirs for a night, or more—however long it took for reality to set in. I was fat. I was unpopular. I was too smart. They were ashamed of me and their desire for me.

Despite their shame, there were many boys, both black and white, who passed me notes in the halls, or smiled at me during class, or struck up conversations with me after school. There was no such thing as interracial dating at St. Gabriel's, but those rules didn't apply to illicit sexual encounters that ranged from simple petting to sex in the backseats of cars.

I brought none of them home, of course. I had refused to speak to Aunt Gillian for a week after Will stopped coming around, somehow blaming her for what happened. She neither asked about him nor mentioned his name again, but it rankled that she had seen through him in a way that I couldn't. I wouldn't give her the satisfaction of being right again.

When I graduated high school and went away to Georgetown, little changed. I was still fat, and I still needed to feel wanted. My methods, and those of my suitors, became more sophisticated, and casual sex was more acceptable on the college campus than it was at my provincial Catholic high school. Until senior year of college, I convinced myself that I was in charge of my own sexuality, that I was taking what I needed just as the men were. This, I told myself, made me a feminist, liberated, strong. This, I told myself, was why I had few women friends, none close; they were not as enlightened as I.

Francisco Alexander and Monica Coleman changed my mind.

CHAPTER 10
"The Latino Agenda"

By the spring semester of my senior year, I had fulfilled the requirements for my English and literature degree. I wanted to take something different, so I enrolled in a women's studies class called "Twentieth-Century Feminism: Still Battling the Sexes." I wasn't sure what the class would be like, or even what the title meant, but it sounded interesting. It was January 1993. I was twenty-two years old. It was my first class of the day, on the first day of the semester.

I noticed Francisco right away because he was the only man among the fifteen people sitting around the seminar table. If I had been the only woman in a class full of men, I would have been nervous. But he looked comfortable, slouched down in his chair and wearing the slightest smirk on his face. I looked around and saw the other women noticing him, too. I had experienced this phenomenon before, having a man invade what is a woman's space—and even in 1993, men were infrequent visitors to the Women's Studies Department. It was often in a beauty salon, where a man would be getting an ill-advised perm or some other kind of treatment normally reserved for women. Or it was in an aerobics class, where the men had one of three goals: 1) get in shape, 2) ogle women in leotards, or 3) make fun of the institution of aerobics.

At the start of "Twentieth-Century Feminism," we all wondered whether Francisco was here to learn, to gawk, or to antagonize.

He was there for all three, as it turned out, although I wouldn't realize that until much later. Francisco Alexander was Colombian, which we knew because he made sure to mention his family in Bogotá at every opportunity. He insisted on being called Francisco, not Frank or any other shortened version of his name, because, as he told us on the first day of class during introductions, "I was named after my great, great *abuelo* Francisco, who lost his life fighting for freedom."

He was the kind of person who peppered his speech with Spanish words, although he had no discernable accent except that common to inhabitants of Reston, Virginia, where he and the other freedom-fighting Alexanders had settled. This bothered me from the very beginning, but I told myself I was being unfair. Spanish was his native language, I told myself. Why shouldn't he retain it in his everyday conversation?

Francisco was dark haired and fair skinned, handsome in a wiry, lithe way. He wore a uniform of faded jeans, black suede Pumas, and either a bright-colored sweater or t-shirt, depending on the weather. He topped this with an ancient leather jacket that looked as if it had belonged to a World War II pilot. He seemed to glide along instead of walking (later, I would think of it as slinking), and he felt as if he belonged in any setting. He had an unshakable confidence; he could not be convinced that he and his views were anything other than right. Some people called it arrogance, but his conviction captivated me.

What made him most interesting was his passion. Francisco did nothing without giving it his full attention. When he read our first assigned book, *Sex, Art, and American Culture* by Camille Paglia, he devoured it, quoting it from memory as if opening the book would take too much energy away from the point at hand. Then he went on to read many of Paglia's other works in order to contextualize her writings. He made sure we all knew he had read them, and none of us could question him on those, since we hadn't read them. I supposed the professor had, but she tended to let you hang yourself with your own rope, so to speak, so she never stopped Francisco from holding court in class.

He ate every meal with the graceful manners of the upper-middle class, and he enjoyed each bite as if it were his last. He made love as if he meant to savor each movement, to remember each curve along my skin. He always had a new idea, and he was spontaneous. One day he would whisk me off to a Brazilian restaurant, and the next day we would drive four hours so we could see a Broadway show. On Broadway.

He was romantic and generous, exciting and challenging. Francisco was a living, breathing example of how to live in the moment.

We spoke for the first time during the discussion of Paglia's book, which was a collection of essays examining contemporary feminism and popular culture. The professor began the class by asking what we thought of the book.

I suspected that most of the class would want to refute Paglia's assertion that women's studies was "institutionalized sexism," if only to justify our presence in the classroom. But I was interested in her take on women in pop culture, so I spoke before anyone else had the chance.

"I think she's right about Madonna. She's a feminist, a role model. She's sexual, and she controls her sexuality and how it is portrayed. It's a performance-based marketing strategy, true, but it's interesting and admirable."

I looked around the room. This was not long after Madonna released her book *Sex*, and people weren't sure how to react to it. She'd placed women in a bind. If we called ourselves feminists, could we applaud what seemed like raw porn in places, even if it came from a woman? If we didn't like it, were we prudes?

The professor, a tiny woman with short blonde hair and a booming voice, looked around, waiting for someone to respond. She didn't wait long.

"Madonna cheapens sex, making it into a spectacle instead of a sensual experience. She is not a feminist. She is a joke." Francisco's tone left no room for dispute. I heard a couple of the other women gasp. It wasn't proper academic form to speak in this way. We'd been taught that college was about debate. Francisco saw no reason to debate what seemed obvious.

After he spoke, we looked at each other, and I almost smiled. I liked him.

The class rolled on, with several women defending my view (more because they disliked Francisco than out of any sense of agreement with me, I suspected). At several points there was shouting before the professor turned the discussion to what I knew she would zero in on—the validity of women's studies. I kept quiet, watching Francisco throw himself into that discussion with a vigor I admired (and would later loathe). We had our first date two days later, and it wasn't long after that we were spending every free moment together.

Francisco loved my Rubenesque body (he had been an art history major before choosing political science). The fact that he saw beauty where I saw fat made him even more appealing to me, and I began to see me the way he did. Not perfect, but appealing in my own right. When we talked about our pasts, he told me that he couldn't imagine sex without love, and he declared his love for me in the same breath. I was suspicious of this, so I halved the number of men I'd slept with and told him nothing about my reasons for doing so.

He was greedy for all types of cultural enlightenment, so we saw foreign films, went to art galleries, and listened to poetry at local slams. I soaked it all in, happy that I'd found someone who shared my love of Chinese films and Thai food. Francisco had an opinion on everything, and he seemed to know it all, arguing with me until I conceded that he was right.

Some nights, we would go to the theater and then out for a late dinner, and I would agree with him only because I knew we wouldn't eat until I did. We did what

Francisco wanted, and I went along. I let him have the last word most of the time, not because I thought he was smarter than I was (he was the only one who believed that) but because when he was happy, he was charming, intelligent, and exhilarating. I loved being around him when he was in a good mood, and good moods came to Francisco only when he got his way. So in the beginning, I did my best to avoid conflict.

But soon, his need to be right took a toll on me. After two months of constant exposure to his views on everything from the best ethnic cuisine (Bangladeshi) to the correct brand of toothpaste (Aquafresh), I'd had enough and the arguments began.

We argued over politics. I was a Democrat, a quite liberal one, but Francisco felt that Clinton wasn't doing enough to help the poor and to promote what he called "The Latino Agenda." Not one to bother with details, he never specified what that agenda was, and when I joked that I'd like to get a hold of the Latino Manifesto so I could peruse the details of The Agenda, he refused to return my calls for three days.

Francisco claimed that Clinton's plan to focus more on health care, welfare reform, and other "bourgeois" issues was a coward's way to avoid the reality of millions dying in bloody African civil wars and imperialist America doing nothing to stop it. I joked that he was the only twenty-two-year-old Georgetown student who sounded like Ché Guevara. He cancelled our Valentine's Day plans and instead spent the weekend at his parents' house in Reston. When he told me he was going, I con-

sidered pointing out the irony of his retreat to a bourgeois enclave of privilege and wealth where he was known
as "Frank," but I decided not to push it.

When Clinton proposed the "don't ask, don't tell"
rule for gays in the military, I said it was silly but better
than nothing. This sent Francisco into a frenzy. It came
up on a Sunday afternoon in March as we were reading
The Washington Post coverage of the impending congres-
sional hearings. We were at my tiny apartment near
campus, where we spent most of our time together, since
his roommates alternately blared "Beavis and Butthead"
on the television and fake reggae/hip-hop on the stereo
by some white guy named Snow.

Francisco's filibuster on the absurdity of Clinton,
rampant homophobia, and my "hopelessly naïve" political views lasted for twenty-nine minutes, at which point
I got up to make myself a roast beef sandwich. I sat at the
table listening to Francisco's shouting, eating my sandwich and wondering how long it would take him to
either leave or shut up. For the record, it took twelve
minutes for him to come into the kitchen and ask me to
make him lunch.

One of Francisco's passions was poetry, but it was the
only one he kept a secret. At least he kept it secret from
me. When I asked to see his poems, he claimed that he
was too sensitive about his art to expose it to the likes of
me. I wouldn't appreciate it, he insisted, not if I thought
that Freud was wrong about the unconscious. I shrugged
and said nothing. I would do many things for Francisco,
but I drew the line at endorsing Freud.

At the end of March, three months into our relationship, I noticed advertisements for a poetry reading on campus. Francisco hadn't mentioned it, but he became very busy writing and I deduced that he would be reading from his own work. I was anxious to hear the one thing Francisco wouldn't talk about, and I also wanted to show him that I was a supportive girlfriend, even if I did doubt the veracity of penis envy as a guiding theory of behavior.

I arrived just late enough to the reading so that the room would be filled and I could hide in a corner where Francisco wouldn't see me. I wanted to surprise him with my praise and support after the reading. I was a huge fan of poetry, and I already had plans to write my master's thesis and dissertation on some form of poetry. I looked forward to hearing local writers, and I was not disappointed by the first three people who read, two women and a man, who were interesting and talented. Francisco's name was announced next as a newcomer to the group. I held my breath.

He slinked out to the microphone and without acknowledging the crowd's polite applause, began reading.

I can no longer remember Francisco's actual words, but the specifics of the poem aren't important. The important thing is that his first poem was one of the worst pieces of writing I'd ever heard. The topic was war or love, maybe both, I couldn't quite tell. What I could understand of his writing was didactic and melodramatic.

I felt as if someone had punched me in the stomach. It never occurred to me that Francisco had kept his poetry a secret because it was terrible. I suppose on some level I believed him when he said that I was the reason for his reticence. I swallowed my horror, and then I felt an almost irrepressible urge to giggle. Laugh. Chortle. Bend over holding my sides with tears in my eyes. The poem and Francisco were that bad. And that funny.

I knew right then that it was over between us. I could be with someone who wrote bad poetry, but I couldn't be with someone so full of himself, so self-righteous, so obnoxious. It took hearing him read his poetry for me to see him as he was. What I saw made me sad. Francisco, and his poetry, somehow helped me see that I didn't have to accept what men were willing to give. I could, and should, demand more.

He finished reading his second poem, which I didn't even hear, and the crowd clapped its polite thanks. I joined in, trying to figure out how soon I could leave without being spotted. Then, I saw him walk over to another woman, familiar from the same women's studies class where we had met (which Francisco eventually dropped, claiming the professor was a reactionary). He embraced her with a passion that I should have suspected wasn't reserved just for me.

I felt little more than a bemused interest in this exchange, and I was relieved that breaking up with him would be much easier. I remembered her name, Monica Coleman, but not much else. She was quiet in class and said little, and until now, I hadn't noticed how much she resembled me. Round figure, dark skin, short hair, pretty face. I laughed to myself as I snuck out before Francisco saw me. At least he had been honest about liking a Rubenesque woman.

I broke up with Francisco the next morning. Five days later, Monica Coleman stopped me after class.

"Can we talk?"

I looked around for an escape. She seemed nice enough, but it was a beautiful April day, and I was in the midst of the most pleasant, relaxing week I'd had since I met Francisco. I was in no mood for any kind of drama.

"Please." She smiled, and something about her smile reassured me.

I looked at my watch and saw what my stomach already knew—it was noon. "How about lunch?"

Neither of us had any more classes that day, so we walked over to a nearby Indian restaurant and ordered samosas and spicy chicken curry. The poetry reading had been the last straw for Monica, too, and she and Francisco broke up that week. She made the mistake of calling his poem charming, for lack of a better word. He went ballistic and called her an ignorant cow.

"Charming?" I smiled at the thought of Francisco's reaction.

Monica shrugged, laughing. "It was all I could think of. That, and 'absolute dreck.' "

We ordered beers and compared notes. She'd started seeing him last August, and I marveled that she had lasted that long.

"Well, I'm nothing if not persistent. And masochistic."

I told her about his parents leaving a message for "Frank" on his answering machine. We made fun of him, and ordered more beer. It turned out that Monica Coleman and I had more than looks in common—she was also from the Midwest (Chicago) and was fighting a parental mandate to be a doctor. She was pre-law, had already been accepted at Maryland, and was delighted at her parents' dismay. We fell into that type of platonic, all-encompassing friend-love that only women can share. We've been friends ever since.

CHAPTER 11

"I knew an easy bet when I saw one"

I knew Jack for a year before I let Monica meet him. Or before I let him meet Monica. I wasn't sure which one of them might embarrass me more. Jack could tell stories of my baggy swimsuit. Monica could tell stories about college, about Francisco. Either way, worlds would collide, and I wasn't sure I was ready.

Of course, Monica wanted to meet him the moment I told her we had a date. She volunteered to fly down from Atlanta the next day if necessary. I discouraged this. I told Jack the basic details of the Francisco story, including the fact that I and the woman who was now my best friend were dating him at the same time. I did make some small adjustments, making myself sound much less vulnerable to his charms and making his bad poetry sound even worse.

Jack was intrigued.

"I have to meet the woman who could bond with you over a cheating man."

"Maybe someday," I told him. At that time, we had only known each other for a few months, and I was not sure we would develop the type of relationship in which we met each other's friends.

After a year, I couldn't fight off Monica anymore.

"Are you ashamed of me?" she asked. She put just the right amount of melancholy in her voice to make me feel guilty. I knew it was a ploy, but I couldn't resist.

"Of course not. You're my best friend."

"Am I? Then why wouldn't you introduce your best friend to your new boyfriend?"

"He's not my boyfriend. I told you, we're just friends."

She pounced. "Then why are you hiding him from me?"

I put up a fight. "You live in Atlanta."

"It's an hour's flight away. I'm going online now to make reservations. How does next month sound?"

It was over. Worlds would collide. I could only hope that the two most important people in my life would like each other.

"Next month sounds perfect."

Monica picked a bad weekend to come to Florida. It was Super Bowl weekend, and Jack, a Panthers fan, was rabid because Carolina was playing the Patriots and he believed, against all reason and evidence, that his team would win.

Football was one of the things Jack and I shared. We watched games every week, even during the preseason, and until he got TiVo, we argued over which games to watch when two good matchups were on satellite at the same time.

My love of football went back to high school, when I tried to develop hobbies that would distract from the fact that I was fat. I couldn't play any sports, but I learned everything I could about football. For a while, I thought it would get me dates, but then I realized that most guys don't even want to watch football with their girlfriends. Football and sex occupy separate worlds for guys, and the less crossover the better.

But sex was not on the agenda for me and Jack (at least, I didn't think it was on his agenda), and when he found out I liked football, he was impressed. We were at the pool and I mentioned plans to watch on Sunday.

"You like football?"

I smirked. "What, I'm a woman so I can't like football?"

"No, it's just, most women don't."

"Well, I'm not most women."

He laughed. "So I'm learning."

From then on, we made plans to watch together, usually at his house because his television was bigger and he subscribed to a service that let him see any game he chose.

On Super Bowl weekend, 2004, Jack and I had money on the game. He mistakenly believed that the Panthers would beat the Patriots, and while I wasn't a fan of New England, I knew an easy bet when I saw one.

"Why are you even a Panthers fan, anyway? You're from St. Louis. You live in Florida," I asked as we decided the terms of the bet.

"Not that it's any of your business, but I went to the University of North Carolina for undergrad."

"State school, huh?"

"Just like Maryland. An inferior ACC opponent, by the way."

I feigned shock. "Inferior? Please. You're in trouble when college hoops starts."

"Hoops? Aren't you hip."

I raised my eyebrows. "No one says 'hip.' "

Jack waved me off. "Whatever. What's the bet?"

I pretended to ponder, even though I already knew what I wanted.

"If New England wins, you have to cook and serve me dinner for a week. If Carolina triumphs, I cook for you."

He smiled as if he was getting the better end of the bargain. "All I can do is cook spaghetti and make sandwiches. And I prefer a more gourmet palate. I'll find some recipes for you. Sucker."

I shrugged. "Whatever you say."

He was the sucker. Either way, I got to spend every night for a week with Jack.

The stakes were high that weekend, and Monica had chosen it as her weekend to visit, mostly because she knew nothing about sports. By the time I realized what she was planning, the tickets were bought.

"Why would you come on Super Bowl weekend?" Monica had called to tell me her plans.

"What's the difference?"

I sighed. She was such a girl.

"The difference is, Jack and I will be watching the game. We have a bet. This is important."

Monica clicked her teeth. "It's just a game, Tina. I can't believe you want to put baseball ahead of me."

She always played the guilt card, probably because I always fell for it. I gritted my teeth.

"Football, Monica. The Super Bowl is football. Seriously."

"Whatever. I'll watch the game with you," she suggested, her voice bright. "So it's all settled."

There is nothing a true sports fan hates more than watching an important game with someone who knows nothing about the sport. I decided not to tell Jack about Monica's ignorance. He would be distracted by getting to meet her.

"You just have to promise not to embarrass me by asking dumb questions."

"Like 'where are the bats?'"

We laughed. "Exactly."

It was a perfect winter day when Monica arrived in West Palm Beach. It was cooler than normal, giving Floridians a chance to wear all those sweaters we didn't need eleven months of the year. When Monica saw me waiting at the baggage claim, she burst out laughing.

I looked around. "What?"

"You actually own a leather jacket?" We both thought of the high-school guy I dated, the one with the leather jacket that my aunt hated. Well, my aunt hated them all, but this one offended more, his leather symbolizing a fatal character defect.

"Guys can't wear leather. For women, it's fine."

Monica snorted. "Forget about that high-school guy, who probably was evil. You live in Florida."

"A Floridian can't have leather?" I spread my arms wide. We both looked around, and at least five of the people waiting were wearing leather jackets.

Monica shook her head. "You people are insane. It can't be less than fifty degrees out there."

I grinned at her. "Forty-seven today."

Monica arrived Friday afternoon, and I asked Jack to come over for dinner that night. We would go sightseeing Saturday, since Monica hadn't spent much time in South Florida, and Sunday was the game. I planned a full itinerary to cover all bases: If Monica and Jack liked each other, the weekend would be fun. If they didn't, well, we would all be too busy to think much about it.

My main worry was the Super Bowl. Jack could be blunt, and so could Monica. He might make a comment about her football ignorance, or she might say something about his football obsession, and we would have a war on our hands. Neither was one to back down, and I wasn't sure how I might mediate without taking sides.

All this ran through my mind as we drove back to my house. Monica had her window open, and I alternated between worrying about the weekend and telling her it was too cold.

"In Atlanta, this is like spring."

I leaned over and turned on the heat. "We're not in Atlanta. It's January in Florida, and this qualifies as cold."

Monica rolled her eyes. "Aren't you from the Midwest? You've gotten soft."

I shrugged. "True. Now can we close the window?"

Afterward, I decided that it didn't make sense to worry about Monica and Jack meeting. It was going to happen, and now all I could do was hope it would work out. They were both too important to me.

Monica and I spent the early evening cooking and laughing, remembering all the reasons why we had hit it off from the moment we met. She had a dry sense of humor and a way of cutting right to the heart of an idea. Even though Monica used to be overweight just like me, she had never suffered from the lack of confidence that I still struggled with. I always thought it was because of her family, her mother. She came from a close-knit clan that held raucous family reunions each year, where they wore matching t-shirts and told family stories over and over. I never had anything like that, and I always believed that was the reason why the fat devastated me in a way it didn't hurt Monica.

We couldn't agree on the kind of food we wanted (she wanted Mexican and I wanted Italian), so we compromised and made Asian. Monica concocted a Chinese stir-fry, I made Pad Thai, and we found a bottle of organic sake at the Whole Foods. We couldn't find fortune cookies, so we agreed that peanut butter was always a good cookie option, no matter what.

When Jack arrived, he carried a bottle of white wine in one hand and a bunch of flowers in the other. Monica insisted on opening the door and I hung back, watching their faces for first reactions. When Monica noticed the flowers, her face brightened a bit, and then more when he handed them to her.

"For you. I'm so glad to finally meet you, Monica." Jack was on his most charming good behavior. I think Monica might have been blushing.

"So sweet. How did you know I love calla lilies?"

She glanced at me and I shrugged. "I guess he's psychic."

Jack stepped inside.

"Not psychic. Just well mannered, thoughtful, charming, intelligent . . ."

"We get it." I stopped him or else we would be standing there all night.

Monica laughed. "Is modest on the list?"

"My father always told me that when you're trying to sell yourself, modesty has no place."

"He sounds like a wise man." Was she batting her eyelashes at him? She gave me a teasing look. I knew what it meant—if Jack and I were just friends, why would I care if they flirted a little? I sighed. She always was a bit of a troublemaker.

"Actually, he was, and is, a jackass, but it's probably too early in our relationship to trade family stories."

He and Monica spent another moment beaming at each other. I finally had to step between them.

"Okay, he's thoughtful and you're flattered. Can we agree that you guys like each other and go eat? I'm starving," I said. I made my voice stern, giving them both a mock frown. Inside, my muscles unclenched, and for the first time since Monica announced her visit, I was relaxed. Until that moment, I hadn't realized just how important it was to me that my two best friends get along. I valued Monica's opinion, and I had for years. Now I realized how much I valued Jack's as well.

"And by the way, you never bring me flowers," I informed Jack.

He struck a dramatic pose and looked off into the distance. " 'Keep love in your heart. A life without it is like a sunless garden when the flowers are dead.' "

Monica was impressed. "That was beautiful," she gushed.

"That was Oscar Wilde. Add literary thief to your list of accomplishments."

Jack grinned at me. "So what's for dinner?"

Super Bowl Sunday couldn't have been better. The Patriots won, I won my bet with Jack, and from Jack's perspective, seeing Janet Jackson's nipple during the half-time show made the loss worth it. More important, Monica had spent some time learning the basics of football. When she wondered what the offensive coordinator would call to counteract the blitz, I never loved her more. She smiled at me. She was a good friend.

CHAPTER 12

"Happily ever after is important"

During that first week taking care of Aunt Gillian, I developed an intense appreciation for the work of medical professionals. And there were days, more of them than I liked to admit, that I wished I was at the university, teaching summer classes to students who thought that cramming fifteen weeks of instruction into six would be easy. That seemed like a vacation compared to caring for my aunt.

It had been so long since I lived with Aunt Gillian I had no idea what to expect. When I was a kid, I spent my days at school, and I never had any idea how she spent hers. She napped a lot, which I assumed was normal for an older person, but when she wasn't sleeping, she puttered around the house starting what she called projects. In my house, these were items or situations that she first criticized, and then insisted on fixing.

"Where did you get those curtains?"

"I don't know, Aunt Gillian."

"Well, they're tacky. I'll sew you a pair that is more tasteful. Lord knows you never had any taste."

So I bought her an inexpensive sewing machine and took her to pick out fabric. She sewed one side of a curtain, declared she was tired and never touched the sewing machine again. I left the loose fabric out, thinking she would come back to it when she was ready. At the end of the week, she frowned at it as if she had never seen it before.

"You need to clean up around here. I know I taught you better than to keep house this poorly."

Then things started getting lost and showing up in weird places. We spent one whole morning looking for the remote before I found it inside a box of cereal. The next day, my aunt spent fifteen minutes looking for her glasses until I pointed out they were perched on top of her head. I must have said this with a note of sass.

"Don't be a smart-mouth, Ernestine. It's not becoming."

Aunt Gillian had always been moody, but I noted now that her moods were unpredictable and often inexplicable. She was excited when I suggested we go to the salon to get our nails done, something I knew she liked to do. But when we got there, she complained that the girl doing her nails didn't speak English, and she told me not to leave a tip. I left double the normal tip while my aunt wasn't looking and apologized to the technician, who was Korean but spoke perfect English.

I decided that I needed to adjust my thinking and treat my aunt more like a patient and less like a normal family member joining the household. There was a certain irony in this. My aunt had always wanted me to be a nurse, like her. Being like my aunt, deliberately or otherwise, was the last thing I wanted. And aside from wanting to oppose her, I never wanted to be a nurse. I wasn't one of those people who grew up wanting to help people. I had little interest in medicine, even less in the gritty details and precision of biology classes. The smell of blood has always made me queasy. I hate needles.

What I loved was reading. When I was nine years old, I spent the summer reading every book in the Cleveland City Library's children section. I did not discriminate; Judy Blume was as fascinating to me as R. L. Stine. It wasn't the subject of the books that mattered; it was the feeling I got when I read. Books helped me escape the reality of my neighborhood, which was by that time well on its way to being run-down and forgotten. When I read, I could play in distant cities, countries, worlds, instead of riding my bike up and down the block in front of our house, staying within my aunt's range of vision. Books took me away from home and the disapproval that was punctuated by icy silences instead of yelling. Books allowed me to be someone other than Tina; between the pages I was as pretty as Deenie, as funny as Ramona, as clever as Nancy Drew. Books saved me.

What I really wanted was to be a writer. I always thought I could write a children's book, one about a girl like me, an overweight girl, who finds her value in what's real, not just the superficial. It would be a book about loving oneself not in spite of differences but because of them. The main character would not run from imperfection but would embrace it. And she would have a family, a mother and a father, brothers and sisters. A big, loving, messy family in which no one kept secrets or told lies.

I knew it was self-indulgent, maybe even far fetched. But it was still my dream. I even did the research. I read all the children's books I could, studied the illustrations, thought about plot and narrators. I made lists. First, I started with the basics:

1. Keep it simple
2. Use humor
3. Use made-up words and rhyme
4. Show, don't tell
5. Use words kids can understand

I kept adding to my lists, getting more detailed and specific:

6. Develop interesting characters
7. Make an outline; have a general understanding of the beginning, middle, and end of the story—and of how the characters will interact and evolve.
8. Conflict: A good story usually has some sort of conflict or obstacle that the main character has to resolve
9. Happily ever after is important

Sometimes the lists were more complicated, more like self-encouragement than guiding principles.

10. Start writing today
11. Write every day
12. Believe in yourself
13. Find illustrator

Her name would be Brianna. It was the kind of name I'd always wanted for myself. Her challenge would be something simple, like wanting to join the volleyball team but being told she was too slow and too fat for sports. She would practice until she was so good they had to take her, fat and all. People would see beyond her outside and look at what she could do, what she was, as a person. Brianna might not even be skinny, but she would be a great volleyball player.

I thought it was a great story. I thought that someday I would write this book, and it would be the start of a whole series of books about Brianna and her friends, all of whom had to overcome something in order to find their place in the world. I even wrote out a rough draft, but I never showed it to anyone because I was afraid it wasn't good enough. I wasn't ready to give up the dream, so I couldn't let anyone tell me my idea wasn't a good one.

I kept the draft on my desk at home as a reminder that someday I had to take that next step. I didn't even know Jack had seen it until he presented me with a folder on my thirty-second birthday.

"I usually like jewelry," I said, looking at the folder with mock disdain.

"Just open it."

I did, and I found drawings of a girl inside. She had deep brown skin and a wide smile. Her arms and legs were plump and she had a little pot belly. She held a volleyball and wore a uniform shirt with her name on it. Brianna.

I looked up at Jack, my mouth open. He held up his hands.

"I know you shouldn't go through the stuff on someone's desk. But I was using your computer one day and I happened to see your story. It was right there out in the open."

I still couldn't speak.

"Anyway, it's a great story, and I thought you might need some illustrations to go with it."

Jack watched me, worried that I was angry. I was in shock that another person had read my book, that he liked it. Most of all, I couldn't believe he had taken the time to make illustrations. I flipped through the pile. They were perfect.

I felt tears coming, but I didn't want Jack to see me cry. I cleared my throat.

"I didn't know you could draw. Like this. They're beautiful."

His face brightened. "So you want to use them?"

I did. But that would mean I'd have to actually write the book, for real, not just a draft. And that prospect was still scary. Jack was my friend. Of course, he was supportive. Maybe the rest of the world wouldn't be.

I tried to explain this to him without sounding like a wimp. He nodded.

"Well, whenever you're ready, I am."

According to Aunt Gillian, writing wasn't a career. She said the only way she would help pay for me to go to college was if I chose a sensible career. When I was a senior in high school, I pleaded with her. I could be a librarian, an editor, a reviewer, even a writer, I told her. She suggested medicine and Howard University, thinking I would be a prominent black doctor, or at the very least, marry one. I chose Georgetown and an English major. I got a scholarship, maintained a perfect GPA, and ignored Aunt Gillian's complaints. I went to graduate school for longer than my aunt felt was appropriate, becoming Dr. Jones after all. Aunt Gillian came to watch me receive my Ph.D. from Maryland, although she made it clear that a Ph.D. was *not* as good as an M.D. in her book. Through it all, books and the fat around my waist and thighs were my constant companions.

When I began my job at Mizner University in West Palm Beach, I found another love: teaching. I soon realized that many of my colleagues were writers who taught. They spent most of their time outlining essays and books, plotting to become the next Henry Louis "Skip" Gates or Harold Bloom. I too wrote and had published articles in my specialty, African-American poetry of the nineteenth and twentieth centuries. But I did so under duress. I was a teacher who wrote.

Before my first class, I worried that I would feel uncomfortable with so many people sitting there, staring at me, staring at my fat. But, after those initial classes, my students related to me in a warm way. I listened to them talk about their other professors, and I realized that my classes were different, more relaxed. It took me months before I realized that they didn't like me in spite of my imperfections; they liked me because of them. My weight took me down a few notches, from vaunted professor who could do no wrong to professor who was more like a regular person, with problems just like everyone else. Many of my colleagues would balk at being pushed off the careful pedestals they constructed for themselves, but I welcomed it. I wanted my students to be engaged and talkative during my literature classes, and if my weight was helping me reach that goal, well, it had finally proven to be good for something.

And I loved being on campus. Mizner University occupied premier waterfront property, right on the Intracoastal in West Palm Beach, just blocks from my house. Named, as so many South Florida edifices were, for architect and benefactor Addison Mizner, the University was one of Mizner's designs. The original buildings dated back to 1920 and were lovelier when you learned that Mizner had no idea how to draw blueprints and had no formal training. What he had was his vision of Florida as a tropical Mediterranean, filled with barrel tile roofs, terra cotta stucco, and projecting understated elegance. The University was a collection of one- and two-story buildings spread out over more than one hundred acres, with the most high-profile departments and administrators in buildings facing the water and the rest creeping inland. It was located not far from downtown West Palm Beach, but once inside the gates, the school was a like a green oasis, both at one with and separate from the hustle of the city.

I loved the look of the campus, where the breezeways opened at either end into arched doorways and every window arched as well. I loved the muted mustard tones of the buildings on the outside, and the noninstitutional décor inside. I even loved the man-made lakes dotting the campus, because although they paled in beauty compared to the Intracoastal and the ocean, they were surrounded by leaning palms and tropical vegetation.

My own small office was spare and severe in many respects. There were only three pieces of furniture: a long, narrow desk, the leather chair I sat in, and another, less comfortable chair for guests. The walls on two sides were lined with ceiling-to-floor bookshelves, and a large window took up nearly the entire wall behind me. I sat with my back to the window so that I faced the door and could see any visitors right away. I'd taken down the blinds from the window, so the office was bathed in light even on the cloudiest days. The walls were white, but I planned to lobby for permission to paint them a more soothing color after I received tenure.

There was something about Mizner University that felt like home to me, and it was where I was closest to being the Tina I wanted to be. It wasn't perfect, but if there was one thing I had learned about life, it's that being a perfectionist, like my aunt, wasn't all it was cracked up to be.

CHAPTER 13

"Go get me some cigarettes"

I longed for the classroom during those first weeks with Aunt Gillian, and the fact that she had gotten her way was not lost on me. I'd found myself playing nurse that summer, caring for a cranky, ungrateful patient who lived in my home and sometimes surprised me by forgetting my name. It turned out that Aunt Gillian's dementia was more advanced than I had thought, and I was at a loss for ways to deal with it. The only bright spot in those first few days was that my aunt was much nicer to me when she thought I was a stranger.

I could always tell when it was one of those times when she forgot our history.

"Good morning," she chirped at me when I came into her room. Then she would give me instruction on the handling of her laundry, her meal requests, and a few pointers on cleaning so that the room was truly clean.

At first, this annoyed me, but I soon realized that Aunt Gillian was a lot nicer when she treated me like a servant. It wasn't polite to be rude to the help. Family, now that was an entirely different story. Aunt Gillian was at her nastiest when she remembered who I was and why she was in my home.

"This chicken is terrible, too rubbery," she complained one night. "You always were a terrible cook."

Food was a recurring theme in both her complaints and compliments. I had made her the same meal the week before and she loved it. Of course, she thought I was her personal chef that day.

"I'll try not to make it too rubbery next time, Aunt Gillian."

She tsked. "Why bother? Just bring back that nice woman who cooked for me last week. She knows how to make baked chicken."

I soon realized that it was futile to point out that I was that same woman who had cooked for her last week.

The fascinating thing was that she always recognized Jack. Or at the least, she was always happy to see him. After a while, I wondered if she remembered who he was, or if it even mattered. When Jack came over, she acted as if he was her date, batting her eyelashes and flirting. I always cringed, embarrassed, but Jack always went along with her moods.

"Be careful, or you'll end up married to a seventy-year-old woman," I joked.

He smiled. "I always wanted a sugar mama."

I met Aunt Gillian's demands for complicated and unhealthy meals, changing her outfits according to her whims, chauffeuring her to various doctor appointments, and acting as her own personal servant. She had been with me ten days when things came to a head.

"I need my cigarettes."

I was running a bath for her when she spoke from the doorway of the bathroom. This was the first time Aunt Gillian had mentioned the cigarettes. I had never admitted to finding them, and I had assumed that she had accepted my denials. It was hard to tell whether she remembered all that now, but I'd had just about enough of being ordered around in my own home.

"Pardon me?" I turned, plastering a courteous look on my face to hide my annoyance. I had heard her, because she had shouted her demand. As usual, she wore only one of the two hearing aids she needed.

"Go get me some cigarettes."

I couldn't stop the frown that creased my forehead when I heard this revised demand. I hoped she would forget about the supply of cigarettes we found (and threw away) in her house, since as far as I knew she hadn't had any in weeks.

"Cigarettes?" Maybe if I kept playing dumb, she would let it go.

"You heard me."

I turned back to the tub and shut off the water, feeling with my hand to make sure it wasn't too hot. I considered whether I should contribute to a bad habit, and then she said it.

"You heard me, you old cow. I need my cigarettes!" Now shouting, my aunt swayed in the doorway as if she were about to lose her balance. I jumped up to grab her so she wouldn't fall and she swatted me with her purse. I caught it midair with one hand and turned her around with the other, guiding her back toward the sitting area.

I guided her into the soft leather recliner and ignored the indignant look on her face.

"Now look, Aunt Gillian," I began, holding up a hand to silence her. "I'll cook for you, bathe you, welcome you into my home. I'll even let you call me an 'old cow,' since we're family. But I will not have you smoking in my house. I don't care how old you are and how long you've been smoking—you're not going to do it anymore. Not as long as I'm in charge."

She glared at me, and I wondered which part of what I'd said had stung the most.

"You're not in charge," she said, her lips curled, her nostrils flaring. But her voice was weak and too soft to match her words.

I wanted to smile, but didn't. "Oh, yes, I am. And the sooner you get used to it, the better. You have to let someone else take care of you for once in your life." I softened my voice so she would know that my words weren't motivated by spite. "And that someone, like it or not, is me."

There was a long pause, and she looked at the wall for what seemed like forever. Then she cleared her throat and struggled to her feet, waving off the arm I offered as support.

"You've always been bossy. And stubborn. Can I take my bath now, or do you want to yell at me some more?"

I laughed. "Do you want bubbles or not?"

Another important element of my new life as Aunt Gillian's nurse was time. I had lots of it on my hands, more than I'd ever had in my life. I was left to my own devices between meals and caretaking. Under normal circumstances, my own devices would lead me to lounge and read, or to grade papers when I was teaching. But whenever I sat down with a book, the birth certificate I'd found in Aunt Gillian's house called to me. Or, at least, that's what I told myself when I unfolded and looked at it every day.

Lily Jones was born on February 28, 1960, in Milwaukee, Wisconsin. No one had ever mentioned anything about us having family in Milwaukee, but then again, no one had ever mentioned Lily at all. This didn't seem like the kind of thing that would slip someone's mind, especially if that someone was my aunt and she had had a real daughter out there somewhere to mold into the debutante I would never be. It was obvious that Lily was just another secret that my aunt had kept from me. But this was so big that it made me crave the answers to the questions I'd always had. If Aunt Gillian never told me she had a daughter, what else had she kept from me? About my parents? About me?

Every time I touched the delicate parchment paper, I wanted to ask Aunt Gillian about it, to shake her awake if need be to get answers. But I knew that wasn't the way to get information from my aunt. Lily's birth certificate had my mother's and Aunt Gillian's maiden name, which raised even more questions. I knew my aunt had been married by that time, but I didn't know when she got divorced and changed her name from Gillian Jackson back to Gillian Jones. The father was listed as unknown.

Each time I unfolded the paper, I thought of more questions without answers. It wasn't long before I tried to change that.

One Saturday afternoon, I called Jack. I wanted him to help me, but he was less than enthusiastic.

"I hate to say this, Tina, but maybe you should just leave well enough alone."

I frowned. "Why? Don't I have a right to know?"

"Doesn't your aunt have a right to her own secrets?"

Jack was infuriatingly sensible.

"I'm not trying to force her to give up her secrets. I just want to know if I have a cousin out there some-where."

I did plan to confront Aunt Gillian with whatever I found out. But this wasn't just about her secrets. This was my family, too.

"Are you sure you just don't like the idea of unraveling a real-life mystery? Maybe you've got too much time on your hands." I could hear the smile in his voice.

I snorted. "Can you blame me? You try spending all day at home taking care of a cranky old lady."

"No thanks." He paused, and his voice turned serious. "You know, you could hire someone to take care of her. Since you won't put her in a home, I mean."

"I can't do that. She needs me."

He cleared his throat. "You don't think you deserve to have a life, too? One that isn't limited to cooking for your elderly aunt?"

I sighed. "What life?"

"Dating, being young, enjoying yourself."

Dating whom? I thought. Jack and I never talked about our romantic lives. I didn't have one, but I was sure he did. Sometimes, when I called him at night, he didn't answer, and when I asked where he had been, he acted cagey and vague. Sometimes he smelled of expensive perfume, and sometimes he disappeared for entire weekends. If I'd asked, he would have been honest and told me everything. That was his way. But I didn't ask. I didn't want to know. I liked to think of Jack as mine, even if it was just a fantasy.

I held up my hand, as though he were in front of me. "Okay, truce. Let's get back to the birth certificate. Let's say you're me, and you planned to ignore the sensible advice of your sensible friend. How would you go about finding out more about your cousin Lily?"

With a resigned sigh, Jack replied, "Well, you don't have enough to go on to get anything useful off the internet, and you probably don't want to spend money on a private investigator just yet. Have you looked through that old trunk you've got in the attic? Maybe there's some information in there."

"For someone whose policy it is to leave well enough alone, you sure know how to be nosy."

He laughed. "Call it a gift."

One of the only times Aunt Gillian had ever talked to me about my parents was when she gave me an old trunkful of my father's things.

"Most of the time, it's the women who keep a hope chest," she told me when I was fifteen years old, pulling an old trunk out of an unused closet at the back of the house. "But your father was the one who liked to save everything."

I was sitting cross-legged on the floor next to the closet, examining the battered trunk. I rolled my eyes at her use of the outdated term "hope chest." Aunt Gillian clicked her tongue.

"If you don't want it, then I'll keep it."

I jumped to my feet. I craved information about my parents, and I regretted challenging my aunt.

"I want it."

She nodded. "Good. Your father would have wanted you to have it."

It was an old Army trunk, battered and scuffed, covered with stickers and strange markings. My aunt had always kept it in the closet, saying she didn't want to be reminded of sad times. I'd always been fascinated by the trunk. A few years before Aunt Gillian gave it to me, I had discovered it in the back closet one day when I was snooping around, looking for some clue that my aunt had once been young. Its lock was old and rusted and held fast until Aunt Gillian gave me the key. I hoped it would hold secrets, information or mysteries that would reveal who I was and how I'd come to be. But it held a small metal box with a sturdy lock I couldn't pick no matter how hard I tried. My aunt claimed she had never seen the smaller box and refused to speculate as to its contents. Once the trunk was mine, I filled it with my own childhood secrets: a perfect white marble that I found at the park playground, the diary I'd gotten for my eighth birthday but had never written in, the wrappers from the Twinkies I was forbidden to eat.

I'd forgotten about the trunk until now. I once again thought the small metal box it held might hold answers to my questions. I kept the trunk in the attic over the garage. It was a Friday, and I waited for Aunt Gillian to go down for her nap before I went looking for it.

I had a thing about spiders and ants, any kind of bugs, so I felt more than a little revulsion as I pulled down the attic ladder and climbed up. My need for answers outweighed my squeamishness, so I held my breath and flipped the light switch. I hadn't been up there since I moved into the house years ago, and I'd forgotten what I'd deemed so unimportant as to be stored with the bugs and critters. Storage containers were stacked against the walls, and although the attic air was dusty and stale, I saw no signs of life beyond spider webs.

I found the trunk under bins marked "Tina's old clothes." The words were written in Jack's handwriting. Months ago, we had argued about me keeping the clothes after I had lost all the weight.

"You've lost all the weight, and kept it off," he said, ever reasonable. "You should throw all this stuff out."

I had nodded as if I agreed with him, and, in theory, I did. But every time I tried to put those old clothes in a bag for Goodwill, something stopped me. I couldn't explain it to Jack. They were a part of me, a reminder of how far I'd come. I couldn't let them go.

"I need them."

"You need to throw them away and embrace being thin and healthy."

I shook my head and tried to smile, but instead I burst into tears and ran out of the room. When I came back later to find Jack and apologize, he and the clothes were gone. He'd left a note on the kitchen table.

"Sorry," it read in his neat block print.

I couldn't resist peeking inside the storage bin. When I opened the top, it was as if the ghost of my former self floated out. I pulled out an old lavender sweater and held it up to my body. I could fit two of me in it now. There were huge pairs of jeans in there, folded as if they were waiting for me to bring them back to their rightful place on my closet shelves. I touched my waist, now taut from daily workouts, and I felt like crying.

I closed the container of clothes and moved it aside. The trunk was built solid and had always been heavy, no matter what was inside, but I managed to drag it down the ladder, through the garage and into the kitchen. There I stood, brushing off my hands and looking around for a place to keep it, a place where it would remain private, at least until I'd had a chance to look inside.

Before I could settle on a place, sounds of Aunt Gillian stirring came over the monitor. I shoved the trunk back out into the garage before hurrying down the hall.

CHAPTER 14

"Ten weeks is a long time"

My failed liaison with Jack was typical of my adult dating disasters. I'd grown smarter about many things in my life as I aged, but men and relationships were not among those things. Four months before I went to see Aunt Gillian, I was in the middle of my Slave Narratives seminar when I felt the prickle of discomfort that told me I was being watched. Of course, in a class of twenty-five students, I was always being watched by those listening with intensity and those pretending to do so. I was used to that kind of scrutiny. But I was aware, and always had been, of being watched in a more personal way. I'd learned the hard way back in high school that it was better for people like me to fly under the radar—there was less chance of ridicule and harassment that way. Now I still felt most comfortable when people looked through me rather than at me.

Without missing a beat of the lecture, I looked around the small seminar room filled with long tables and uncomfortable chairs, wanting to find the culprit and at the same time wishing he or she would just go away. But high school had also taught me that knowing the enemy was better than being surprised. I saw the usual faces, whose names I had yet to learn, and none of them would meet my gaze. Except one.

He sat straight in his seat, a sharp contrast to the others who sloughed in various poses of indifference. He was a tidy dresser, wearing a golf shirt tucked into his jeans. Jeans that were *pressed*, I noted, with sharp creases up the middle of the legs. I wondered at this. What college student wore golf shirts and creased jeans?

He looked young, maybe twenty or twenty-one at most. The seminar was available to juniors and seniors, and I had found that only the most ambitious of seniors took the class because I required too many papers. So he was a junior, I figured. Perhaps an overachiever, I thought, glancing again at his creased pant legs.

He sported a shock of wild, curly hair that surrounded his head like a fluffy brown cloud. He nodded as I lectured, his hair bobbing away as he moved his head up and down. There was a sweetness in his face, with clear, honey-brown skin and cheeks filled out in a way that reminded me of the way boys looked before they sprouted mustaches and muscles.

I was disconcerted by the way his gaze never wavered when I looked at him, looked away and back again. I wanted him to look away, to be embarrassed, to stop watching me as if I were fascinating. I didn't want to be fascinating. I just wanted to be left alone.

I frowned at him and continued my lecture, refusing to look back at him for the rest of the class, even though I could feel his eyes on me the entire time. When the class ended, I looked up just in time to see him smile at me as he handed in his paper. Andrew Hopeman. I nodded at him and turned to the next student. Andrew Hopeman wanted something from me. The question was, what?

Later that day, I had a number of student conferences scheduled. When the last student left, I returned to the paperwork on my desk, wanting to get out of the office as soon as possible. It was a beautiful February day, the kind of day that reminded me why I lived in South Florida. I thought I might go for a run, or convince Jack to join me for dinner at an outdoor café on the water.

I was alone for just a moment before I heard the door creak open. I looked up to see Andrew Hopeman smiling down at me.

I looked down, shuffling the papers in front of me. I always got flustered when people were interested in me, for whatever reason. It was a residual of being fat, or being an outcast. Too much attention was never a good thing for a fat girl. It meant ridicule was on its way, sooner or later. Even though I was no longer overweight, my thinking hadn't caught up with my body.

After a few seconds, I looked up, smiling my best I'm-in-control smile. I gestured to the seat in front of my desk and waited as he adjusted his body to the uncomfortable chair. I was determined not to speak first, lest I reveal my discomfort.

"Hi, Dr. Jones. I'm Drew Hope," he said, holding out his hand. I shook it, noting that his hand felt soft and cool.

"What can I do for you, Drew?"

Drew's smile broadened. "I need a tutor."

We looked at each other for a moment. I pretended to mull over his request, but I wondered why he called himself Drew rather than Andy or Andrew. Did this say something about a person? I knew a guy named Drew in college, and I hated him. He was in my freshman-year political-science class, he was a Republican and I had recently discovered that I was among the most liberal of Democrats. One day he proposed that people on welfare were lazy. I had called him a fascist.

This student neither looked nor sounded like that guy; still, the name rubbed me the wrong way.

"You want me to find you a tutor?"

He shook his head. "I want you to tutor me."

I raised my eyebrows. "I don't usually tutor my own students, Drew. If you need help with something specific from class, well, maybe I can direct you to one of the graduate students," I said. His smile faded.

Drew cleared his throat. "Well, that's the thing, Doctor. See, I want to study slave narratives in graduate school, so I wanted to talk to someone with a lot of experience so I can do well in this class and get ideas for my senior thesis." He rushed his words together, and for the first time since he had entered my office, Drew looked as uncomfortable as I felt.

His excuse didn't hold up. A graduate student could help him. But he wanted me, whether for tutoring or something more, I wasn't sure. In most cases, I would simply refuse and direct the student to one of the more capable graduate students in the field. I would chill him with my coldest leave-me-alone look. But there was something about Drew that made me feel anything but normal. He seemed needy and vulnerable under the surface. I was a sucker for vulnerability.

"I'll help you."

His smile returned in earnest, and I wished I could take back my words. I felt as if I'd agreed to something more important, something I might regret. Before I could think of a way to rescind the offer, Drew made an appointment to see me next week and left the office in a purposeful rush. I turned back to my papers, trying not to think of Drew at all.

Later that day, Jack and I sat on my back porch drinking white wine and eating pizza. I didn't realize that I'd had too much wine until I heard myself telling him about Drew.

Jack frowned and set down his glass and leaned forward on the wrought iron chair.

"Let me get this straight—this student who's what, nineteen, twenty—"

"He's twenty-one." I'd looked up his records.

"Oh, right, *twenty-one*. Anyway, you're interested in a 21-year-old kid? A *student?*"

I felt my cheeks flush. "I'm not interested in him."

His eyes showed his disbelief. "That's not how it sounds. You know, there are policies against this kind of thing, Tina. I don't want you to risk your career."

"He just wants a tutor." Even as I said it, I knew it was a lie. I wasn't quite sure what Drew wanted, but I didn't think it was as simple as tutoring.

"He wants *you*. Believe me, I know. I'm a man." Jack just stared at me until I looked away.

"If he wanted sex, would he be so obvious about it?"

Jack laughed. "Tina, it amazes me how little you know about men."

We sat without talking for a moment, contemplating this truth. This was one of the reasons I thought it was good that Jack and I had ended up as friends instead of something more. He let me peek into the psyche of men and would always tell me the truth, no matter what.

"It's hard. I still see myself as fat, as ugly. I can't trust my own instincts."

He nodded. "Men *do* like you, and it has nothing to do with your weight. But you're always pushing them away."

"I don't push them away, they leave. They don't like me because I'm not pretty." Self-pity and chardonnay were making me feel light-headed.

Jack sighed. "You don't really believe that, do you?"

"You don't understand. Women fall all over you because you're gorgeous. I'm just plain."

Jack laughed. "Have you looked at yourself lately? You still see yourself as an awkward teenager, but you're not that girl anymore." He jumped up and left the room, returning a moment later with a hand mirror. Standing behind me, he held it up to my face.

I looked, at first focusing on Jack's familiar smile behind me.

"Stop looking at me. Look at you."

I saw the short hair I'd always had, the brown skin, the wide mouth. But I also saw high cheekbones and long, sweeping eyelashes.

"You're beautiful."

I blinked, not sure if I could believe Jack, not sure if I could believe the image in the mirror. I felt tired, my limbs heavy. I turned around and hugged him.

"You're a good friend. The best."

He pulled away and seemed embarrassed.

"It's late. I'd better go." Jack walked into the house toward the front door, and I followed. Before he opened the door, he turned to me.

"Be careful, okay? With this Drew kid. Be careful."

I shooed him away. "Don't worry about me."

He shrugged. "Good night, Tina."

⁂

The first tutoring session was scheduled for a Tuesday afternoon in February. Most days I wore the same thing when teaching: A tailored pantsuit with a crisp white shirt, sensible yet stylish black or brown loafers, pearl earrings or tiny gold hoops. I didn't wear makeup. But today, I found myself wondering if I should wear a blue shirt. Maybe a skirt? Peering into the bathroom mirror, I noticed a series of fine lines at the corners of my eyes, and considered whether some eyeliner might be in order.

The trouble was that I didn't own any eyeliner, which meant I'd have to go buy some at the drugstore, which meant I'd have to examine my impulse to spruce myself up for a tutoring session. So I put on my white shirt and settled for lipstick, which I told myself was meant to protect my lips from chapping in the Florida sun.

I didn't teach on Tuesdays and spent those days at home, grading papers or hanging out with Jack, who also had the day off. But today, I went into my office an hour before my meeting with Drew. I brought a thermos of coffee, and as I sat in my seat, the coffee tasted sweet but also made me feel jumpy. I read the same paper three times, smudging its corners with my damp fingers and not retaining a word. After a while, I gave up, pushed the pile of papers away and sat back, thinking of what Jack said. The tutoring session, the whole Drew situation started to seem like a terrible idea, and I looked at my watch, hoping I could call him and stop this before it ever got started. I was typing at warp speed, trying to call up his student records on my laptop, when Drew knocked on the door and poked his head inside. He was early.

His hair was even more unruly today, and he looked harried, as if he had run from the dorm to my office. It was no surprise to see one of my students looking as if as if he had been up all night, studying or something else, but Drew carried a pile of books and a sheaf of articles, one of which, I noticed, bore my name.

"Hi, Dr. Jones. I'm sorry I'm early, but I didn't want to be late."

Apparently, just being on time was not an option he had considered. I was annoyed that I hadn't been smart enough to just say no to his tutoring plan in the first place.

"Hi, Drew. Did you read that?" I pointed to the article that I'd published in graduate school on *Incidents in the Life of a Slave Girl.*

He nodded. "I'm using it in my senior thesis. You had a lot of good ideas on voice in there."

I could have taken this as an advanced version of brownnosing, but he sounded so sincere that I gave him the benefit of the doubt. Before I could reply, he pulled out a typewritten memo that he pushed across the desk to me.

"I hope you don't think this is out of line, but I developed a plan for our sessions," he said, fingering the books he still held on his lap.

"A plan?" I hadn't even considered a *plan*, nor had I considered the fact that there might be enough of these sessions to warrant one.

"Yeah, you seemed a little taken aback by me asking for tutoring, and I didn't want this to create extra work for you, so I outlined all the areas in which I need help. I think we can cover it all with weekly sessions for the next ten weeks."

"Ten weeks?" I knew I sounded idiotic, repeating his words, but he released the words in such a barrage that I couldn't think of more appropriate responses.

Drew leaned forward, running his hands through his hair in a gesture that revealed why it was so mussed.

"Is ten weeks too much? I can modify the plan."

I shook my head. I was impressed that he had given this so much forethought—it was like something I would have done as a student. Yet, as far as I could tell, Drew wasn't an outsider as I had been. He managed, as far as I could tell, to be smart and popular, despite the creases in his jeans.

Before I could stop myself, I asked the question that weighed on my mind.

"Why me?"

Drew frowned. "What do you mean?"

"Why me? Why did you pick me for tutoring? Why not Dr. Gaston or Dr. Ferrer? Both of them are tenured professors, they have been doing this a lot longer than I have. In fact, they've both written books on slave narratives, not just articles. So why pick me?"

I still wanted to believe that he really needed tutoring and was not, as Jack claimed, angling for some kind of illicit *thing* with me. So I had to ask. I couldn't spend the next ten weeks wondering. A little voice, which sounded like Jack's, said that if he wanted to date me, he wouldn't just come out and say it, not if I asked. I dismissed the voice.

He placed his stack of books on the desk and sat back, looking around my office for the first time since he had gotten there.

"Doctor, if we're going to be here for ten weeks, is it okay if I call you by your first name?"

I nodded, feeling as if I were sacrificing my last and most tenuous hold on student/teacher decorum.

"It's Tina."

"Like I was saying, you just seemed like the right person. I could tell right from the beginning of the semester. I was meant to be here, with you."

I wondered if he was one of those people who believed in God and karma and destiny and fate—the ideas people use to explain the inexplicable. I was not one of those people.

He looked at me and shook his head. "I'm not crazy, and I don't mean to be melodramatic. I just mean, well, this feels right."

We stared at each other for a long moment. It was starting to feel very wrong to me, but I couldn't think of a way to say this without seeming to overreact to what might be a legitimate request for help.

I looked down at Drew's plan. Ten weeks was a long time.

<hr/>

I was packing my briefcase when Jack came to my office later that afternoon. He plopped down in the chair across from me and began drumming his fingers on my desk.

"That's annoying."

He ignored me and kept drumming. "So? How did it go?"

I closed my eyes and rubbed my forehead. I hadn't told Jack that I was tutoring Drew today.

"How did you know I was meeting Drew?"

"*Drew*, huh? We're on a nickname basis now?"

I glared at him and he smiled, holding his hands up in surrender.

"Okay, okay. I came by earlier, saw him walking in."

I frowned. "How do you know what Drew looks like?"

Jack's grin broadened. "Research, my friend. You didn't answer me. How was it?" Jack leaned forward with his chin in his hands, as if I was about to reveal everything—as if there was anything to reveal.

"He's a good student."

He raised an eyebrow, waiting.

"He had a plan for our sessions, all typed up. He says he and I were meant to meet." I wished I'd left off that last part.

Jack's demeanor changed from joking to serious in an instant. "See? That's weird. What does he mean by that?"

I shrugged. "I thought it was kind of creepy, too. But now, how do I get out of this? He has a ten-week plan."

"Ten weeks is a long time."

The next time I met with Drew, we went to a coffee shop just off campus. I still hadn't figured out a way to get out of the tutoring sessions, but meeting outside my office would be better, less intimate. I noticed that he was more dressed up than I'd seen him before. He wore khaki slacks and a dark green button-down shirt that was wrinkled, as if he had had to search long and hard to find his nice clothes.

We met midmorning, so the coffee shop was busy but not overcrowded. We found a table in the back corner, away from the noise of the cappuccino maker and the chattering students, and I sat at the wrought iron table while Drew got us coffee.

Looking around, I felt a kind of nostalgia for my own college days. The Mexican tiled floor, the walls covered with student art, and the smell of expensive coffee beans reminded me of the hours I'd spent in coffee shops just like this one, studying for exams, writing notes for papers, or just sitting and watching the world pass by the bay windows. But I wasn't like these cheerful girls, leaning in to giggle with my friends, chatting about classes and dates. I'd never had those kinds of close female friendships until I met Monica Coleman, and that wasn't until senior year.

Drew's return interrupted my reverie.

"I got you a latte—I hope that's okay."

I hated lattes, preferring regular coffee to the trendy, milky drinks.

"That's fine, thanks."

He settled himself into a chair and looked around the room. "When I was younger, I never hung out in places like this. In Cleveland, there aren't all these coffee bars like down here."

I was startled. And suspicious. Did he know I was from Cleveland, too?

"I'm from Cleveland, too." I watched him for signs of surprise. There were none.

He laughed. "I have to admit, I knew that. That's one of the things we have in common."

We sat there for a moment, staring at each other. He was smiling. I was trying not to grimace. I didn't like the idea of him checking on me, on my background, and it just occurred to me that his interest coincided with my weight loss last year. I was alarmed but tried to keep things easy and neutral.

We talked about Cleveland locales we both knew, and I tried to reveal as little as possible about myself, about my family, while appearing to be friendly. After we exhausted our lists of favorite Cleveland places (mine was shorter than his, since I hated Cleveland), he paused and then dug into his backpack.

"I brought you something."

The knot already growing in my gut tightened. For the first time, I felt nervous. Gifts could not be a good sign.

"Drew, I don't think you should give me anything. It's my job to help you with your studies." I used my most formal official-sounding tone.

He pushed a small wrapped package across the table to me. "It's not really a gift. Okay, well, I guess it is. I just saw it in a used bookstore and I thought you'd like it."

I didn't want to touch it, but I knew I had to. I watched his face while I opened the package. He looked thrilled, almost like a kid.

It was a first edition hardcover copy of *Incidents in the Life of a Slave Girl*. It was weathered and worn, the title was difficult to read, and it smelled musty. But the cover was sturdy, and it had all its pages, which was amazing for a book dating back to 1861. I was in awe, forgetting Drew for a moment as I examined the book. It was a treasure, the kind of thing a book collector dreams about. It must have cost a fortune. "It's gorgeous." I looked down at the book again.

"I knew you'd love it."

I held the book out to him. "But I can't accept it. It's too much."

144

He shook his head and pushed the book back toward me. "It's perfect for you. More coffee?"

He rushed off to get us refills while I sat there, desperate to escape. When Drew came back, he launched right into his study questions and never said another word about the gift. The book sat between us on the table.

About an hour passed, and I looked at my watch.

"I'm late for a meeting," I said, even though it wasn't true. I just needed to get away from Drew. The word "stalker" began to scream in my head. I made a mental note to listen to Jack the next time he gave me advice.

We stood up at the same time and I moved toward the door as fast as I could, calling good-bye to Drew over my shoulder and leaving the book on the table.

The next day, when I arrived at my office, the book was propped against my door with a note from Drew.

"Maybe next time we can have dinner."

I shivered and placed the book in a desk drawer. I didn't hear from Drew the rest of the week. Friday, I was in the office later than normal to finish some overdue grading and plan for the next week's classes. I worked all afternoon, and when I took a break, it was after six o'clock and the February evening was already dark. There was a knock on my door, and without thinking I assumed it was Jack. We had made plans to go to the YMCA for a swim, like the old days, and then have a late dinner.

"Are you ready for a swim?" I looked up after I spoke. It was Drew. He was holding two white take-out bags.

"I thought we would have dinner instead."

I felt panicked. This was weird. I was not overreacting. I was rarely, if ever, in the office this late, which means Drew was following me. Or watching me. Or both. I prayed that Jack would come soon.

"What are you doing here?" I was tired of trying to be nice to Drew.

The smile on his face faded. "Dinner. Didn't you get my note?"

"How did you know I was here?"

He shrugged. "Lucky guess."

I didn't answer. He stood in the doorway, both of us waiting for the other to say something. He set down his bags and walked closer to my desk. I stood, not wanting him standing while I sat at a physical disadvantage. If he was capable of spying on me and checking on my background, who knows what he might do.

I found out soon enough. Moving in one smooth motion, he was standing next to me before I could move away.

"I love you." Then he gripped my arms in his, hard, so I couldn't wiggle free, and he kissed me. I squirmed and fought, and then Drew was pulled off me. I rubbed my arms and ran to the phone while Jack held Drew down.

It turned out this was not the first time Drew had done something like this. He'd left his first school rather than be expelled, and at least two other local women held restraining orders against him. I didn't want to think about what might have happened if Jack hadn't come to my rescue. Here I was, once again depending on him, needing him in a way that I have never needed a man before. I was lucky he was always there for me, although I didn't realize it until later. It was as if we knew our roles without having to rehearse. I was in trouble, and he was my rescuer. It was a variation on the damsel-in-distress fairy tale in which the prince swoops in to save her from evil. The only problem was, I wasn't much of a damsel, and by all counts, Jack wasn't my prince, no matter how much I might have wanted him to be.

He might not have been a prince, but he was a good friend. He took me home and listened as I told him the whole story. Jack was nice enough not to say I told you so that night. In fact, he never said I told you so, but I shouldn't have expected any less. The prince never blamed the damsel for getting herself into trouble.

CHAPTER 15
"Old age is not an illness"

It took less than a month for me to realize that I couldn't care for Aunt Gillian on my own, and I was worried that her memory lapses and bad tempers were more than garden-variety dementia. In her first month, I often had to remind her where she was and why she was there.

"But I live in Cleveland."

I knew it was important to be patient, but I grew tired of having the same conversation over and again.

"You did live there for many years, but then we thought it would be nice for us to live together."

I took the opportunity to craft a more pleasant history than the one we shared. It was the one advantage of Alzheimer's disease. Revisionist history was often necessary, or at least tolerated, because the listener, my aunt, sometimes didn't know the difference.

"You hated living with me. We argued all the time." Aunt Gillian flashed in and out of reality, so I could never be sure when she would pick up on one of the white lies I used to placate her.

"No. We're family."

She grunted and told me she wanted to take a nap.

This was another problem: napping. For someone who claimed she didn't need much sleep, she was spending much of her time doing just that. At first, I chalked this up to being older, but my aunt had always been a bundle of energy. Throughout my childhood, she rose before the sun every day, and by the time I awoke she had done the laundry, cooked breakfast, and written out a list of chores I needed to complete that day. Even last Christmas when she came to Florida, she had bustled around my house, making sure there was no dust lurking in the corners and rushing to refill Jack's water glass before he even asked.

Now, it was July and she could barely be bothered to get out of bed in the morning, and when she did, lethargy clung to her every move.

What was most worrisome was her attitude toward me. She could be nasty at the most unexpected times, but more often, Aunt Gillian was sweet to me.

"You look nice today," she had told me on a recent morning when I came in to make up her bed.

I looked down at my torn jeans and the ancient Georgetown t-shirt I wore. I had covered my hair with a scarf and I wore no makeup. I couldn't remember the last time Aunt Gillian had complimented me, but I was pretty sure I wasn't dressed like a cleaning lady at the time. But instead of deriving pleasure from her acceptance of me, I became alarmed. I resolved that day to take her to the doctor for a full evaluation.

I read up on dementia and Alzheimer's. There was a ton of information online, including a pamphlet from the Alzheimer's Foundation of America. The website was informative and well organized, but the information on warning signs scared me. "Alzheimer's disease is a progressive, degenerative disorder that attacks the brain's nerve cells, or neurons, resulting in loss of memory, thinking and language skills, and behavioral changes." This I knew. But I felt dizzy as I read the familiar symptoms. There was one line that cut me to the core. "Personality changes can become evident in the early stages of Alzheimer's disease. Signs include irritability, apathy, withdrawal, and isolation." Irritability was nothing new with my aunt, but since she had been in Florida, she didn't put up much of a fight about most things. She ate the food I cooked, and her complaints that my cooking wasn't up to par were halfhearted. She spent too much time in her room, often claiming fatigue. She didn't seem to care much about her appearance and had rejected my suggestion that she schedule a regular appointment at the hair salon as she had done back in Cleveland.

I took her to the medical center at Mizner University, which was renowned for its work with the elderly. The tests were scheduled over several days, and I was so nervous the first day I begged Jack to come along with us. He and Aunt Gillian were still getting along well, and I wanted a buffer at the doctor's office, just in case.

My aunt was silent the morning of her appointment. I'd waited until the night before to tell her about it. When I'd explained to her that she needed a complete physical, she had protested.

"I'm fine. Old age is not an illness."

"I know. But everyone needs a physical, and I just want to make sure everything's all right." I never directly referred to her dementia, because I wasn't sure how aware of it she was.

"Why wouldn't everything be all right? I don't take any pills. There's nothing wrong with me. Is there?"

We were in the middle of dinner, and I chewed and swallowed before answering.

"I'm sure everything will be fine."

I expected more arguing from her in the morning, but she said little as she dressed and ate her oatmeal, the same breakfast she had eaten for as long as I could remember. She finished the entire bowl, and I wondered if this was her way of showing me that she was in perfect health.

Jack met us in the waiting room at Dr. Ortiz's office, where we were the only people waiting. The room was spacious and elegant, painted a warm, dusty rose and decorated with sleek, modern furniture and accessories. One wall was covered with his framed degrees. After I got Aunt Gillian settled into a seat with a magazine, I wandered over for a closer look. Dr. Ortiz's pedigree was impeccable, and I was further buoyed when I saw that he had attended Georgetown University a few years ahead of me. I took it as a good omen and sat down next to Jack, who was flipping through *Cosmopolitan*.

"That seems like an odd magazine choice for a doctor who deals with older patients," I said.

Jack smiled. "Mature women need to know 'Ten Ways to Please Your Man in Bed,' too. Right, Gill?"

Aunt Gillian gave Jack a stern look, but I thought I saw just a hint of a smile before she looked back down at her magazine.

"Gill?" I whispered to him. I'd never heard anyone refer to my aunt as Gill.

"Jack and Gill. It's why we get along so well," he teased. "Maybe if your name was Jack, you two wouldn't argue so much."

"Yeah, right." Just then the nurse called my aunt's name.

Dr. Ortiz was a lanky man who spoke English with just the slightest Spanish accent. His skin was honeyed and smooth. He looked like someone who spent his free time outside playing tennis and swimming. His manner was soothing, and I sensed that whatever the diagnosis, we were in good hands.

"Ms. Jones, we're just here to check you out and make sure everything is fine. There's nothing to be afraid of; the tests we'll be doing over the next week won't hurt, and I'll tell you exactly what each one checks for so you'll know what's going on."

His eyes never left my aunt's, and I could tell that she liked Dr. Ortiz right away. I hadn't told Aunt Gillian that the testing and examinations would mean that we would be seeing him several times over the next week, but when Dr. Ortiz smiled at her, she didn't seem to mind.

He then explained that he would take a medical history to gather information about my aunt's current and past health problems and a family history of illnesses. He would interview me as well to get a good idea of how Aunt Gillian was doing.

This was where his spell broke. Aunt Gillian frowned. "Ernestine can't tell you anything more than I can. I'm not a child, you know." She shifted in her seat and pulled her purse closer to her, as if Dr. Ortiz had suggested she hand over its contents for scrutiny.

I tensed up and stole a glance at Jack. *It's okay,* he mouthed at me.

"It's just standard procedure, Ms. Jones," Dr. Ortiz said in a soothing voice. "We know that you know yourself better than anyone."

Aunt Gillian sighed and leaned back. "Just as long as you don't take her word over mine."

"Take my word about what?" I couldn't help interjecting. I knew part of this was the dementia talking, but then again, she had always treated me this way. Nothing I had ever done was good enough, not even bringing her into my home and care when she needed it.

Jack and Dr. Ortiz shot me warning looks. I pursed my lips to keep them closed. They were right—I needed to try to act like an adult. This wasn't about me. It was about my aunt's health.

"Your word is the most important, believe me." My aunt nodded and started rifling through her bag. I prayed she wasn't looking for cigarettes, and while she was occupied with the contents of her purse, Dr. Ortiz flashed me a reassuring smile. I felt my facial muscles relax and I smiled back.

He went on to explain that he would ask Aunt Gillian a series of question, and although he didn't say so, I knew they would be used to evaluate her mental status, memory, and sense of time and place.

"Of course, we'll do a routine physical, with some specific neurological tests added to make sure we're covering all of our bases. And after all that is done, we'll come together and go over the results."

Aunt Gillian stopped rummaging in her bag, coming up empty-handed and seeming upset about it.

"Can I get you something, Ms. Jones, or help you find something?"

"My cigarettes. I can't find my cigarettes." Her voice was irritable, and I could feel my cheeks heat up with embarrassment. I started to speak, but Jack took my hand and I managed to stay quiet.

"Ernestine, did you take my cigarettes?"

I said nothing. I kept my lips pursed and occupied myself with admiring my own restraint.

Dr. Ortiz smiled at the mention of cigarettes, as if he was glad she had mentioned it.

"Ms. Jones, this is a nonsmoking facility, you know." He raised a conspiratorial eyebrow at her as if to indicate the foolishness of the bleeding-heart liberals who'd created such a policy.

"Why don't you come with me? I'll walk you over to the examination rooms down the hall, and we'll see if we can't get you comfortable there."

He offered his arm and Aunt Gillian took it after shooting a self-satisfied smirk my way. Dr. Ortiz winked at me over her shoulder as they left the room.

I looked at Jack, and we burst into laughter.

Jack left to get some air, and I wandered over to the cafeteria for coffee. I was stirring in skim milk when a man standing next to me spoke.

"That's not good for you, you know."

I looked up at him. "Milk?"

"Coffee. I should know. I'm a doctor." He grinned when he said that, giving the line just enough irony to keep it from being cheesy. "May I join you?"

I shrugged and nodded, doubting that this guy was all that interesting and feeling almost certain I wouldn't like him. But I needed a distraction, and he seemed to be just as good as any.

"I'm Marvin Brunson," he said in a booming voice as we sat down.

"Tina." I decided not to give him my last name. I had no plans to take our chance meeting further. But I was intrigued. He didn't look like a Marvin, not with those camouflage green eyes, caramel skin, and chiseled shoulders covered by a tailored jacket. His sandy brown hair was cut short and curled just enough so it didn't look too perfect. He was tall, a full head taller than me, and his skin was smooth and clean-shaven. Everything about him was well-groomed and expensive, and I felt downright frumpy in my jeans, t-shirt, and plain black cardigan.

He asked why I was at the hospital and I told him. But I didn't want to talk about me.

"So, you're not a chiropractor, I hope."

"Plastic surgeon."

"So you do boob jobs, then?" I was feeling antago-
nistic because he seemed smug. But Marvin seemed prepared to take it.

"Breasts, tummy tucks, face lifts, the whole spectrum.
I would ask you if you're interested, but you don't look to
me as if you need any improvements."

I shook my head. "Nice. I'll bet you say that to all the
girls."

Marvin raised his eyebrows. "Would you rather I suggested Botox?"

Marvin was insulting, a jerk who was enamored with
himself. He was the adult version of the boys who had
hurt me back in school. And he was just the kind of man
I knew to avoid.

"Do women really fall for this stuff? And, more
important, do you pick up a lot of women in the hospital
cafeteria?"

He shrugged and smiled. "I'm not spending my
Saturday nights home alone."

Even though I didn't approve of him, he was vaguely
charming. I had to smile, raising my cup.

"To Botox." He touched his cup of orange juice to
my coffee cup. Then I looked at my watch.

"I have to get going."

"Can I see you again sometime? Maybe we can meet
here for corned beef sandwiches on Thursday," he joked.

"I don't eat corned beef. It's not good for you."

He grinned. "Maybe you want to give me your
number and I can take you out for something you *do* eat."

I tilted my head and looked at him. I couldn't say that I liked him, but I was intrigued. I scribbled my cell phone number on a piece of paper and gave it to him. I didn't think it mattered. He wouldn't call.

After Aunt Gillian's initial tests, we drove to my house, where I'd promised to make Jack lunch as a reward for spending the morning in a doctor's office. Aunt Gillian was tired and went to her room to watch television, saying she would eat lunch later. I offered to help her but she pushed me away.

"I'm not an invalid, you know," she called back over her shoulder.

I looked over at Jack and shrugged. I had been trying all day to pretend that this was just like any ordinary day, business as usual, such as it was since Aunt Gillian had come to live with me. Jack knew better.

"It's going to be okay, you know. No matter what Doctor Feelgood says, things will be okay."

I raised an eyebrow. "You didn't like Dr. Ortiz? I thought he was great."

"I could tell. He had you and Gill charmed."

"What's wrong with a little charm?"

He didn't answer. I watched him fiddle with his silverware. He sounded jealous. This wasn't the first time I'd heard him use this tone. If it had been anyone besides Jack, I would have recognized it as clear jealousy, but this was Jack. We were friends. Just friends. I had always wanted more from our relationship, but after five years, I wasn't sitting around hoping that our friendship would be anything more. Was I?

"What, you're worried that he'll take your place in Aunt Gillian's heart?" I poked Jack with the cheese I was preparing to slice for his sandwich, but he didn't smile.

"Yeah, right." He seemed to realize that he had been rolling the cloth napkin between his fingers and put it down. He looked up and offered a wan smile that didn't reach his eyes. "Where's my sandwich? You dragged me into a hospital—"

"It's a medical center, actually."

"—*Medical center*, where I spent half the day. As you know, I hate *medical centers*. The least you could do is give me the sandwich you promised."

His act was unconvincing, but I was too worried about Aunt Gillian to keep arguing.

"Okay, your highness. Turkey or ham?"

CHAPTER 16

"Strange fruit"

After lunch, Jack fell asleep on my sofa and I sat down with a novel from the pile I'd been meaning to read. I was ten pages into it when the telephone rang. I jumped up to answer it so another ring wouldn't wake Jack or Aunt Gillian. The caller ID showed Cleveland Police Department. I felt my shoulders tighten as I said hello.

Aunt Gillian's house had been broken into, the detective on the line told me. We had left the house locked up and in the care of a local realtor, who agreed to check on the place in exchange for the listing whenever we were ready to sell. The police got my number from the realtor.

The place was vandalized and ransacked, but according to the realtor, there didn't seem to be much missing from the things we left there when we moved my aunt to Florida. The detective sounded weary and apologetic when he told me that there wasn't much chance of catching the burglars. He thought it was someone from the neighborhood looking for cash. I didn't begrudge him a lack of interest in the case. I knew how overtaxed Cleveland's police department was, and I understood that a break-in at a near-empty house wasn't top priority.

"Someone needs to come here and see to things," the detective told me.

"I'll be there tomorrow."

We made an appointment to meet Tuesday afternoon and I hung up. Only after did I consider the situation. I needed to go to Cleveland, and Aunt Gillian needed to finish her testing. Even if we put off the tests, I didn't relish the idea of traveling with her, especially not back to Cleveland. I thought it might give her ideas about staying up there, and that was not an option. And there was the matter of the house. It should be sold, but I needed my aunt's permission before that could happen. My head began to ache and I set down the book that I'd been clutching.

"Jack," I whispered, not wanting to startle him.

He slept on, and after a few more attempts to wake him, I poked his chest. I leaned over and put my mouth next to his ear.

"Jack." I said it loud enough to jolt him awake. He sat up so quickly we bumped heads.

"Why are you yelling?" He rubbed his head and squinted at me.

"Wake up."

He sighed and slumped back against the couch, glancing at his watch.

"I was only asleep for half an hour."

"My aunt's house was burglarized. In Cleveland," I added when he didn't react right away.

"I know where she lived." He rubbed his eyes and thought for a moment. "You have to go there."

I nodded and stared at him. I hoped he would volunteer without my having to ask.

He stared back until he couldn't stand it anymore. "I can't give her baths and stuff like that. You'll have to hire a nurse, at least for a few days."

I nodded. "Of course. I won't be gone long. Two days, three at the most."

He sat forward now, taking over the planning. "I'll have to get a sub for my classes, and take her to all her tests. Those shouldn't be canceled. We'll go grocery shopping today, and I'll order in all of that comfort food she likes, because I've never cooked cornbread in my life."

I couldn't suppress a smile. "You've never cooked anything besides spaghetti in your life."

"How would you know? You rejected me before I had a chance to invite you over for one of my gourmet dinners."

I stopped smiling. "Rejected *you*? What?" The way I remembered it, he had shown no interest after the first date. What I thought of as our second date—the night at Dean Goldman's house—probably wasn't even a real date.

He thought for a moment, and then waved his hand as if to dismiss his own words. "Never mind. We'll talk about it another time—"

I held up my hand to stop him. I thought I heard something coming from my aunt's room. "What's that sound?"

Jack listened for a moment, his head cocked toward Aunt Gillian's bedroom.

"Singing?"

I stood up and walked down the hall, keeping my steps soft. I put my ear to Aunt Gillian's door. Her voice was a high and clear soprano. I'd never heard my aunt sing before, not once. She had a beautiful voice, and it made me sad that it had taken all these years for me to hear it. I was about to knock, and I realized the song she was singing was one made famous by the woman Aunt Gillian's father had hated all those years ago. My aunt's version of "Strange Fruit" was nothing like Billie Holiday's. Aunt Gillian didn't imbue the words with a lifetime of weariness tinged with hope. You couldn't hear the smoke of a thousand clubs in my aunt's lungs. But from her lips the song sounded just as lovely.

She finished and started another song, a hymn this time. It was an unfamiliar one with melancholy lyrics.

"I'm but a stranger here, heaven is my home
Whatever my earthly lot, heaven is my home;
And I shall surely stand there at my Lord's right hand.
Heaven is my fatherland, heaven is my home."

Aunt Gillian wanted to come with me to Cleveland. "It's my house. I want to go. I have a right to go."

She was standing in the living room, her hands on her hips. This was the most animated she had been in weeks, and it was nice to see the old Aunt Gillian surface, even if she was arguing.

I didn't want to travel with her for a few reasons, most of which were selfish. I wanted to see the condition of the house and deal with the police without the emotion I knew she would attach to the process. Also, I knew that selling the house was a necessity, and I didn't think convincing her would be easy. I wanted to put off that conversation until I'd had time to strategize.

The reason I was most ashamed of was also the simplest. I wanted some time away from her, from the medical tests, from everything. I'd spent the past two months focused on my aunt, and I hadn't stopped to realize how tired I was. Sitting there listening to my aunt fume, I felt the exhaustion settle into my neck and shoulders. I looked over at Jack, hoping he could rescue me. He was so good at being my rescuer, and I knew it wasn't fair, but I needed him to do it again.

He caught my look and understood. He stood up and led Aunt Gillian to the rocking chair she liked. Her back stayed rigid even as she allowed him to seat her.

"Gill, you're right in the middle of your appointments with Dr. Ortiz. Let's call him and ask him what he thinks."

Before my aunt could formulate a reply, Jack picked up the phone and dialed. He then proceeded to have a conversation that was entirely made up.

He hung up after a few minutes and looked at Aunt Gillian.

"He says it's best that you do all your tests at once to make sure the readings are accurate."

I thought she would never buy this vague explanation that didn't explain anything. What "readings?" But my aunt looked at him for a long moment and then nodded.

"Well, Dr. Ortiz would know best, I suppose." She turned to me and frowned. "Can you take care of things back home?"

I offered my sweetest smile. "I'll be back in a few days, and Jack's going to stay with you while I'm gone."

She nodded again. "I trust Jack." They smiled at each other, and I went into my room to pack. I didn't know whether to be relieved that she had given in again, or annoyed that the only person my aunt didn't seem to trust was me.

I loaded up my smallest suitcase with just enough clothing for four days. I hoped I wouldn't be in Cleveland any longer than that. Just before I zipped the case, I decided to put the birth certificate into an interior pocket. As I did it, I had to admit that looking for answers about the past, about my parents, about Lily were the real reasons I didn't want my aunt to come with me to Cleveland.

CHAPTER 17

"The most important things"

Here's what I knew about my parents. They married young, when my mother was eighteen and my father was twenty. They eloped. It was 1968, three years before I was born, a little over two years before they died. Aunt Gillian was much older than my mother, her sister. She was already sixteen years old when my mother was born, making her thirty-four years old when my parents eloped. My parents were Ernest McElroy and Brenda Jones-McElroy. I was named after my father. My aunt said they died in an accident when I was six months old.

I always wondered what my life would have been like if I could have remained Tina McElroy, daughter of Ernest and Brenda, instead of Tina Jones, niece and legal ward of Gillian Jones.

When I was a kid, I used my parents as fodder for my imagination, inventing personalities and scenarios to take the place of the real lives that were cut short. I never wrote down my ideas, preferring to lull myself to sleep at night by replaying the vivid memories I'd created in my head.

My parents were conscientious students like myself, who had planned to attend Case Western right there in

Cleveland until they found out I was on the way. They were happy about this development, of course, and planned to bring me along to their classes in a baby carriage. Or they were lovers at first sight who met each other at a community dance and never looked back. Or they were forced to elope because Aunt Gillian, who was like a mother to mine, disapproved.

Maybe none of these things was true. Or maybe they all were. My aunt was reluctant to talk much about my parents. Her reticence seemed to me cruel and spiteful. All I wanted was to know who I was, where I came from, and she denied me even that small gift.

"Living in the past will get you nowhere," Aunt Gillian told me whenever I asked about my parents. "We can't change what's already happened, so we have to look forward to the future."

I always resented the use of 'we,' because it seemed to me that it was *I* who suffered, not *we*. I was an adult before I considered that I wasn't the only person who had lost something, someone, when my parents died in June 1971.

To be fair, my aunt did provide some information after I begged and harassed her. She claimed not to know how my parents met, or why they eloped. When I was thirteen years old, she told me that she and Brenda were apart for a long time. She had known her sister as a baby, and then as a young woman. Their own mother was not around for most of Brenda's childhood, having been committed to a mental hospital in their hometown of Baltimore soon after her second daughter was born. She died there, my grandmother, not long after she was committed. My aunt claimed not to know why her mother was committed, or how she died, but I knew she was lying.

She went on to say that my mother was spoiled and difficult, which sparked an argument between us. I accused her of being cruel and unfeeling; she accused me of asking for the truth but being afraid to hear it. We were both right.

When I was sixteen years old, she told me that my father was a poet and worked in a restaurant. Just before I left for college, Aunt Gillian told me that my father was a wonderful, sweet man whose love was easy and complete. This seemed like an intimate thing to say about one's brother-in-law, but I was so happy to hear any details about my parents that I soaked it up without question.

I had two photos of my parents. One must have been taken the day they got married at Baltimore City Hall. She wore a pink suit in imitation of Jackie Kennedy, complete with a small pillbox hat and white gloves. She was pale, like my aunt, and her curly hair tumbled to her shoulders. Her smile was bright and genuine. She looked like a kid trying to be an adult.

My father's eyes bore straight into the camera without smiling. He looked serious and a little scared. He, too, was dressed up for the occasion, wearing a dark suit and a crisp white shirt with a maroon striped tie. His dark skin had an eggplant sheen, and his hair was close-cropped instead of the afro style of the time. They both looked more like civil rights volunteers from the 1950s and 1960s than members of the Black Power generation of the late sixties and early seventies.

Here's what I didn't know about my parents: The sounds of their voices. Her favorite breakfast cereal. His dream car. The looks on their faces when they were happy, sad, angry, bored. Their smells. Their laughs.

The most important things.

I took the Tuesday morning flight from West Palm Beach to Cleveland and I rented a car at Hopkins International Airport. I hadn't made hotel reservations before leaving Florida, and when I called around, most hotels were booked. It was early August, a time when people came north to visit family, catch an Indians game and visit the Rock and Roll Hall of Fame before the start of the school year. My flight had been full of families coming from Florida to enjoy the cooler Cleveland weather. They reminded me that my own classes would soon begin. This trip was to be the last break I would have until Thanksgiving.

When I couldn't get a room at the more moderate-priced hotels, I was faced with a choice: stay at my aunt's house while I sorted things out, or take another look at my budget to see just how much I could afford to spend on a hotel.

Two hours after my plane landed, I was soaking in a bathtub the size of a small swimming pool at the Ritz-

Carlton on Third Street. The only suites available cost more than I'd ever paid for a hotel in my life. But taking a long bath at ten o'clock in the morning while I waited for room service to deliver eggs Benedict, I decided it was all worth it. I had never treated myself like this. I'd always dreamed of this kind of luxury, but when I was fat, it somehow seemed like a waste.

Soaking in the bathtub, I couldn't quite let go of the feeling that I was impersonating someone else, that the body my fingers touched wasn't mine. When I lost weight the first time, there had been none of this uncertainty. I didn't stop to think about how different I felt on the inside because of the changes on the outside. Maybe, I thought, as I poured Perrier into a wineglass, that was part of the reason I'd gained the weight back.

After a lazy morning, I decided to go to Aunt Gillian's house and get the worst part of my journey over with. The police officer I'd spoken to said I just needed to itemize what was missing and file a report. I drove to East Cleveland, dreading what I might find at my aunt's old colonial. My dread wasn't a result of sentimentality, since I'd never felt at home there. I just wanted to sell the house and move on, although I suspected that things wouldn't be as simple as I hoped.

For one thing, there was the problem of ownership. Aunt Gillian and I had never talked about power of attorney, and even if she was able to make this kind of decision on her own, I wasn't at all certain that she wanted to sell her home. She'd lived there for more than half her life, and she still referred to the house, and Cleveland, as home.

When I got to the house, I saw the boarded-up window where the vandals broke in. On the first floor, I found broken lamps and the books strewn around the rooms. Unintelligible writing was spray-painted on the dining room wall, and framed prints lay broken on the floor. Upstairs, all the bureau drawers in my aunt's room were opened and the medicine cabinet was torn off. But that was the extent of the damage. I figured the police were right, that this was the work of locals looking for cash. Apparently, they gave up when they found nothing. My room and the upstairs guest room were untouched. Standing there, I shivered and said silent thanks that my aunt was safely in Florida.

I called a cleaning service to come put the house back into shape. They agreed to come right away, so I decided to look around a bit while I waited. When we moved Aunt Gillian in May, we packed the essentials but left most everything else, figuring we would be back one way or another. I stepped into the guest room, which we left intact during my aunt's move. There were boxes labeled *photo albums* in the closet. I thought this was strange, since Aunt Gillian had taken many photo albums to Florida. The ones she had insisted could not be left behind contained photos of her parents and a few of me, and they included my high school and college graduation ceremonies. These photos, she had told me, were the records of her entire life, everything that was important to her. I had to wonder what the photo albums she left behind contained. I dragged out the nearest box and sat on the floor to look inside.

I found photos of my aunt when she was a young woman, just out of her teens. Many showed her standing next to a building or in a field, smiling and shading her eyes with one hand. Other showed her posing with her hip jutted out as she looked directly into the camera, confident and proud. I was starting to wonder why Aunt Gillian had so many pictures where she was the only one in the frame. Then, near the end of the album, I saw the first photo of a young man.

His hair was combed into silky waves. His skin was smooth and pale and he wore a thin mustache and a graduation gown flapping open, under which a suit and tie was visible. He looked straight into the camera, and although the photo was in black and white, I could see how light his eyes were. Hazel, or maybe ocean blue. This, I concluded, must be Jeremiah Jackson, my aunt's ex-husband. When I was a child, before I'd learned that getting information from my aunt was impossible, I used to ask if she had ever been married, and if so, what happened?

Her answer was the same every time. Her face contorted into a polite grimace, and she hissed his name through clenched teeth, adding, "It's always best, if one has nothing nice to say, to say nothing at all."

It was an unsatisfying answer, but it was all that I'd ever gotten. I took the photo from the album and turned it over. On the back, written in my aunt's handwriting, was a notation: *Jeremiah 1952.*

That was the year my aunt had graduated from Howard, gotten married and moved to Cleveland, Jeremiah's hometown. I tried to imagine Aunt Gillian as a twenty-two-year-old woman, fresh and hopeful, but I couldn't reconcile this version of my aunt with the one I'd grown up with. I wondered about Jeremiah. They'd gotten married in 1952, but by the time I was born, he was out of the picture.

I stood up and stretched, still holding the photo of Jeremiah. My uncle. I took it downstairs while I dug in my bag for Lily's birth certificate. I set them side by side on the now-ruined dining room table and I studied the dates. Lily was born in 1971, the same year as my birthday. Was Jeremiah still around then? I pulled out my cell phone, and without thinking about the ramifications, I called information and asked for listings of Jeremiah Jackson. While I waited, I figured there might be too many to sort through. There must be tons of listings for J. Jones, I figured, so I decided not to bother with those. Not yet, anyway. I was on hold for so long I started to lose hope and was just about to hang up when I heard the operator's voice.

"We have one Jeremiah Jackson listed. Please hold for the number."

Before going to the police station to fill out paperwork on the burglary, I headed over to the downtown library on Superior. I wanted to check past editions of *The Cleveland Plain Dealer* to see if I could find out anything about my parents. For whatever reason, this had never occurred to me. Perhaps out of fear, I had always simply accepted the nuggets of information my aunt chose to provide.

But I was thirty-four years old, and it was time to find out more about my family. I ignored the fluttering in my stomach as I sat down to the computer and clicked on *The Cleveland Plain Dealer* icon. I already learned from the reference librarian that the newspaper had computerized its archives back to 1965.

When I typed in my mother's name, just one item came up. I closed my eyes for a moment and took a deep breath before clicking on the link. It was an obituary for my mother. Gillian Jones was listed as the surviving relative. It noted the date of her death, June 1, 1971, and her age, nineteen. But no cause of death was provided. There was no mention of the accident my aunt always referred to when she spoke of my parents' deaths. I had always assumed it was a car accident, but now I realized that Aunt Gillian had never described the accident. I wondered why I had never dared to ask. What kind of person was I that I never asked?

I didn't bother looking up my father's obituary, assuming it would be much the same. I tried a few more searches, using my father's name and then my aunt's, but there was nothing more. I entered Lily's name. Again, nothing.

I sat at the computer for a long while, thinking. What I had found didn't answer many questions. I already knew my parents had died when I was less than one year old. The provided information created more questions. How did they die? Why wasn't I with them? And why didn't the obituaries mention me?

I printed the obituaries and put them in the envelope with Lily's birth certificate. Discouraged, I headed out to the police station. It was getting late and I was tired. All

I wanted was to eat nice meal, lie down, and forget about the past, at least for one night.

The next morning, I got an early start and was headed toward the Shaker Heights address listed for my uncle. I considered calling first, but I wasn't sure he would want to see me. I didn't know what to expect, but I imagined that seeing me might trigger unpleasant memories of my aunt. I knew almost nothing about him, and I had to assume he knew nothing about me. We were strangers. We were family.

I turned into a quiet neighborhood filled with stately brick homes. The expansive lawns were precise and neat, and every house featured bursts of colorful flowers around the front entries. Although it was a Tuesday afternoon, there were Mercedes sedans and BMW sport-utility vehicles in several driveways, making me think this was a neighborhood populated by either stay-at-home moms or retirees of some means.

A white Lexus sat in the driveway of Jeremiah's home. It was a two-story Victorian with yellow and white tulips in clay planters on either side of the door. I parked in the long driveway and took a look at the hundred-year-old oak that shaded most of the grass. I got out and walked to the door, looking inside the Lexus as I passed by it, hoping to find clues about its owner. Two plastic CD cases sat on the passenger seat. I couldn't see who the artists were, but I decided against a closer look. I didn't want the neighbors, or Jeremiah, to catch me peeping into his car.

Bricked steps led up to the door, and a flowered welcome mat lay spotless at the doorway. It occurred to me that the tulips, the mat, and the car all seemed very feminine. Maybe I had the wrong house, the wrong Jeremiah. Maybe he didn't even live here. I rang the doorbell and felt an urge to run back to my car and leave. After a moment, I decided to do just that. Then the door opened.

The man who stood there was tall, well over six feet. His hair was cropped close to his head, but I could still see that it was brown flecked with white. He wore wire-rimmed glasses and a neat mustache and beard, which, unlike his hair, were gray. His skin was the same pale shade that I'd noticed in the photo at Aunt Gillian's house, and it occurred to me for the first time that with his patrician features and skin tone, Jeremiah could pass for white.

Unlike some older men, he didn't stoop. His posture was erect and relaxed at the same time, and he was casual, dressed in soft khaki slacks and a button-down oxford shirt that looked comfortable and expensive. I knew he must be at least seventy years old, or maybe older, but he looked ten years younger.

He held a rolled-up newspaper in one hand and he held out the other. I took it and he led me inside. It wasn't until I was standing on the polished wood floors of his foyer that he spoke.

"You're Gillian's daughter. You look just like her."

I was taken aback. "What? No. I'm her niece. Ernestine Jones. Tina. But she raised me. How did you know?" I was babbling. No one had ever told me I looked just like Aunt Gillian. I had found the right Jeremiah Jackson.

He raised his eyebrows and smiled. "Niece? You're named after Ernest McElroy?"

I nodded, wondering why he seemed to find this so surprising.

"He was my father." I figured he must already know that, but his question seemed to demand a response.

He nodded. I had the feeling he was agreeing to let something go for now.

"So I guess you know who I am."

I nodded again. I had lost my voice. He looked at me for a moment, still smiling.

"I read about Gillian's house in the newspaper." He answered my question before I could ask. "It wasn't a big story, just a little blurb, but I read the paper every day. Cover to cover."

He gestured with the rolled-up newspaper. We stood in the foyer a few moments longer, and I grew embarrassed at my silence. I was a college professor, a grown woman, and I couldn't think of a thing to say to my uncle.

"Why don't we go to the living room? I'll make some tea."

"That would be nice."

I followed Jeremiah down the hall to the back of the house, where the hallway opened out into a spacious living area. I sank into a deep sofa and looked around the room. The walls and the sofa were all pure white, complementing the cherry wood floors. The room was large and open, with a cathedral ceiling and tall windows along one wall. The white linen sheers were pulled closed, but through the gauzy fabric I could see an enormous back-yard. I was struck by the simple beauty of the house, and I wondered how a man with such refined sensibilities could have loved Aunt Gillian, even all those years ago.

The room was sparse: two sofas, two comfortable-looking chairs, and floor-to-ceiling bookshelves along two of the walls. Like me, Jeremiah was a reader. I got up to look at the books. I have always believed that you can tell a lot about a person by the books they read. Jeremiah's shelves were filled with history books and paperback mysteries. I was wondering what this said about him when he returned with a blue and white ceramic teapot, teacups, and a plate of small butter cookies on a silver tray.

After he poured the tea, I decided to tell him the simple truth.

"I know it's strange for me to just show up here. I just want to know more about my family, and I thought you might be able to help."

"And Gillian won't talk about the past."

At that moment, I relaxed. We had Aunt Gillian in common.

"You know how she is. Or you did know at one time, anyway. That's one of the things I wanted to ask you about—if you don't mind."

Jeremiah titled his head to the side and looked toward the windows. After a while, he turned back to me.

"I don't mind your asking. I'm an old man, living alone. It's nice to have company." He paused. "But maybe you could answer a question for me before we start."

"Of course. I should tell you about myself before interrogating you, Mr. Jackson. I'll answer any questions you have."

"I just wondered about Gill. How is she?"

There it was again. "Gill." The way he said it was familiar and gentle, and I knew then that he still felt something for my aunt.

"She's good. She's okay, I mean. Getting older. She lives with me in Florida." I didn't want to tell him about her problems. Not yet.

He smiled and sat back in his chair. "Call me Jeremiah."

CHAPTER 18
"She was more beautiful than ever"

It wasn't love at first sight. Jeremiah felt he was in a position to avoid such entanglements. In September of 1952, the Korean War was still going on, but Jeremiah had been back in the States for several months. He'd joined the Army out of boredom rather than a true desire to serve his country. He was not so naïve as to believe that America was a black man's country. But joining was what young men did, and so Jeremiah went.

He was lucky in that he never got near any actual military conflict. He was stationed in Seoul with a unit that wrote Army-approved dispatches that purported to tell the truth about the conflict. He had no parents, having grown up in a Cleveland orphanage, and so there was no one to whom he could write letters about the spoils of war, which, for Jeremiah, meant sheltered Korean women who yearned for the kind of carefree sexual excitement he was happy to provide.

He remained in Seoul for more than two years before another stroke of luck befell him. He was injured in an automobile accident involving several American military vehicles. He suffered a broken leg and collarbone, and these injuries were just bad enough to earn Jeremiah a medical discharge but not bad enough to cause permanent damage.

When the third stroke of luck occurred—his acceptance to Howard University based, as far as he could tell, on his status as a former soldier, Jeremiah concluded that he was in fact a very lucky person. There had always been evidence of this. Despite the fact his mother died giving birth to him and he had never known his father, his life in the orphanage had not been unpleasant. This was due to his instinct, developed early on, that capitalism was the key to self-preservation. He learned to steal extra treats from the communal lunch tables and then barter them to other children who were hungry but not as brave as he. As he grew older, Jeremiah figured out how to get other items in high demand—cigarettes, the occasional beer, candy—and he sold them to all takers. He operated this miniature black market until he was seventeen, when the nuns who operated the orphanage found him out and gave him a choice: discontinue his enterprise and stay another six months until his eighteenth birthday, or find his own way out in the world. The next day, Jeremiah lied about his age and joined the United States Army.

When Jeremiah arrived on Howard University's campus in the fall of 1952, he was twenty years old, a bit older and much wiser than most other freshmen. He was among the first of the servicemen returning from Korea to continue their education on the GI Bill. He and the others honored an unspoken agreement not to congregate together or discuss their war experiences. When he saw another former soldier, who were always recognizable by a slight flatness in their gazes, Jeremiah nodded but kept going. They did the same.

He had been on campus for five days when he spotted Gillian. She was standing near the biology building, standing erect in a crowd of giggling girls. Gillian was the only one not giggling. She was gazing at some spot outside the group—Jeremiah couldn't tell what. There was a small, sardonic smile on her face. It occurred to him that she was the leader of this group and they vied for her attention. He suspected that she parceled out her attention in bits or not at all.

He was about fifty feet away, strolling toward the biology building for his one o'clock class, when she turned to look at him. Her eyes were black, in sharp contrast to her pale-honey skin. Her dark hair fell in a straight curtain down her back, and she wore a straight skirt and a cashmere V-neck sweater that emphasized her curves. She reminded him of the women he had known in Seoul. The shared the same confidence and held themselves apart from emotional entanglement with Jeremiah, as if they knew they would be hurt if he got too close.

Jeremiah held her gaze until he passed her to enter the building. Just before he pulled open the door, he turned to see if she was still watching him. She was, with one of her eyebrows raised a bit. The smile still played on her lips. He was laughing at him, mocking him for turning back. This made him smile.

It was not love at first sight. Jeremiah found himself in demand among coeds, and he had no plans to limit himself to just one, however shiny her hair and devilish her smile. He made his lustful way through the entire chapter of Sigma Mu Beta sorority and was working his way through their arch rival, the Thetas, before he spoke one word to Gillian. She was not a sorority girl, and since these girls had been his initial focus (they were well organized, making for easy targets), it was three months before he had the opportunity to meet Gillian.

It was just before Christmas break, and the crowds on campus were thinning out as students went home to families in and outside the Washington, D.C. area. Jeremiah had no plans to leave, since there was no home to return to. Instead, he intended to find an apartment off-campus where he could entertain his conquests with more privacy. He would also need a part-time job to pay the rent. After his first semester, he had decided that studying was overrated and he dropped his biology classes in favor of history classes that came easy to him. He'd always had a mind for dates and stories, and history was nothing if not a collection of stories. He considered economics, but he decided that he had learned all he needed to know about commerce at the orphanage.

Switching to a history major gave him more time to pursue young women, many of them fresh from high-school cotillions in their small Southern hometowns. He liked these small-town girls best. They were the most impressed by his fabricated war stories. Having his own apartment would only help him sweet-talk these innocent young girls (who were later not so innocent), and he was on a mission.

He was walking across campus, intent on finding a newspaper with local real estate listings when he saw her. She was sitting on a bench on the quad, wrapped in a heavy winter coat to fight off the forty-degree chill that drove most everyone else inside even though the sun offered a bit of warmth. She wore no hat and her hair rustled loose in the wind, strands flying their own way at random. He noticed that she wore black wool pants under her coat, a rarity for women on campus, who wore skirts and full makeup whenever they were seen in public. She was reading a book that was too small and narrow to be a text-book. He sat next to her on the bench and she looked up.

He offered his most charming smile and waited for her to respond. She watched him smile for a long while, a slight frown on her face. He took her silence as an invitation to speak and tried not to be dismayed by the fact that she did not seem the least bit charmed.

"I'm Jeremiah." This had been his simple, standard opening approach to his college conquests. He thought it made him seem older and more mysterious than his younger competition, who stuttered and gave away their intention before they spoke a word. This approach had worked. First, the young women returned his smile. Then they took the hand he offered, and he held their soft hands just a few beats too long. It was enough.

But Gillian ignored his hand and didn't smile.

"I know who you are."

His smile broadened. "You say that like it's a bad thing." He paused to offer her the opportunity to banter back. She remained silent.

"You're Gillian, right?"

Although they had never met, Jeremiah had made it his business to find out all he could about her. She was studying to be a nurse, a bookworm who managed to be one of the most popular—and least attainable—women on campus. For that first semester, Jeremiah was quite busy with his sorority girls, but he always knew that he and Gillian would cross paths.

No one on campus seemed to know much about Gillian's family, only that she had a sister who was much younger and that she still lived in her hometown, Baltimore, commuting in a shiny 1949 Ford sedan rather than living in a dorm. This lack of a clear pedigree bothered the class-conscious crowd that was desperate to have Gillian as one of their own. They loved her pale skin and long hair, but her refusal to play the Who-Are-You game frustrated them. Jeremiah, who had no interest in such things, having no pedigree of his own, suspected that this was how Gillian kept herself aloof from the crowd.

He thought she would be impressed by his efforts to find out about her.

"Why are you asking me my name when you clearly already know it?" she snapped at him and looked back down at her book. He tried to see the cover, but she held it so he couldn't read the title.

Her coldness annoyed him, but he was not one to shy away from a challenge.

"Just trying to be friendly. You should try it some-time." He said this in a mild, teasing tone and sat down on the bench next to her. She moved as far away from him as was possible.

They sat there for a while, she pretending to read, he pretending to be unbothered by her reticence. She exhaled a heavy sigh, closed the book and put it into her bag.

"Why?"

"Why what?"

"Why are you being nice to me? Why should I be nice to *you*?"

He didn't care for the emphasis she placed on "you." He also didn't have an answer to her direct question, which felt more like an accusation. Jeremiah's specialty was seduction, and one of his rules was the less talking, the better.

He blushed and felt something unfamiliar—confusion. Jeremiah had been to war (sort of), had suffered terrible abuse in an orphanage (depending on your definition of abuse), and was struggling to put himself through college (struggle is a relative concept). He did not blush.

Seeing the pink in his cheeks was what got Gillian to smile. Jeremiah was unable to think of a comeback that would salvage his dignity, so he stood up and left without another word.

One thing Jeremiah did not do was lie to himself. He knew that Gillian's rejection of his charms, her apparent lack of interest in him, was not without cause. He did not placate himself by deciding she was in some way deficient. She was the first woman he had met who saw through his act, who saw weakness where most others saw strength. And he knew she was right. Why should she be nice to him? He had proven himself unworthy of her attentions by approaching her as if she were just another conquest. She deserved more, and he knew it.

He was prepared to be honest with himself, but he had no intention of changing. Weighing his options, he decided that Gillian, however beautiful, however intriguing, could not be his. She understood him, without even knowing him, and that was a problem. Jeremiah did not want to be understood. He wanted to have fun while he still could, before he was forced, by age or by circumstance, to be responsible.

More than three years went by before he and Gillian spoke again.

By April of 1956, Jeremiah and Gillian's class was preparing to graduate from Howard University. She was considered the best nursing student in her class, and he was known, once again, as the man who could get you whatever you needed. He didn't deal in contraband, since college students had access to the cigarettes and liquor that orphans did not. Jeremiah dealt in desire and weakness: the desire for academic success and the mental weakness that made this impossible for some.

He had discovered that the college was full of the progeny of the growing black bourgeoisie, the sons of teachers and businessmen who were expected to go on to be doctors and lawyers. It was their birthright. They were the talented tenth that W.E.B. DuBois believed would lead the black masses. They had vast economic resources, relative to the general black population, and impeccable social standing.

There was just one catch. Many of them, Jeremiah realized, were just plain dumb. No one knew better than he that money and class can't buy intelligence. But someone had forgotten to let the bourgeois progeny in on this secret. So they floundered in their classes and risked both expulsion and social humiliation until Jeremiah came along. He was the savior they could not acknowledge, and they paid him for it. He wrote their papers, helped them cheat on tests, and crafted their presentations. He had a natural ability in many subjects, and he was not stingy about sharing it. As his customers' grades rose from below average to exceptional, Jeremiah's reputation grew, along with his savings.

This lasted until Jeremiah, and many of his customers, were due to graduate the next month. Jeremiah didn't have enough fingers to count the men who would be graduating because of him. If he had placed ads in the newspaper, he would have emphasized his ninety-nine percent success rate. It was the one percent that got him into trouble.

Jon Johnson was a student who was born and raised in Washington, D.C. He looked the part of the privileged, and he spoke the part as well. He told people that his family was descended from Frederick Douglass, and he earned a solid reputation around campus based on his famous ancestor. Jeremiah alone knew this was a lie. He had written a research paper on Frederick Douglass for Jon just three months ago, and he supposed that if Frederick Douglass was Jon's great-great-grandfather, he would know something about him.

Jeremiah didn't care, of course. He was a hustler, and he was happy to let other hustlers conduct their business in peace if they offered him the same courtesy. But he could see that it bothered Jon that someone saw through his attempts to impersonate the black middle class. Their dealings had always been strained, and Jeremiah considered this further evidence of Jon's lack of pedigree. The true bourgeoisie didn't care what Jeremiah knew—he was a means to an end.

There was also another thing, so insignificant that Jeremiah forgot about it. The first time they'd met, which had been at the beginning of their senior year, Jeremiah laughed when Jon introduced himself.

"Your parents named you Johnson Johnson? They must not have liked you much." Jeremiah was joking, but he could see the fury building in the other man's eyes.

"It's Jonathan," he said, his voice tight. "My parents named me after the famous writer Jonathan Swift. But you probably don't even know who that is."

Jeremiah stopped laughing and looked at Jon, who he was certain *was* named Johnson Johnson. What he saw was a flawless presentation, the right clothes, the right hair, the right mannerisms. And he knew that Jon was not what he appeared to be. He was trying too hard.

Jeremiah, always the savvy businessman, held out his hand as a peace offering.

"Hey, Jonathan, I'm sorry. I was just joking around a little, letting off some steam. Friends?" Jeremiah smiled and waited. After a brief hesitation, Jon shook his hand. The inevitable small talk ensued before Jon asked how much Jeremiah charged for his services.

Jeremiah nodded and winked at Jon. "Well, Jonathan, let me make you a modest proposal."

One of the things Jeremiah had always regretted was not heeding the warning signals Jon Johnson gave off. He thought him a harmless phony, not worthy of serious consideration. In one of the last transactions of his college career, Jeremiah wrote a poem for Jon's creative writing class. He'd been clear that poetry was not his forte, preferring short stories and essays based on characters he had known in the Army. But Jon had insisted that he needed someone to write the poem, and Jeremiah agreed to do it, although in private he thought that imagination and creativity were certainly qualities possessed by a man who told people he was named after an author whose work he hadn't even read. Jeremiah had even gone so far as to offer Jon a reduced rate, since poetry was not his specialty. Jon insisted on paying full price, which did not raise Jeremiah's estimation of his intelligence. But he accepted the money and delivered the poem.

It was not one of his best efforts, Jeremiah thought. But it was good enough for Jon Johnson. He wrote it out carefully on a sheet of paper and delivered it on time.

You are a spoiled plum
Dark and soft
Yielding to my touch
Your scent is syrup, mild
After the first bite I taste the truth
Fleshy and weak
Fetid and bitter

Hating you
Is dark chocolate melting in my mouth
At winter's dusk
I shouldn't do it
It's not good for me
I'll be sorry later
Lick the outside
Sink my teeth into the middle
It feels so fine
Heavy and decadent
A pleasure to rival the feel
Of a woman's lips on my thigh
You are not what I expected

Two weeks later, Jeremiah was walking across campus one night around eight o'clock, intending to hit the library for a couple of last-minute jobs. As he walked, he considered the campus and knew that he would miss this time, these buildings, even the people, although he didn't call anyone a true friend. Jeremiah was a loner by nature, and he was okay with that. After graduation in May, he planned to return to Cleveland, which he thought of as home even though he had never had a real place to call his own there. He'd heard from an old Army buddy that real estate was cheap there, and he planned to open a legitimate business with the money he had earned in college. He was smart enough to know that hustling came in all shapes and sizes, and he also knew there was one thing people always wanted: to forget. So he planned to open a liquor store, and he envisioned it becoming a franchise down the line.

He was mulling over what to call his franchise when Jon stepped out from the shadows of the health-sciences building, a new edifice that now housed premed and nursing students.

"Hey, Jonathan, what are you doing out so late? Past your curfew, right?" Jeremiah was disconcerted by the way the man had appeared as if from nowhere, but he didn't show it. He'd found that his dealings with Jon were best if he teased the other man just enough to let down his guard. Most times, it worked.

"You fucked with me." Jon looked sweaty and agitated.

Jeremiah frowned, trying to remember if one of his recent conquests had belonged to Jon. He didn't think so.

"What do you mean?"

Jon had been standing a comfortable distance from Jeremiah, but he stepped within a foot. Jeremiah wanted to push him away, but there was a wild look in Jon's eyes that worried him. Instead, he took two steps back as Jon spoke.

"You fucked with me."

"You said that. But I don't know what you mean." Jeremiah wished he had resisted the urge to be sarcastic, but it didn't seem to change Jon's demeanor in any way.

"I got an F. You fucked me." Jon's voice had risen in volume and pitch, and he reaching into the pocket of his jacket. This, more than anything, concerned Jeremiah. The jacket was suitable for skiing and was much too heavy for the pleasant spring night. He tried to stall.

"An F? On what?"

"On the stupid poem you wrote. Now I'm not going to graduate." Jon's right eye twitched, and now he was yelling.

Jeremiah had only a second to consider his options. Try to talk his way out of this, or run. He ran.

He couldn't say how far he got when he felt the bullet tear into him. He didn't know where he had been hit, just that the bullet was in him, somewhere, and it was the worst pain he had ever experienced. He screamed and fell, and then there was darkness.

When he woke up in the hospital, he felt groggy and his vision was fuzzy from the pain medication. He didn't know where he was or why. He looked around the room and saw Gillian standing next to his bed. In his haze, she was more beautiful than ever, and for a moment he believed she was an angel.

After a few moments, he remembered the sound of the shot, and the blackness. Jeremiah didn't know why she was there, but he was happy to see her.

"I love you," he said. The blackness returned.

CHAPTER 19
"Think positive"

When I returned home from Cleveland, I had a week to prepare for all my classes. I had spent the summer dealing with Aunt Gillian and the past, and I had not thought about myself at all. In the past, this would have been a perfect opportunity for me to gain back all the weight I had lost, using my busy schedule as an excuse not to take care of myself. But now things were different. I was different. Instead of eating more when I was distracted, I ate less. When I stepped on the scale, I saw that I had lost another ten pounds without even trying.

"You look skinny."

Jack sat at my desk, sipping coffee. It was our tradition to meet in the mornings, chatting before we got on with our day.

I had arrived early, leaving Aunt Gillian's care to the temporary nurse Dr. Ortiz recommended.

"It will be a while before we have an official diagnosis, but I don't think it's best for you to try to handle your aunt's care alone."

He had taken me aside at our last visit, the day after I returned from Cleveland. Jack distracted Aunt Gillian while we spoke.

"Best for whom?"

He smiled at me, and I noticed for the first time that he had deep dimples in both cheeks.

"For both of you."

Our eyes held for just a moment longer than necessary. I wondered if he was flirting with me.

"Well, thanks, Dr. Ortiz."

"Please, call me Tim."

Aunt Gillian had surprised me by being receptive to the idea of professional help. It was clear that Dr. Ortiz—Tim—was right. We both needed some time apart, and she needed better care than I could provide.

Back in my office at the university, I felt more like my old self than I had since Aunt Gillian moved to Florida. It seemed like a lifetime had passed since I'd taught a class, read an article, sat and enjoyed a cup of coffee with Jack.

I smiled at him. "Thin? I'll take that as a compliment."

He shrugged. "Well, don't overdo it."

"You can't be too thin or too rich, right?" I laughed, but he didn't join me.

"You have to be *healthy*."

"I'm not going to waste away, worrywart." Despite his nagging, I was overjoyed to be thinner than I'd ever been. It was nice not to be afraid to look in the mirror.

"So, how's Gill adjusting to the new nurse?"

"She doesn't say much, but I take that as a good sign. She seemed happy to have me out of the house, actually."

Jack laughed. "At least her spirits are up. When will you find out about her diagnosis?"

Neither of us liked to say the word *Alzheimer's*. If we said it aloud, that made it real.

"Well, Tim said it would probably be at the end of this week."

Jack's expression darkened. "Tim?"

"Dr. Ortiz."

"I know who you meant. I had no idea we were on a first-name basis with *Doctor* Ortiz."

I busied myself, opening drawers, looking for a pen even though I had nothing to write.

"He asked me to call him Tim," I mumbled, my head down as I examined the stapler and paper clips in my top drawer. I could feel Jack watching me, but I wouldn't look up. If I met his gaze, he would see that I had been thinking about Tim as a lot more than my aunt's doctor.

"I'll bet he did." Jack's voice was sarcastic, bordering on nasty.

"What's the big deal? He was just being nice."

Jack was silent until I could no longer resist looking at him. He sat still, watching me, his brow furrowed.

"What?"

"Just make sure Doctor Feelgood doesn't get too friendly. He's Gill's *physician*. Remember that."

I offered a laugh that was meant to sound casual but came across forced.

"I have no interest in Tim, except as a doctor," I lied. "Why do you care, anyway?"

He looked uncomfortable. "I want Gill to get the best care possible, and if this guy is hitting on you . . ."

"Well, he's not." I cut him off and stood up. "I'm going to get more coffee."

Without asking him if he wanted any, I snatched his half-full cup off my desk and stomped off.

When I returned, we changed the subject by tacit agreement. It was my first opportunity to tell Jack what I'd learned in Cleveland, and I gave him an abbreviated version of Jeremiah's story. Jack listened with the same fascination as I had to the tale of Gillian as a young woman.

"So what about Lily?" he asked when I finished.

I shook my head. "That's the thing. When I asked about her, he just said, 'I don't know any Lily.' But I got the feeling that he was lying."

"About all of it?"

"No. Just about Lily."

My week was filled with faculty meetings and refining syllabi for my fall classes. I would be teaching a class on African-American poets, a first for me and the university. I was up for tenure at the end of this academic year, and I knew I would be evaluated, in large part, based on the success of this class. If I could draw lots of students, it would go a long way toward supporting my tenure candidacy.

I studied black poetry in graduate school, but Mizner University wasn't as progressive as it could be in terms of offering a diverse selection of courses. People who favored the traditional Western canon argued that students were more comfortable with what they called "established tradition." They claimed classes on African-American poetry wouldn't attract enough students. I argued that true literary tradition reached beyond Dickens and Dickinson. I spent a large part of the last academic year campaigning to add a new class as a test case. The administration had relented, if only to shut me up. I didn't care why they'd added the class. I was thrilled to have the opportunity to teach something different, something close to my heart.

I spent all day Thursday deciding which poets to include and which to leave out. The class outline was broad; I had pitched it as a survey class in order to garner support. But I wasn't sure that was the best way to engage the students. I'd decided to focus on the twentieth-century poets to make the material more accessible to the students. Now it was just a matter of picking from among some of my favorites. Langston Hughes, Gwendolyn Brooks, Sonia Sanchez, June Jordan, Rita Dove. They were givens. I also wanted to include some lesser-known poets, and I spent a pleasant morning browsing through my books looking for good candidates.

It was almost noon, and my stomach had just begun to protest when the telephone rang. Dr. Ortiz's assistant wanted to schedule appointment for me and Aunt Gillian for the next morning. Her test results were back, and the doctor wanted to discuss them.

I made the arrangements and hung up, feeling a churning in my belly that reminded me of my childhood. I'd felt this same churning on the first day of school when

I looked forward to a new year and a new start, but I knew that nothing would change, that I'd still be the fat girl, the smart girl, too, but always the fat girl. The cute, popular girls would treat me as if I were a part of the background, as if I were nothing more than an uninteresting poster on the wall. It was that indifference that hurt. I would have almost preferred outright cruelty because it would have been a validation of my existence. The churning lasted for the first few days of a new school year, the physical manifestation of hope and dread.

I had a lot more work to do, but I couldn't concentrate, and whatever hunger I had been feeling was gone. I packed up my books and papers and left the office. I found myself driving south on A1A, looking at the ostentatious mansions next to each other across from the beach. In Palm Beach there were no high-rises on the east side of the street. The town was elitist and self-sufficient, enabling it to resist the pull of money-makers like condos right on the beach. If you lived on Palm Beach and you had a beach view, there was at least a road in between your home and the sand, and sometimes vegetation remained to further separate you from the Atlantic Ocean.

In South Palm Beach, east of Lake Worth, there was no such distance between humans and nature. Condos dotted both sides of the street, and majestic homes gave way to convenience and practicality. You could drive along A1A in Palm Beach without seeing a soul for miles (the really rich people frolicked in private), but the walkways just a bit farther south were dotted with people out for exercise, even in the middle of the day in hot South Florida summer. These people were not the snowbirds who populated the island during the fall and winter months. These were hearty holdouts who had given up their northern homes, out of financial necessity or optimism, and lived here full-time. These people called their two-bedroom units in the high-rise buildings home year-round, and their dark, leathery skin attested to their determination to live out the rest of their lives in the sun, even if it beat down on them without mercy in the ninety-degree dog days of August.

I couldn't blame them for not wanting to stay inside under the protection of coolness. Despite the architectural sterility of many of the condominium buildings, South Palm Beach was lovely. In certain places, the island of land between the Intracoastal and the ocean was so thin that it was a wonder that anyone ever felt confident building on it at all. I always marveled at the nerve it took to build an entire town on a strip of land less than a mile wide. It was a good thing the development of Florida had not been in my hands, or else it would still be a swamp.

I drove on, turning up the air-conditioning as I watched those brave souls walking in the humid air, not thinking too much about Aunt Gillian or school or anything of import. I just wanted to clear my head, and being close to the water always did that for me. Whenever it got too hot, or I felt too lonely, I always went to the water to remember what was magical about this place, about life.

I soon found myself going through Ocean Ridge, east of Boynton Beach, then Gulfstream and Delray Beach. This was, in my opinion, the best people-watching beach in the area. It combined a long, wide public beach area with a variety of small restaurants on the west side of A1A and room for in-line skaters, runners, and dog walkers to enjoy the scenery. I decided to stop at Café Luna Rosa, just south of Atlantic Avenue, for the lunch I'd forgotten I needed until the fragrance of focaccia bread and cappuccino reached inside the cool cocoon of my car.

I parked in the public lot and walked back to the restaurant, which was crowded even on a Thursday afternoon in August. After ordering a turkey and provolone panini and iced tea, I pulled a folder out of my bag. I had been collecting information on Alzheimer's, dementia, and caring for elderly parents ever since Aunt Gillian came to live with me, and I wanted to look over the research to prepare myself for whatever tomorrow's appointment would bring. I had two options here: become an emotional mess at the prospect of my aunt's possible illness, or treat it like a project. I chose the latter.

The first paper I pulled out was titled "12 Ways to Boost Caregiver Success." I had gotten it from the Alzheimer's Foundation of America, and until now, I hadn't done more than glance at it as I pulled it off the printer. The page contained a list, and as I read it I checked off the things I had done:

1. Educate yourself about the disease.
2. Learn care-giving techniques.

3. Understand the experience of your loved one.

4. Avoid caregiver burnout.

5. Maintain your own physical and mental health.

6. Discuss the situation with family and friends.

7. Do cognitive stimulation activities with your loved one.

8. Foster communication with physicians.

9. Take care of financial, legal, and long-term care planning issues.

10. Smile.

11. Think positive.

12. Reach out for help.

I figured I had number one, two, five, six, eight, and twelve under control. I placed numbers three, four, seven, and nine at the top of my to-do list. Number eleven seemed like a stretch, and I wasn't sure I was capable of number nine. These last two seemed to require a closer, more intimate relationship than Aunt Gillian and I had ever enjoyed. I wasn't sure we had the time or the willingness to change that now.

I closed the folder and looked out past the beach to the still water. I had never thought of my aunt as a mother, even though she was the only one I'd ever known. She had always been a reminder of everything I wasn't. She never stopped showing me in ways obvious and less so that I was a disappointment. Now she had taken over my life, and I had to admit that I resented it. My career was going well, I had lost the weight, and I was settling into a comfortable, if sometimes lonely, routine.

Then she fell, moved to Florida and became the center of my world. I wished that everything could be the way it was, but I knew that was impossible. What I didn't know was how I was going to face the future, which most certainly would include Aunt Gillian. She and I were connected by blood and by necessity.

Until this moment, some part of me had thought of Aunt Gillian's moving in with me as a temporary solution. I hadn't considered what the permanent answer would be, but a combination of warm, salty air, the smells of an Italian café, and a twelve-item list from a web site made it clear that Aunt Gillian was here. For good. The question was, now what?

Aunt Gillian was quiet the evening before our appointment with Dr. Ortiz. I had been trying to improve her diet, cooking meals that combined something sinful (fried chicken, meatloaf, buttery mashed potatoes) with more healthy fare (salads, steamed vegetables, whole-wheat pasta). When she was feeling ornery, my aunt complained about the healthy food and said it tasted like cardboard. When she was feeling charitable, she tasted small amounts of it and left most of it to the side. Tonight, I had forgotten to stop at the grocery store, and all we had in the house were tomato soup and the makings of a salad. I served this without comment, waiting for Aunt Gillian's negative reaction.

We sat down and she began to eat.

"You like tomato soup?" I knew I should have left well enough alone, but her calm alarmed me. I wanted to pick a fight so she would get back to being her cranky self.

She just shrugged. "It's as good as anything, I suppose."

"When I was a kid, you *hated* tomato soup."

She didn't even raise her head to look at me when she spoke.

"That was a long time ago."

There had not been many times in my life when Aunt Gillian refused to take the bait for a fight. I changed tactics.

"How was Elaine today?"

Elaine St. Cyr was a home-care nurse recommended by Dr. Ortiz. She was young, just twenty-five years old, but she had an air of efficiency that I'd liked when we interviewed her. She charmed me when we met, with her light Haitian accent and her tendency to laugh with her mouth wide open and her head thrown back. When she arrived at our door, I vowed to call Dr. Ortiz for another recommendation, mostly because Elaine was gorgeous. She was tall and I had to look up at her. She had the kind of creamy caramel skin my aunt had always admired (while expressing dismay at my own dark complexion), and her long, braided hair was sandy at the roots.

Elaine looked as if she could have been on the cover of *Vogue* instead of standing in my foyer in bright pink scrubs and Nike sneakers with a matching pink swoosh. Add the fact that she had perfect teeth and model-quality cheekbones, and I was prepared to loathe her.

But she won me over. When Aunt Gillian came into the room, her look of disdain and superiority at the ready, Elaine won her over as well by complimenting her on her drab housedress and asking her about the old days at Howard, where, it turned out, Elaine had always wanted to go to college.

While I quizzed Elaine from my long list of interview questions, my aunt beamed at her, and I soon surrendered to their girlish bonding. I had expected Aunt Gillian to resist the idea of a day nurse, but she was receptive to Elaine. I suspected that she saw herself in the young nurse. In many ways, Elaine was the person Aunt Gillian had planned to be, before she met Jeremiah and everything changed.

Elaine had been with us for about a week before we saw Dr. Ortiz. When I mentioned her name, Aunt Gillian raised her head and smiled.

"Elaine is a lovely girl. She went to Howard, you know."

I debated whether I should correct her or not. At our first meeting, Elaine told me that she had *wanted* to go to Howard, but her family had no money to send her, and she couldn't quit her job to return to school. There were brothers and sisters left behind in Haiti who battled daily to find food and safety amid the civil unrest there. They needed her.

I decided it didn't matter. If it made Aunt Gillian feel good to believe certain things about Elaine, what harm could there be?

"Yes. She's very smart. Is she nice to you?"

I made a point of asking my aunt about Elaine each day. I had heard so many horror stories about how home-care health providers could abuse their patients without family members even knowing until it was too late. I had a good feeling about Elaine, but it didn't hurt to double-check.

"She's nicer than you. She wouldn't make me eat tomato soup, knowing I hate it," my aunt snapped.

I smiled. "Good. That's good."

Jack had asked to come with us the next day, but I told him I thought it would be better for my aunt if just the two of us went. In truth, I thought it would be better for me, since there was still some tension between Jack and me since our tense exchange about my calling Dr. Ortiz Tim. I knew this wasn't supposed to be about me, that I should be thinking about my aunt first, and I knew she would be fine having Jack there. But I wasn't quite that selfless, and I asked him to stay away.

CHAPTER 20
"Sweet dreams"

The actual moment of diagnosis was anticlimactic. It confirmed what we already knew, giving a name to what we already lived with every day.

It was the early stage of Alzheimer's, Dr. Ortiz told us, looking into Aunt Gillian's eyes as he spoke. There were new treatments, ways to slow the disease's advancement. We had options, he said. He handed both of us a copy of the Alzheimer's Foundation of America brochure that I'd already downloaded from the web. I pretended to read it, but Aunt Gillian set hers aside without even glancing at the cover.

"There's no cure."

She held Dr. Ortiz's gaze for a few moments. She wanted him to say it aloud, to utter the truth into the room so it could not be denied. She didn't want to hear about options, treatments that would prolong what was unavoidable. Her back was straight and stiff. I realized that she was more aware of, and perhaps more horrified by, the changes in herself than I'd given her credit for.

"No. No cure."

She nodded and picked up the brochure, fanning herself in a slow, rhythmic motion as if the room had grown warm. We sat there for a long time, listening while Dr. Ortiz displayed a remarkable optimism, outlining all the options he envisioned for Aunt Gillian's care. I was diligent, taking notes and asking the right questions. All the while, Aunt Gillian sat still but for the slow movement of her hand, fanning, fanning.

For the rest of the week after Aunt Gillian's diagnosis, we wandered around without much sense of purpose. It seemed things should change, or that there should be action taken. But I was already doing everything that could be done at that time. Now, I was trying to figure out how I would manage life with Alzheimer's.

On Sunday, Jack called me. I was reading through one of my fall textbooks, and when I answered the phone, I realized I had no idea what I'd just read.

"We should take a trip."

I frowned. "A trip? Now? You want me to leave my aunt after she just found out she has Alzheimer's?"

"No, I mean with Gill."

"So you're suggesting that the three of us go somewhere. Together. Now. Have you been drinking?"

He laughed. "Seriously. We could go somewhere fun. Somewhere we've never been."

"I don't think it's a good idea. I mean, a trip isn't going to change anything."

I knew I was being stubborn, but I felt as if I had no energy since the doctor's visit. It was all I could do to just cook and keep my aunt on some kind of schedule. I couldn't imagine planning a trip.

"Of course, it won't change anything. But it would take your mind off things for a while." He paused. "It would take her mind off things."

Selfish. That's what I had been these past few days, thinking only of how this affected me, not focusing on how devastating it must be to my independent, head-strong aunt.

"So it's not just about me, then?" I tried to make a joke, but it fell flat.

Jack's voice was soft. "It is about you, and Gill. I think the trip will be good for both of you."

I didn't answer.

"Come on, Tina. I'll plan everything. I'll even pack your luggage."

I had to laugh. "Sounds like an offer I can't refuse."

Jack developed the list of criteria for our trip: on the American continent; reachable within four hours; somewhere none of us had ever been; reservations could be made to travel within the week; and it had to be fun. Niagara Falls was the only place that fit.

I objected. "Isn't that kind of touristy?" I said when Jack showed me the brochures.

"We *are* tourists."

Aunt Gillian clapped her hands like a girl when we told her.

"I always wanted to go to Niagara. Jeremiah promised to take me, but he never did. But you're a better man than him, so you'll take me. And I think I'll ride in one of those barrels."

Jack and I exchanged skeptical looks. The idea of my aunt going down the falls in a barrel was both horrifying and hilarious. He smiled at her.

"So Niagara Falls it is!"

I shook my head and looked at the top flyer. It advertised the *Oh! Canada Eh? Dinner Show*. I read aloud.

"You'll meet singing Mounties, lumberjacks, and Klondike Kitty. Klondike Kitty sounds a little dirty, doesn't it?"

Aunt Gillian swatted at me. "Keep your mind out of the gutter, Ernestine. Jack is not that kind of man."

He cackled and I shook my head.

"This is going to be a fun weekend, right, Gill?"

She wound her arms through his and gave me a smug look.

"Right, Jack."

He planned our trip down to the hour. It was to be a quick trip, just a weekend. We both thought it best that we keep it short, since Aunt Gillian could be unpredictable. The next Friday, we flew from Miami to Buffalo, then drove to Canada. We decided first-class would be a better option, albeit expensive.

On the airplane, Aunt Gillian slept for the first hour of the trip. Then she awoke, wondering in a loud voice where she was and why it was so noisy. We had taken a late flight, thinking she would sleep in the dark. The airplane was completely quiet before she awoke. I couldn't meet the eyes of the other passengers seated near us as I tried to calm her down. In desperation, Jack flagged the flight attendant, ordered a vodka and orange juice, and fed Aunt Gillian sips until she nodded off.

After the crisis was averted, Jack resumed the position he had adopted as soon as we sat down. Stiff arms ending in hands grasping both arm rests, eyes narrowed and staring straight ahead, teeth clenched.

"You're afraid of flying?" I leaned across the aisle, whispering.

His shoulders twitched. I thought it might be a shrug.

"I wouldn't say I was afraid."

"What would you say?"

He glanced at me. "I get airsick."

I considered this. When he came to Cleveland to help me with my aunt, we had taken separate flights. But on our first date, he had planned to take me up in a small plane, a plane so small it had a propeller. If that didn't make him sick, I don't know what would.

"What about that little plane you used to have? What did you call it? Elsie? Ellen?"

He frowned at me. "Eleanor. That's completely different."

"How so?"

He sighed. "When I got sick in Eleanor, no one was there to see it. This plane is full of witnesses."

I laughed. "And I thought you were mad at me for throwing up all over Eleanor."

He managed a tight smile. "I was just glad you threw up before I did."

Something occurred to me. Jack was the one who had suggested this trip. A three-and-a-half-hour flight, all for me and Aunt Gillian. He knew he would feel ill the entire time, and he never once said anything. And then all he had to look forward to was a weekend with a sick old woman and me, struggling to figure out what to do about it all. Any other man would have run the other way. But Jack was here, the skin on his knuckles taut, his teeth grinding, buying drinks to pacify Aunt Gillian.

"Why are you staring at me?" he growled.

I looked over at my aunt, who was snoring softly, slumped back in her seat. I looked back at Jack.

"Thanks for this."

"For what?"

"The trip. For always knowing the right thing to do."

Our eyes met and held. I thought he might say something to explain why he was always there when I needed him. I let myself daydream that it was about more than friendship. He looked away first.

"It's no big deal. I always wanted to see the Falls."

Since we booked our trip at the last minute, we didn't have many choices for hotels. We chose a Victorian bed-and-breakfast near the Horseshoe Falls because it was the only place that had two rooms available. Each of the rooms had only king-sized beds and seemed to be designed more for couples on a "special getaway" than a woman, her platonic male friend, and her senile aunt with an attitude problem. Under different circumstances, the house, with its bright yellow paint, heavy red velvet drapes, and aged wood floors might have been romantic. In our case, we just agreed that Aunt Gillian and I would share a bed. We put away our clothes and went out to see Horseshoe Falls.

When we woke up Saturday morning, the sky was cerulean and the air was crisp and cool. It was a welcome change from Florida in August, where humidity was the rule and we spent summer days hopping from one air-conditioned location to another. The Florida sun was bright but brutal, lulling me into the hope of outdoor relaxation, then slapping me in the face with its heat.

That late summer day in Niagara, the sun seemed to make a promise it would keep, vowing to warm us under the sixty-five degree air and the mist from the falls. We awoke early that day, and it was a good day for Aunt Gillian. She was talkative and smiling, even though she kept insisting that she wanted to ride the falls in a barrel.

"Before we look into the barrels, how about a visit to the botanical gardens?" Jack suggested.

"Do they have roses? I love roses. That's Ernestine's middle name, you know."

I frowned at the use of my full name and Jack grinned at me.

"Ernestine, could you check to see if they have roses?"

I snatched the sheaf of papers from his hand.

"The visitor may schedule an overall view of a great variety of gardens in an afternoon self-guided tour, or may linger for days or even weeks to savor the subtleties of the plant world as seen in the herb garden, the vegetable garden, the rose garden, or the splendid arboretum, embracing one of Canada's finest collections of several hundred trees and shrubs," I read from the tourism website printout.

She nodded. "I knew it. Jack always knows the best places to go." She grabbed her purse. "Well, Ernestine, are you ready?"

I stuck my tongue out at Jack. "I'm ready, Aunt Gillian."

I was not the kind of girl who knew the names of birds and flowers, who knew the cuts of diamonds, who understood the difference between taffeta and satin. So I was surprised at how much I enjoyed the botanical gardens. Aunt Gillian went straight for the roses and Jack and I wandered off to the nearby herb garden, which smelled of oregano and basil, reminding me of a sumptuous Italian meal, maybe angel-hair pasta in an olive oil and herb sauce, or a many-layered lasagna smothered in marinara.

Jack took a deep breath. "Smells like an Italian restaurant here," he said, closing his eyes. "A good one."

I smiled. "All we need is some garlic bread and a bottle of red wine."

"Merlot?"

"Shiraz."

Jack bent over to look at one of the batches of herbs. He breathed in, closing his eyes again, and I watched him for a moment. He looked so peaceful, the lines of his jaw relaxed.

He held out his hand behind him.

"Come smell this."

He wiggled his fingers, so I took his hand and let him draw me closer. His citrus smell mixed with the fragrance of the herbs. I held my breath for a moment, wanting to savor the feel of his hand against mine. His palm was smooth and his fingers tangled firmly with mine.

"Isn't this great?"

I knew he was talking about the herbs. I let out my breath and nodded.

"Yes, it's great."

Then we heard Aunt Gillian calling. "Jack. Come see these tea roses."

We walked toward her voice, our hands still entwined.

That night we ate at Mamma Mia's. Aunt Gillian's mood turned sour. She berated the server for bringing too much bread.

"Ernestine can't eat all that bread. You should know that," she told her.

When the confused waitress walked away, I excused myself and followed her.

"I'm sorry about that. My aunt, she's . . . not well." I found it difficult to say my aunt had Alzheimer's.

The waitress nodded and smiled when I handed her a twenty. It was a preemptive strike, since I knew that when Aunt Gillian got like this, it got worse before it got better. We could leave, or I could pay off the waitress.

"For your trouble."

She smiled. "Thanks. My grandmother had Alzheimer's, so I know how old people can get sometimes."

Hearing the word out loud made my stomach clench.

"Thanks. For understanding."

She nodded. "My mom took care of Grams up until the end. It was hard." She paused and I could see tears welling. "But my mom, she stayed strong."

I nodded. She gave me another fleeting smile before dashing off to the kitchen. I hurried back to the table, hoping my aunt hadn't caused more trouble.

Aunt Gillian ordered penne pasta. When it arrived, she claimed she had ordered eggplant. Jack placated her by offering to trade his chicken parmesan for her penne. She traded plates with him, took one bite and complained that the food was cold. I could see steam rising off the plate, but I knew better than to argue with her. She was loud, and I could feel the eyes of the other diners on us as her voice grew more strident. I wondered what they were thinking, but I didn't have the nerve to meet their eyes. I kept my eyes on my plate or on my aunt. Jack did most of the talking to Aunt Gillian. She never seemed to get mad at him, whereas she disagreed with everything I said.

Jack just agreed with all of her demands and offered solutions that caused a minimum of fuss. We ate quickly and left a large tip on the way out.

Things only got worse when we arrived back at the bed-and-breakfast. As we were getting ready for bed, Aunt Gillian glared at me.

"I don't need a baby-sitter."

"What?" I was in the middle of changing into my pajamas. My body felt sore and weak, as if I had spent the day in physical combat. I was starting to think this trip had been a mistake.

My aunt was already in her nightgown. She slipped into the bed and lay right in the middle.

"I'm perfectly capable of sleeping alone."

"But Aunt Gillian—"

"Get out!" she demanded.

I weighed my options. I could argue with her and sleep upright in a chair. I didn't think it was a great idea to leave her alone, but I could take the room key and remove anything that could hurt her if she got up in the night.

I looked over at my aunt. Her eyes were closed and I thought she was asleep.

"Stop staring at me and get out."

I sighed. I made a brief reconnaissance trip around the room, taking a few possibly dangerous items with me, and left. I went next door and knocked. After a few moments, Jack answered, his face half-covered in shaving cream.

"You shave at night?"

He looked down at the razor in his hand. "You knock on men's doors at night wearing your pajamas?"

I shrugged. "Touché. Now can I come in?"

He stepped aside.

"Aunt Gillian kicked me out."

He laughed. "So now you're homeless?"

"Just roomless. Can you take in a poor waif?"

He pretended to consider it for a moment. "I suppose so. But the waif has to agree not to criticize the generous benefactor for shaving at night."

"The waif agrees." I sat down on a chair while he went into the bathroom to finish shaving. Sniffing the air, I now knew why he always smelled of lemons.

I looked around the room while I waited. My gaze fell on the king-sized bed, and it occurred to me that unless someone slept in the chair or on the floor, Jack and I would have to share a bed.

He appeared in the doorway of the bathroom. He was wearing just a t-shirt and shorts, and I became aware of how little clothing we were both wearing. I wore light cotton pajama pants and a tank top. We had seen each other in bathing suits, but somehow this seemed more intimate.

He looked over at the bed.

"So."

"So."

There was a long pause. I tried to read his expression but couldn't. He cleared his throat.

"Maybe I should sleep in the chair," he suggested.

I was sitting in the chair. It was stiff, okay for a brief stay, but I couldn't imagine spending eight hours in it.

"I couldn't let you do that. It's too hard." I weighed my words, not wanting him to think I was coming on to him. If it was a come-on, he would have to respond somehow, and I was afraid his response would be no, thank you. Or worse, hell no.

"Maybe we could sleep in the bed together? I mean, not *sleep together*, but in the same bed. It's big enough. We wouldn't have to touch. I mean, well, you know what I mean."

He held up a hand to stop my babbling. "I know what you mean, Tina. It's not like you came over here to seduce me."

Maybe I did want to seduce him. Maybe I could have argued with Aunt Gillian, or just waited for her to fall asleep, and then crawled into bed with her as we had arranged. Maybe I did mean this all as a come-on. But Jack didn't even seem to think that seduction was a viable possibility.

I shook my head. "Right. So, good night, then?"

We moved toward opposite sides of the bed. I raised the duvet and slid in, and Jack did the same. We hugged the edges of bed, careful not to let any parts of our bodies brush.

Jack clicked off the lamp and the room plunged into darkness. There was just the sound of Jack's breathing and the smell of his shaving cream. I wondered what he was thinking.

"Sweet dreams, Tina."

"You too, Jack."

His breath grew deeper and more regular. I thought I would never fall asleep lying this close to Jack, wanting to touch him but afraid to. I lay there, listening for sounds of Aunt Gillian next door, wishing the night would pass faster so we could go home and the torture of lying inches away from Jack would end.

But I must have fallen asleep, because I started awake just after dawn. I was facing the window and I could see the night haze fading into daylight. As the fog of sleep cleared, I realized that Jack's body was pressed against mine, his arm thrown over my side. I thought about moving away, not wanting him to wake up and be embarrassed or regretful. But I didn't move. Instead, I memorized the feel of his chest against my back, the feel of our thighs touching, the feel of his breath on the back of my neck.

When I woke again, the sun was up and I heard the shower going. Jack was singing an off-tune version of "Staying Alive." I smiled and missed his body next to mine.

CHAPTER 21

"Sometimes, not knowing is a gift"

After our Niagara Falls trip, our daily lives didn't change much in the wake of Aunt Gillian's diagnosis. Elaine became our permanent nurse instead of temporary caregiver. She worked days, and it wasn't long before I stopped thinking of her as an employee and started thinking of her as a friend.

I was fifteen years older than she, and the more we talked, the more I saw that we had led very different lives. If she had been born in America, she would have been Homecoming Queen, one of those girls who are popular with guys because of her beauty and popular with girls because they knew all the guys. She had gone to high school in the States, but being an immigrant had made her afraid to immerse herself in the frivolity of American adolescence. She could not forget that most of her family remained in Haiti. No matter how few new outfits she had each school year, her family had even fewer back home.

So she had studied instead of dating, and we had that in common, though our reasons for doing so were different. Also, we both had been raised by aunts. Elaine was sent to the States by her mother, who stayed behind to care for five younger siblings.

Elaine's aunt had died years ago.

"That's why I like Miss Gillian so much. She reminds me of my Auntie Hermione."

We were sitting on the back patio, enjoying one of the first cool breezes of the season. It was October, and the cool air was the first hint that summer was giving way to what passed for fall in these parts. It was Columbus Day, and I had decided to celebrate the day off by grading no papers, writing no articles, and returning no phone calls.

My aunt was napping, so I'd asked Elaine to share a pitcher of iced tea and enjoy the late afternoon air.

I smiled at the idea that Aunt Gillian would inspire fond memories. As they had become more comfortable with each other, Elaine and my aunt had settled into a familiar routine that I envied. But lately, the more help Aunt Gillian needed, the more she asserted her independence. She'd even insisted on cooking us dinner one night. Jack, Elaine, and I spent the meal choking down sugary, overcooked rice, underdone boiled chicken, and a salty peach pie.

"Your aunt Hermione must have been an interesting person."

Elaine gave one of her wide-mouthed laughs. "She had good spirit. Like Miss Gillian."

"Spirit. I suppose that's one way to look at it."

This time, we laughed together.

The next day, I felt rejuvenated when I returned to my office and classroom. By this point in the semester, the college community was settling into its routine after the relative freedom of summer. My students in particular seemed more relaxed than they had been at the beginning of the semester.

Back in August, I had noticed that many of my students were reticent, watching me with what seemed like suspicion. I had become an unknown quantity and they weren't sure what I was up to. This seemed odd to me, because I'd been teaching at the university for years and most students knew me by sight, if not by experience. It took a week for it to sink in: Many of them hadn't seen me since last winter, when I'd lost all the weight. I'd been on campus during the spring, but it made sense that the weight loss wouldn't have registered if they hadn't been in one of my classes. Also, students tend to see their professors as extensions of the classroom, not as human beings with personal lives. Being fat had been a part of who I was as a teacher, and I did not compute as a thin person.

All of this occurred to me at the end of the first week of classes, when a student in my black poets class made an offhand comment as she was leaving the room.

"You look good."

She had stopped in front of the desk where I was stuffing papers and books into an old leather messenger bag I'd had since college. I looked up at her and smiled. She was a senior, I remembered, one of a group of black students who sat in a group near the front of the class. From what I could tell about her in the few class meetings we had had, she seemed interested but not eager. She had been attentive in my early lectures, but paid just enough attention to her friends so as not to come across as a complete nerd. She was petite and walnut-skinned, with a long tangle of curly hair that looked like a very expensive, well-maintained weave. She was pretty in a serious way, and I had wanted to like her.

I smiled at her words, although I wondered whether it was appropriate for a student and a professor to comment on each other's appearance. Then I realized that she wasn't smiling back, and I wondered whether she had meant it as a compliment at all.

Since I had lost the weight, I noticed that not everyone was happy for me. Certain colleagues expressed what seemed like dismay at my weight loss, and I'd overheard snide comments about stomach stapling and starvation diets more than once. Men were happy for me, or didn't even notice my appearance, depending on whether they were looking for sex. But women were all too often critical and seemed disappointed at the prospect of my smaller-sized thighs.

This student seemed to be one of those women. I decided to keep smiling.

"Thanks."

She nodded but said nothing else. The encounter was on the verge of being uncomfortable, so I cut it short.

"Well, have a great weekend." I went back to gathering my things and she left. I shook my head. All my life I'd dreamed of being thin, and now that I was, it was like I was learning about the world all over again. People saw me as a different person, and even though I resisted the notion, I had to consider that maybe they were right.

I soon learned that despite the smooth transition Elaine had made into our lives and the myriad of treatment options Dr. Ortiz suggested, life with a chronically ill person was never calm for long. In late October, we received a form letter from Dr. Ortiz's office, saying that he would no longer accept the health insurance Aunt Gillian had carried for years. When I'd asked about insurance during that first hospital visit in Cleveland, she had told me that Medicare was for poor people and that she, Gillian Jones, was not poor. She paid extraordinary premiums for health insurance, but she claimed it was worth it to be able to avoid what she termed "government-sponsored quacks."

I called Dr. Ortiz's office to explain our situation and find out what our options were. The secretary provided referrals to other physicians for my aunt. She asked me what insurance I had and I told her.

"You know, the best thing would be to get power of attorney from your aunt and put her on your insurance as a dependent."

"Thanks." As I hung up, I was pessimistic about the chances that Aunt Gillian would be persuaded that she was no longer able to handle her own affairs. And I also knew that number nine on the Alzheimer's Foundation of America's to-do list had just risen to the top of mine. "Take care of financial, legal, and long-term care planning issues. Try to involve your loved one in decision-making, if they are still capable of providing input, and consider their wishes related to future care and end-of-life issues." Not only would I have to talk to Aunt Gillian about her finances, but I knew this would involve a trip back to Cleveland.

I obsessed over the perfect way to approach my aunt. Firm and uncompromising? Gentle and persuasive? Acknowledge that this was a big deal? Pretend it wasn't? I couldn't make a decision, and in the end, I was too scared to ask Aunt Gillian about the power of attorney. I let Jack do it. He came over the Saturday after we received the letter from Dr. Ortiz's office. It was an overcast, cool day so he invited Aunt Gillian out for a walk.

She giggled and preened, as she always did when Jack flirted with her. "I'm not as quick as I used to be, you know."

"Well, then, I guess we'll just have to amble instead of walking," he said, grinning as he covered her shoulders with a sweater and took her arm in his.

I spent the entire time they were gone making various deals with a God I wasn't on familiar terms with, but it turned out that I could have saved my prayers for another time.

"Jack and I decided that you should handle all my affairs," she said breezily as she took off her sweater and sat down on the sofa. She sat straight and still, but I could tell the walk had winded her. I reminded myself that, Alzheimer's aside, she was getting older and didn't have the stamina she used to.

"I never liked worrying about all that stuff anyway. Did Elaine make lunch?"

I opened my mouth to ask what stuff she was talking about, since power of attorney means different things to different people. Would she agree to give me full control of her finances and health-care decisions? Or did she envision limitations? As if reading my mind, Jack looked at me and frowned, and I stopped. Aunt Gillian couldn't even remember that it was Elaine's day off—I shouldn't expect her to make a complex legal decision after a twenty-minute walk around the neighborhood.

"Soup and sandwiches for lunch, Aunt Gillian." I said this in my perkiest voice and avoided correcting her about Elaine.

"As long as it's not tomato. I hate tomato soup." Jack and I smiled. I mouthed "thanks" to him and followed them into the kitchen.

The following week I canceled my Monday and Tuesday classes to meet with an attorney Jack knew from his days working at his engineering firm. We'd had dinner with him and his wife a few times, but the last time ended badly after his wife had made a nasty comment about an overweight couple a few tables away. She had assumed that we skinny people were aligned against the fatties. That was the last time I had seen the couple. But Jack's friend was smart and seemed very nice, and he was clearly embarrassed when his wife had made the comment. At the end of our meeting, I wrote him a check for his retainer. He would handle the logistics of the power of attorney and the sale of Aunt Gillian's house. All I had to do was have the remainder of her things moved to Florida. I drove straight to Palm Beach International from the meeting and boarded a flight to Cleveland.

It was rainy and cold when I arrived. I always remembered this about Cleveland: the dreary atmosphere was a prelude to the endless, dank winters. Of course, Cleveland was, and is, more than the sum of its precipitation levels and cloudy days. But in memory, I was always swathed in layers of clothing that separated me from others who were dressed the same. We couldn't speak through our woolen scarves, we couldn't feel through our gloves, we couldn't hear through our hats and hoods. This was the Cleveland I returned to, perhaps for the last time. I donned my seldom-used peacoat and I didn't believe I would ever miss this city.

The movers offered to pack Aunt Gillian's things for me, but I insisted on doing it myself. I wanted to see if there was anything else in her house that would provide clues about the past, about my parents, about me. I didn't find any more photo albums, but I did find a loose photograph at the bottom of a dresser drawer in the spare bedroom. It was a picture of my father and Aunt Gillian, smiling at each other instead of looking at the camera. The photo was a close-up of their faces, so I couldn't see where they were. Their smiles revealed little except happiness, and I figured that my mother must have taken the photo. It was nice to see Aunt Gillian smiling. I slipped the picture into my bag and continued packing.

Later in the day, I called Jeremiah. After thinking about his story, I had the impression that however much he had told me, there was more that he was leaving out. I wanted to know how he had convinced Aunt Gillian to marry him, why they'd gotten divorced, what more he knew about my parents. I wanted to know about Lily, and I knew he could tell me. The question was, would he?

He answered on the first ring, as if he was expecting my call.

"I'm sorry to bother you again. But I have so many questions. I was hoping we could meet again, that you could tell me more about my aunt. About Lily."

I hoped that by mentioning Lily it would somehow get him to admit he knew something about her. I still believed he had lied about not recognizing the name.

He sighed. There was the sound of rustling, maybe a newspaper or the pages of a book.

"I've already told you too much. Why don't you just ask Gillian?"

I paused. "Well, I can't ask her. I mean, I can, but I'm not sure she can answer."

I tried to be vague, but he was too alert.

"I understand if Gill won't answer. But she can't? What do you mean?"

"She's sick. Alzheimer's."

He caught his breath. A long time passed before he spoke again. I wished I had told him before. I wished we could meet instead of being on the telephone.

"I'm sorry for that. No matter what Gillian thought about me, no matter what happened, I always loved her." His voice was sad, resigned. I imagined that my aunt wasn't the first person he had known with this terrible disease.

"So you see why I want to come see you again? I need to find out more, about my parents, about Lily."

"Look, I understand why you want to know. But did you ever stop to think that there were reasons Gill never told you all this? Good reasons?"

"Now you sound like my aunt."

He laughed. "Is that so bad? Gillian Jones was a hard woman in a lot of ways. But she was a smart woman. Smarter than me, smarter than anyone I ever knew."

I was frustrated, sensing that he wasn't going to tell me more.

"So you won't help me?"

Another pause. "Let me tell you about my family. I was an orphan for a long time, and I don't remember much about my family except this. I think I was just three or four years old when my grandmother told me the story of the night my mother was born. It was like a bedtime story to her. She talked about herself, my mother, and my grandfather like they were characters in a play instead of my family."

Jeremiah told his story in a mechanical voice, as if he had never told it before and it felt unnatural on his lips.

"My grandfather's name was Carl," he began. "He was one of those hard men who believed that beating a woman was a necessary element of a marriage. Women needed to be kept in line so they would stay at home and do their jobs. I always asked my granny why she was missing two teeth on the side, and when she finally told me, I was sorry I asked.

"She was pregnant the last time Carl beat her. She had this long dark-red hair, and she remembered that when her head hit the wall, she couldn't tell where the blood was coming from unless she touched the wound.

"Carl kicked her in the stomach, over and over. Granny curled into a ball and stared at her hands. She always remembered how white her knuckles got as she clutched her knees, waiting for the next blow, and then the next one.

"Carl's beatings were more vicious because Granny was what they called a half-breed. Actually, she was probably more white than black, but she didn't try to pass, and somehow this made Carl angrier than he would have been with a brown-skinned woman.

"When the blood started gushing down her thighs, she whimpered for Carl to help her, telling him the baby was coming. He spat in her face and left. She never saw him again, and that night my mother was born.

"Delilah Jones was a ten-pound baby with a head full of curly, reddish-brown hair. She looked just like Carl. Granny was never able to have any more children and she hated Delilah for reminding her of my grandfather.

"When the nurses asked her why she named the baby Delilah, she told them it was from the Bible. It meant that her daughter would always look out for herself first and never let a man control her."

Jeremiah paused. I could hear the heavy sound of his breathing. He sniffed once, and I wondered if he was crying.

"That's all I remember about my family. Some nasty little story about an abusive grandfather, Granny, and a mother who left me in foster care for good."

The sadness settled around my shoulders like a cloak. "Why are you telling me this?"

His voice was impatient. "So you can understand that sometimes, not knowing is a gift."

I started to reply, but he stopped me.

"Good-bye, Tina. Good luck."

The line went dead.

⌇

I didn't want it to end there. I wanted to tell him I was sorry for all he had endured, sorry that his family abandoned him. I wanted to make him understand that I couldn't live with not knowing.

But he was an old man, and he had given me a lot already. I didn't have the heart to bother him anymore. I stayed in the hotel room, watching television with the sound turned down too far to hear until I drifted off to sleep.

⌇

The next day, I made a stop at city hall, where I applied for a copy of my own birth certificate. I must have had one at some point when I was younger, in order to get a driver's license and a passport, but I hadn't needed it in years and I couldn't find it in my files. It was just a piece of paper, but it was a link to my parents. At this point, any connection to them was better than nothing.

On the way to the airport, I drove back to Aunt Gillian's house, surprising myself with a sudden burst of sentimentality. I had spent my childhood here, much of it lonely, most of it unhappy. But it would always be home, and I expected never to see it again. I strolled through each room, lingering in my old room, touching the places on the walls where my posters of Michael Jackson and Prince had been. I remembered Aunt Gillian's horror at Prince's overt sexuality, and how I'd snuck off to see *Purple Rain* behind her back. I remembered the pleasure I took in listening to music in my headphones night after night, escaping into the sounds of that strange mixture of pop, soul, and rock that was eighties music. I remembered Will, and I remembered secret snacks shoveled into my mouth before my aunt could catch me. I remembered the girl I was, and I let myself feel proud of the woman I had become.

I couldn't say I would miss the old house, and I didn't miss the girl who'd lived there. But even the bad memories had a certain sweetness to them. They were mine.

CHAPTER 22
"Tell me about Lily"

The Monday before Thanksgiving, Marvin, the plastic surgeon from the hospital, called. I was off for the week and Elaine had taken Aunt Gillian out to a movie. My aunt had never shown any interest in movies when she was younger. When I was a teenager, she had refused to let me see *The Breakfast Club* and most of the other films that defined my adolescence. She claimed that watching people pretend on screen was a waste of time, that if I wanted to get into medical school, I needed to study. I was already an A student, and I already knew I didn't want to go to medical school, so I sneaked out to see matinees on afternoons when I was supposed to be studying. There was a lot about school that I didn't tell Aunt Gillian, including the fact that the homework was so easy for me that I finished it before the end of seventh-period study hall.

Now she loved going to the movies. Maybe it was the first time in her life that she needed to escape from reality. Or maybe she just liked the taste of the oily popcorn Elaine bought her. Either way, going to the movies had become a weekly treat for my aunt. She often could not recall the movie she had seen, or she recounted the plots of popular 1950s-era movies that were not playing at the Muvico 25. It fascinated me that a woman who, at some point in her life, had loved movies enough to remember every detail of *Imitation of Life,* had spent much of my childhood advising me *not* to go to the movies.

So I was alone in the house that Monday afternoon when my cell phone rang.

"Tina? This is Marvin."

It took me a few moments to remember who he was. I hadn't thought much about him since the day we met. I assumed he wouldn't bother to call me, and I didn't really care. I had been too busy with school and Aunt Gillian to entertain much else.

"How are you?"

There was an awkward pause. He filled it by asking about Aunt Gillian's care. I told him it was nice of him to be concerned and waited for him to reveal the real reason for his call.

"Tina, I know this is out of the blue, but I felt like we had a connection when we met. I wondered if you'd consider going to dinner with me."

I wasn't sure I'd call what we experienced a connection, although he was one of the most handsome men I'd ever seen.

"Dinner?"

"Just dinner."

I went over the pros and cons. Cons: seems like a superficial jerk. Pros: handsome, doctor, wants to take me out; I'm bored and I need to get out of the house.

Before I could talk myself out of it, I decided that Marvin could be just what I needed to take my mind off everything at home.

"Dinner sounds great. Saturday night?"

"Perfect."

Later that day, Jack came over to say good-bye. He was leaving the next day to spend Thanksgiving with his father and stepmother in Phoenix, a trip that he had been dreading for months. Jack's relationship with his father was just as conflicted, in different ways, as mine with Aunt Gillian. He respected his father for raising him alone after leaving Jack's alcoholic mother. But his father had been generous with his financial support and distant with his emotions. When Jack turned sixteen, his father told him he was a man now, remarried and moved to Arizona. He left Jack to live with friends, sent him a monthly stipend and set up a college fund. He told him to fend for himself in all other matters. Jack raised himself through his adolescence and now visited his father only under duress. This time, duress came in the form of a rare plea from the woman who had been his stepmother for twenty-six years but who still was a stranger.

"Your father and I are getting older," she had told him.

"Is Pop okay?"

"He's seventy-five years old. For an old man, he's okay."

Jack wanted to tell her to call him back when his father was not okay, but he was too good a man for that. So he was flying to Phoenix Sky Harbor International Airport the next day.

"I don't even like turkey," he complained, plopping down on the sofa next to me.

What I said next was a mistake, although I didn't know it until after I said it.

"This guy I met at the hospital just asked me out. Marvin." I was still so wound up after talking to Marvin that Jack's anger didn't register for a moment.

"You met a guy at the hospital?" He glared at me.

"What? You always say I should get out more." I was startled by the force of his disapproval. I remembered the argument we had had in my office about Dr. Ortiz.

"At least he's not Aunt Gillian's doctor," I teased.

"That's not funny." He looked away. There was that attitude again, the one that seemed a lot like jealousy. I was pretty sure he dated. Why shouldn't I? Instead of saying that, I told him about Marvin, thinking the story would make him laugh.

"Then he as much as said I needed Botox," I said, trying to laugh and make it all seem lighthearted.

"He sounds like a creep."

"He is kind of a creep. But I just need to get out, do something different. I can't sit here every night. You said I needed to get a life, remember? I deserve to have a life? Well, I'm doing it."

Jack stood up and walked to the door. "I can't believe you." The door slammed behind him. I sat still on the sofa for a while, trying to understand what just happened. Then I called Monica, who was driving down the next day to spend Thanksgiving with me. I told her that Jack was leaving, Elaine was spending Thanksgiving Day with her cousins, and I needed someone to help me with Aunt Gillian. It was true; I did need help in a practical sense, but what I needed even more was her company.

I told Monica about Marvin, the date, and Jack.

She sighed. "Why are you always the last to realize things?"

"Realize what?"

"Jack is in love with you. Tina, tell me this isn't news to you."

But it was. We'd had that disastrous first date years ago, the second date that wasn't really a date, and since then there had been no romantic interest on his part. I was too impulsive, too bookish, too *me* for Jack. Inside, I was still the fat girl, and I couldn't believe that Jack wanted me.

"Jack doesn't love me." I waited for Monica to convince me otherwise. I wanted him to love me so much I couldn't bear any false hope.

"Right. So I guess his hanging around your mean old aunt, going all the way to Cleveland to help you pack her stuff, being there for you whether you were fat or skinny—all that he's just doing for his health. When was the last time he dated anyone?"

I thought about it. "He dates."

"Who?"

A few years ago, I was at Jack's house and noticed an invitation to an engagement party lying on his coffee table. The envelope was made of expensive card stock: sophisticated, elegant, perfect. Tate Newcomb's parents had requested Jack's presence at their perfect party thrown at a perfect hotel in Palm Beach. The heavy cream paper, the embossed lettering, the smooth script—it all rose up from the table, mocking me. You are not good enough, it said. You will never be good enough.

This Tate was getting married to Matthew Miles. I recognized the name. He was a state senator from our district. The newspaper columnists loved him. He was on track toward Congress, the governorship of Florida, maybe even the White House, some people said.

A knot formed in my stomach. The Newcombs must be a prominent family. Was this the type of woman Jack wanted? How could I compete with that? Then I reminded myself that I wasn't competing with anyone—Jack and I were friends, and that was it.

I put the invitation back in the envelope and walked to the bookshelf where Jack kept his photo albums. I picked one out and flipped through the photos. There was one of a woman, a professional shot of her shaking hands with another woman at an event. She wore a sleek auburn bob, which looked like it was created every morning via an hour of careful blow-drying. Her makeup was subtle and she wore a tailored black suit that must have cost a fortune. It fit precisely on her trim, exercised figure. Tall black heels completed the outfit. Her porcelain skin shone with good health and wealth. I pulled the photo out of its sleeve just to make sure. *Tate Newcomb 1999* was written on the back in Jack's handwriting.

I heard Jack walking back into the living room. I put the photo away and turned to look at him.

"Who's Tate Newcomb?"

"A woman I dated. She's getting married."

His voice was casual, as if Tate Newcomb didn't matter. But something in his tone made me suspect he was lying.

"So you're still friends with Tate?"

He shrugged. He was holding a tray of iced tea and cookies. He set the tray down and picked up the invitation. A small smile played on his lips.

"Tate doesn't really have friends. Not in the way you mean."

This was cryptic. "So why would she invite you to her engagement party?"

He laughed. I detected a note of bitterness there. "Probably to show me what I'm missing out on."

"What does that mean?"

He sat down, television remote in hand. "Tate and I used to be engaged."

My jaw dropped open.

"I never knew you were engaged."

He turned on the television, his eyes focused on the screen.

"It was a long time ago. Before I knew you."

He looked at me briefly. "Why are you so interested in ancient history?"

I tried to look as if I didn't care.

"I don't know. It just seems weird that you never mentioned it before."

He changed channels, found the Food Network.

"Yeah, well, it didn't exactly end well. I wasn't good enough for Tate and her parents. Not a senator."

So Tate had broken up with him. Did he still have feelings for her? Creeping jealousy left chill bumps on my arms.

"So are you going?" I could see he didn't want to talk about it anymore, but I couldn't stop myself.

He shook his head. "I already know what I'm missing." His face brightened. "Look, Bobby Flay is on."

I tried to forget about Tate. "Jack, Bobby Flay is always on."

He smiled at me. "And that is what's great about the Food Network."

If Jack dated other women in the time we had known each other, he never told me about it, which was how I wanted to keep it. Don't ask, don't tell. Ignorance is bliss. Whatever. I preferred to think Jack wasn't with other women. I could say with certainty that neither of us had been in a serious relationship since we had known each other. I didn't feel like telling Monica about Tate. I redirected the conversation.

"Jack and I had that date, remember? No sparks."

Monica laughed. "Who said there were no sparks? You made that up to justify the fact that the date was a disaster. And didn't he meet you when you were hauling your fat ass around the YMCA?"

I felt as if I were on trial. I wished I hadn't called Monica.

"If he loves me, why hasn't he said something?"

"He just did—when he practically begged you not to go out with this Marvin guy. Who, by the way, does sound like a huge creep. What kind of guy picks up women in the medical center cafeteria?"

"He didn't pick me up. Whatever." I feigned a casual tone, as if none of this was important. Then I changed the subject.

"So when does your flight get in? I'm making a turkey. We'll eat ourselves silly and pass out afterwards."

I knew Monica wasn't buying it, but she let me off the hook.

"Tomorrow morning, and you'd better not keep me waiting."

Thanksgiving was peaceful. Like me, Monica had never gotten along with my aunt. Since Monica used to be overweight, too, my aunt disapproved of her as well. Unlike me, Monica said exactly what she thought instead of trying to subvert and avoid. They had several tense but polite discussions—everything from politics to

Monica's dress size (back when we were both still over-weight). Monica always said that Aunt Gillian meant well, but that was no excuse to let her get away with murder.

At first, Aunt Gillian showed no signs that she recognized Monica. She treated her with cool civility, as if she were a stranger instead of my first and oldest girlfriend.

"It's just as well," I told Monica while my aunt watched the Macy's Thanksgiving Day parade on television. "There's no sense arguing with an old lady."

During dinner, we were quiet, eating the turkey and trimmings I'd ordered from a gourmet market near campus. Aunt Gillian broke the silence.

"You might be skinny now, but you'll be fat again. I can always tell when someone's going to end up being fat."

I looked up, assuming she was talking to me, but my aunt was staring right at Monica. I tensed, readying myself for battle.

Monica had always bristled at my aunt's barely veiled insults over the years, so I didn't think she would take well to overt cruelty. But instead of fighting back, she just laughed.

"Well, Ms. Jones, we'll see. We'll see."

Aunt Gillian laughed along with Monica, and I just shook my head and dug into my food.

Elaine returned the next day, so Monica and I played tennis in the morning, and then headed out to the mall to battle the Christmas shoppers. Neither of us planned to buy much, but there was nothing like the spectacle of holiday deal-hunters at the Town Center Mall for pure entertainment.

We later sat outside Starbucks sipping coffee.

"So what are you going to do?" Monica loved to start conversations out of the blue, always assuming I'd know what she was talking about. And most of the time, I knew. In graduate school, we used to let off steam with friends by playing Taboo, a board game that was a low-budget version of the *$10,000 Pyramid* game show we all remembered from our childhoods. Monica and I were famous for the time we won for the word "oil." Describing the word to her using only three clues, I looked at her and said: Uter. Light. Beep. Uter was the name of her ancient, baby-blue Volkswagen Golf, which was falling apart and distinguished by a bumper sticker that professed its objection to irradiated foods. Monica tried for months to get the sticker off, having no strong feelings one way or another about irradiated foods. She finally gave up and decided that the faded sticker added to Uter's dubious charm.

Uter was also known for a faulty oil light. At least, the light was faulty that particular day, since it stayed on and beeped at frequent intervals the entire day as we ran various errands.

Unimpressed, our friends accused us of cheating and refused to play with us unless we split up. It wasn't cheating—it was just the uncanny ability Monica and I had to communicate and to remember things that other people never even notice.

But today, I feigned ignorance.

"Do about what?"

"About the doctor. About *Jack.*"

Monica assumed I was avoiding the subject, but I'd thought of little else but what she had said, and about Jack, all week. The trouble was, I didn't have an answer.

"I don't know, Mon. Jack's really mad at me. You didn't see his face—I wouldn't be surprised if he wanted nothing to do with me."

Monica grimaced. "Come on. Don't be melodramatic. You and Jack have been friends too long to let the doc come between you."

She paused to take a sip and tip her head toward a woman wearing a very expensive, very tasteless brown leather jumpsuit.

I smiled while peeking at the woman.

"Do you want to date this guy?"

"I don't know. He's cute. He's a doctor. What more can you ask?"

Monica looked at me. "A lot, Tina."

I nodded. "I have no idea what to do. So instead of sitting here talking about it, let's go see if anything's on sale at Coach."

Monica smiled. "Coach doesn't have sales."

I stood up and grabbed her empty cup. "Okay, then— let's go spend too much money on ourselves at Coach."

Monica followed me, laughing.

Saturday, I received an envelope from Ohio Vital Records. It was my birth certificate. I put it on my desk, left Aunt Gillian with Elaine, and drove Monica to the airport. I was relieved when she hugged me good-bye without saying anything more about Marvin and Jack.

When I returned home, I sat down with Aunt Gillian on the back patio. I felt as if I hadn't spent enough time with her, that I owed her more of me, even though when she was healthy, we had both been happier apart. It was a perfect seventy-degree day, and I poured tall glasses of lemonade for us.

After a few minutes of companionable silence, it occurred to me that my aunt and I had little to say to each other. Most of our interactions before had been arguments; we couldn't even talk about the weather without fighting over which forecaster to believe. She wasn't the same Aunt Gillian she had been, and I didn't know how to handle our new relationship.

My aunt looked happy enough to be sitting there. She had been to the beauty salon the day before and had her still-long salt-and-pepper hair styled. She turned her face to the sun and closed her eyes, smiling at the feel of the warmth on her cheeks.

If I squinted, she looked just as she did when I was a child, lovely and self-possessed. Except on this day, she looked more beautiful to me than she had. There was no disapproval lining the sides of her well-shaped mouth. She began to hum a tune that I couldn't make out, and I was reminded of her long-ago dream to be a singer.

Today was a good day. She was alert and aware but pleasant. I should have been grateful for days like these, days when she seemed happy, but they made me sad.

This was not the real Aunt Gillian. I was never more conscious of her Alzheimer's than I was on days like today.

As we sat there, I ran over the list from the Alzheimer's Foundation of America in my head. One item came to mind: "7. Do cognitive stimulation activities with your loved one. Listening to music, word puzzles, and memory games can easily be done at home."

Memory games. I turned to Aunt Gillian.

"Tell me about my parents. Tell me about Lily."

CHAPTER 23

"She decided to keep the baby"

From the time she was five years old, Gillian knew something was different about her mother. Marianne Graham Jones was a tiny woman, short and curvaceous, like a miniature version of a regular woman. She dressed in the most fashionable clothes of the day, wearing elegant shoulder pads and cinched-waist dresses with sky-high, square-toed heels. Marianne grew up during the 1920s, in Baltimore's heyday. Blacks had been a significant presence in Baltimore since the 1700s, and they fought on both sides of the Revolutionary War because the British offered freedom to escaped slaves. Even though slavery was legal in Maryland, free blacks founded churches and helped slaves escape. Marianne's parents always bragged that there were more free blacks than slaves in Baltimore, and no other Southern city could boast the same.

In Baltimore, there was segregation, just like everywhere else, but the Grahams were among the black elite and owned a drugstore along Pennsylvania Avenue. Her parents were among the 25,000 free blacks who had populated the city in the last century, and her father worked his way up from being a dockworker in Fells Point to owning his store. They were African-American royalty, and Marianne never let anyone forget it.

Gillian was born in 1934, and by the time she was five years old the Great Depression had depleted most of her family's finances and the world was rallying to fight Hitler. But Gillian's mother did not sacrifice even a bit of glamour and style. The world might have been at war, but Marianne didn't think that was any excuse to let herself go. Gillian was a serious child, but she yearned for a mother who would play and laugh. Marianne only laughed at her own jokes and deemed her daughter's games child's play.

"Why don't you go find some friends to play with? But not that little Bell girl, what's her name?"

"Dorothy."

"Right. Dorothy Bell. Her family is rather low class. But find one of the other girls so you can stop bothering me all day."

She had long, light-brown hair that was almost blonde in certain lights, and she wore it around her shoulders, curled under in a romantic pageboy, or tied back and covered with a wide-brimmed hat for special occasions. Her hazel eyes were large and round, always rimmed in kohl and mascara. She could have passed for white, and in fact she had three sisters who did so. Only a slight fullness in Marianne's lips and her olive skin tone hinted that her parents had been among Baltimore's class of free blacks many years ago.

Marianne not only did not care to pass for white, but she in fact married the darkest man in town, barbershop owner Franklin Jones, when she was fifteen and he was twenty-five. Franklin Jones had attended Morgan State University, and there he developed the entrepreneurial spirit and confidence that made him the catch of Baltimore's elite. Marianne was precocious and pretty, so she caught him before any of the older girls had much of a chance.

These were not the most unusual things about Marianne, not the things that made Gillian uneasy around her mother from a young age. Her ever-changing moods were what convinced Gillian that there was something not quite right about her charming mother. She worked part-time as a hairdresser for Baltimore's black elite, claiming she couldn't just sit inside the house and do nothing while Franklin worked all day. He thought it would be more seemly if she did stay home, but Marianne got whatever she wanted, and when Gillian was old enough to attend a private school for black girls of means and reputation, Marianne worked.

Most of the time, she was talkative, sunny, and fun. She was gregarious enough that the women in the salon viewed her as a little sister (since she looked no more than fifteen years old throughout her adulthood) rather than a competitor. But there were other times when Marianne was morose and depressed, taking to her room for days at a time without eating or bathing. No one could, or would, articulate a name for Marianne's problem, but no one was prepared to call her crazy, since the outside world didn't see these dark moods. Only her family knew that everything about Marianne Graham Jones was not as it seemed.

Gillian refused to pretend that everything was normal. She was the only one who voiced the opinion that her mother's dark moods were frightening in the way they changed Marianne into a stranger. But Franklin told her to stop talking crazy, and Gillian learned to keep her distance from her mother, holding her at arm's length and focusing on her studies and pleasing Franklin.

Gillian idolized her father. He was a small man who nonetheless towered over his even tinier wife. He was wiry and muscled, and Gillian loved nothing more than the feel of his arms around her, protecting her, loving her. For many years, she was his only child, his baby girl, and she reveled in that role. Franklin was quiet and gentle, letting his wife do the talking when she was up and caring for her when she was down. His girls, Marianne and Gillian, were his princesses, he told them often, and he treated them as such. Nothing was too expensive, too outrageous, for his girls. His barbershop was prosperous, and he made sure that his wife and daughter were outfitted in the style befitting Baltimore's black bourgeoisie in the nineteen thirties and forties.

In 1950, Gillian turned sixteen and everything changed. During March of that year, Marianne suffered her worst episode yet, ranting and raving through the streets of their neighborhood wearing just her nightgown and a pair of snow boots. Franklin was worried, and Gillian was embarrassed. Marianne was persuaded to go to the doctor, who told her she was suffering from exhaustion due to her busy schedule of clients at the salon and the fact that she was pregnant. Marianne retreated to her bedroom after hearing the news, sobbing. Franklin was thrilled. In November, Brenda Graham Jones was born. That year, no one thought to throw Gillian a sweet-sixteen party as was the custom for her family. Everyone was too busy admiring baby Brenda.

The birth was a difficult one for Gillian's mother. She labored for days, and passed out before she could push the baby out. Brenda was taken by forceps while Marianne slept, and it seemed to Gillian that she never truly woke up again. After coming home from the hospital, Marianne shuffled around the house, looking at the floor or staring into the air, paying little attention to the baby. Consulted once more, the doctor continued to diagnose exhaustion and prescribe tranquilizers, which made Gillian's mother even more of a zombie who could not be persuaded to breast-feed or hold baby Brenda.

When Brenda was three months old, Gillian came home from school and found her mother dressed in her best church dress and heels, sitting on the edge of the bathtub, bathing the baby. Gillian had not seen her mother in anything other than a bathrobe in weeks, nor had she seen Marianne touch the baby in any significant way since coming home from the hospital. Gillian set down her school bag, which was heavy with homework and books, and she stood in the doorway peering at her mother. A closer look showed that Marianne was holding Brenda's head under the water. She would never forget the serene look on Marianne's face as she turned to Gillian and spoke.

"God told me to kill Brenda. He said she is evil."

Gillian snatched the wet baby away from her mother, slammed the door behind her and called her father, who called the doctor. When the doctor arrived, Marianne called him a black devil and tried to scratch his eyes out. She was sent to the best mental hospital Franklin could afford, a place where people sent family members who would not, or could not, behave. Gillian saw it just once, when her father took her to visit Marianne soon after she had been committed.

As she trudged along the hallway, Gillian's chest tightened. She hadn't known what to expect, especially the smell. Stale cigarettes, rancid milk, something coppery and sour that she couldn't identify. She fought the tears that welled in her eyes as her feet reached the door of Marianne's room. She could hear the television blasting in the room.

Gillian wiped her eyes, took a shallow breath and hitched her bag on her shoulder. She brushed her knuckles against the door, waiting to be invited in. When the wait seemed as if it would never end, Gillian realized she had been foolish. Did she really expect her mother to answer the door? Sighing, she pulled open the oak door and stepped inside.

The smells of Ben-Gay, Lysol, and the musk of unwashed bodies flared her nostrils as the door slammed shut. Glancing around the shabby room, Gillian was relieved that her mother's roommate was out, although she had left behind stains on bedsheets that had not been changed.

Someone had tried to make this horrible place a bit brighter. Homemade curtains draped the windows, and the generic pictures of wild flowers were hung on the pale green walls. Still, the room was cramped and airless, more a cell than anything else.

The room was too warm. Gillian shrugged off her wool jacket and set down her bag. She slowly walked toward her mother's bed, being careful not to touch anything. Marianne turned to glance at her, and then returned her gaze to the black-and-white television screen.

Gillian perched for a moment on the edge of the lumpy bed. She was taken aback at the sight of the feeble woman sitting up in the narrow hospital bed. The only trace of Marianne's beauty that remained was her hair, which was still shiny and long despite not having been washed recently.

Her face was creased and her brow furrowed, as if the program on TV was vexing. Gillian unconsciously smoothed her hands over her own slim hips as she took in Marianne's emaciated frame in the pale pink bathrobe she had brought from home.

She watched her mother and searched for something to say. They had never had a normal mother-daughter connection when Marianne was well, and now that she was confined to the sanitarium Gillian had no idea how to talk to her mother, or what to feel. More than anything, Gillian wished she were somewhere else, anywhere else. The smell was beginning to make her feel sick, and she held her breath.

Then Gillian realized that what she felt most was anger. Why couldn't her mother have been like the other mothers? Why had she tried to do something so horrible that Gillian couldn't let herself remember Marianne's eyes when she had tried to drown Brenda? Why was it Gillian's job to stop Marianne?

Gillian hated the sight of her mother.

Marianne ignored her eldest daughter during the visit, instead keeping her eyes glued to *American Bandstand* playing on the television. Gillian never went to see her again.

Gillian did not have the luxury of sibling rivalry, though she resented the way Franklin's eyes lit up when he came home and picked up his beloved Brenda. While Gillian played mother to her baby sister, Franklin focused all the love he had once held for Marianne onto the baby. Gillian had never seen him so enthralled, cooing at the baby, even feeding her whenever he could. Many times, Gillian woke in the night to hear Brenda's cries, but by the time she got to the nursery, her father was already there, holding the baby like a precious piece of blown glass, afraid to break her, afraid to let go.

Franklin used to be proud of Gillian's academic accomplishments, bragging about her rank at the top of her class at the best high school in the city. Now he bragged about how soon Brenda learned to walk, how clear and high her voice was when she called his name, how much she resembled an angel. By the time Brenda was two, she was the spitting image of Marianne, with golden hair, tawny skin, and the ability to charm anyone in her path. Franklin never spoke of his wife to anyone, not even Gillian, although he visited her every week. In the 1950s, it was shameful to have a crazy relative, shameful to be institutionalized. Her disease had a name by then, manic depression, but only doctors and families coping with the disease knew it. Everyone else, especially blacks, saw Marianne's exhaustion as weakness.

Then Franklin's visits to the sanitarium stopped, and Gillian was left to wonder why. After three months had passed, she was home when her mother's things were delivered to their house in boxes. That was when Gillian realized that her mother had died. Her father never said a word. It would be years before Gillian discovered, on her own, that her mother hanged herself with the belt of her bathrobe.

When Gillian was eighteen, she went to Howard University to study nursing. She'd been in the choir all through high school, and she had been told that her soprano was professional quality. But when she had tried to discuss music as a major with Franklin, he had smiled and shook his head.

"You can't make a living being a singer, Gillian. Be a nurse. People always need nurses."

And so it was decided, because however much she resented Franklin's new allegiance to Brenda, she still loved him more than anything and wanted to please him. So she commuted from Baltimore to Howard several days a week in the 1949 Ford sedan Franklin bought for her. While she was in classes during her first year of college, Brenda was cared for by Eloise, a neighborhood woman who seemed to Gillian more interested in Franklin than in Brenda. She did seem to understand that, for Franklin, she would always come second to Brenda. Gillian was not surprised when Franklin announced he would marry Eloise the summer after her freshman year. She was also not surprised that her father seemed to tell her as an afterthought. Gillian knew that she, and Marianne, had been replaced.

"Jeremiah was a dog."

He was not just a garden-variety dog, but the worst, a man who preyed on girls who didn't know better than to be charmed by his good looks and mysterious demeanor. Where the other women on campus saw a noble veteran coming to school to better himself, Gillian saw an opportunist who wrote papers for people for money. He was anything but noble, as far as she was concerned.

She knew all about him for months before they first met. Gillian wasn't the kind of woman who had lots of girlfriends. She didn't spend time giggling over boys and men, worrying about her hair and makeup. But there were many young women who called her a friend, who sought out her opinion on classes, their dates, their clothes. After her father remarried, she lived on campus and learned to enjoy living among girls her own age. Gillian freely gave her opinions on fashion, academics (which she knew a lot about), and men (which she knew nothing about), and she enjoyed their company well enough. But she had no intention of letting them in any closer than was necessary to keep college from being a devastating, lonely experience.

Jeremiah Jackson was one of the most frequent topics of conversation among these girls. They called him a war hero, declared him the best-looking man on campus, and competed for his attention. They ignored the fact that he dated and defiled one woman after the other, without regard for what was socially appropriate, or even what was simply right.

Gillian saw right through Jeremiah, knew him for what he was. And he was the most exciting man she had ever seen. This made it all the more imperative that she keep her distance. And she did so, until the day that Jon Johnson tried to shoot him in the back.

As it turned out, Jeremiah had not actually been shot, because Jon Johnson did not know how to use a gun. Jeremiah had panicked, then passed out as the bullet whizzed by him. When he realized what he had done, Jon collapsed in a heap on the quad, crying. Gillian happened to be walking nearby, heard the shot and ran over to help Jeremiah. She rode in the ambulance with him to the hospital, stroking his hair and smiling when the EMT told her that he had fainted but was otherwise fine. They would take him in just to be safe, but he would suffer no long-lasting physical effects.

She was relieved, much more so than she imagined possible. While she waited for him to wake up, she thought back to the day he had sat next to her on the bench, trying to see what she was reading. She'd felt almost light-headed being near him, the power of her attraction to him so strong that she didn't feel like herself. No man had ever made her feel that way. She was smart in her classes, but naïve in life. She didn't know the difference between love and lust, didn't realize that the warming she felt in her body was about sex, and not much more. She didn't know, and when Jeremiah wanted to make love to her hours after he left the hospital, she said yes. When he asked her if she loved him that same night, she said yes. And when he asked her to marry him the day after they graduated from Howard University, just weeks after he was shot at, she said yes.

The beginning of Gillian and Jeremiah's life together was a whirlwind of change. Gillian's father didn't come to her graduation, telling her by telephone that the baby was sick. Gillian wanted to scream at him that his wife could take care of Brenda, that graduating from Howard was an honor, that she, Gillian, was his daughter, too. She wanted to tell him how proud she was to be at the top of her nursing class, how proud she would be if he would stand in the crowd and applaud her accomplishment. More than anything, Gillian wanted him to know all these things without her having to say a word. So she married Jeremiah at the courthouse and informed her father of her new name in a postcard sent from the road.

Soon after graduation, the newlyweds moved back to Cleveland, Jeremiah's hometown. They took their time finding jobs, living on his savings while they spent their days walking around the then-thriving downtown, fantasizing about their dream house and returning to the room they'd rented to make love on lazy summer afternoons. Gillian felt as if they were the only two people in the world. She believed there was nothing more important to Jeremiah than her happiness. He brought her breakfast in bed. He massaged her feet after their morning walks. He adored her. For the first time in her life, she was a queen.

In gratitude, she made herself up every morning and made sure that Jeremiah never saw her looking anything but perfect. She wore heels and skirts, always the lady Jeremiah was proud to introduce to his city. She never questioned where Jeremiah went on some nights, how he got the money to buy the first liquor store, why he seemed to have so many secrets. Gillian had her own secrets, which she never considered sharing with her husband, so she could not begrudge him his.

Within that first year, they bought a house, the same tall, narrow house where Gillian would live for the next fifty years. Gillian occupied herself with decorating, and when she got bored, she found a job as a nurse. Falling asleep at night, on the nights when Jeremiah slept next to her, Gillian believed she was happy.

She remembered the exact moment when she knew the marriage wouldn't last. It was 1958, and they'd been married two years. Jeremiah was just opening his third liquor store, and he wanted Gillian to stop working as a nurse to start a family.

"Let's have a baby," he said over dinner one night, his voice casual and expectant.

Gillian felt revulsion, and wondered what reaction she was supposed to have. She looked around her bright-yellow kitchen at the utensils in their clay containers and the copper pots hanging from the wrought iron rack she had special-ordered from Marshall Fields. She thought of the neat bedrooms, most of them set up for guests who never came, for family that never visited. She thought of the spacious dining room with its table for eight, twelve with the leaves. She thought of these things, and despite the space they called home, she knew there was no room for a baby.

She was certain that she didn't want to have children, because her research on her mother's manic depression seemed to indicate that the disease was hereditary. Gillian believed she was fine, but she wasn't sure she wouldn't pass on her own mother's craziness to an unsuspecting child. She had no intention of taking the chance.

She pushed her plate away and decided it was time to tell Jeremiah one of her secrets. She told him the story of Marianne's illness, the hospital, her suicide. She could not look at him while she spoke, feeling naked as she recited the facts of her mother's weakness. While she talked, she pictured her mother as she was before the manic depression got the best of her, and the hollow nausea of grief was almost too much to bear.

Fighting back tears, because Gillian never cried, she shook her head and looked up. Jeremiah was finishing the last of his dinner, which meant that he had been eating the entire time she spoke. Anger began to fill the pit in Gillian's stomach.

"I grew up without any parents at all, and look how I turned out." He said this with a smile that Gillian deemed condescending in its kindness. For the first time since she thought he had been shot, Gillian remembered why she had stayed away from Jeremiah for most of their college years.

"Yes, look how you turned out." Her voice dripped with sarcasm, which he chose to ignore. He picked food form his teeth with a toothpick. She watched him with growing malice.

Look indeed, Gillian thought to herself. Jeremiah was already reverting to his old ways, flirting with women, even in front of his wife, and doing God-knows-what with them when she wasn't around. After smelling strange perfume on his clothing for the umpteenth time, it had occurred to Gillian that Jeremiah might have never stopped seeing other women, however much he claimed to love his wife. She thought she could live with his affairs. What she couldn't live with was the idea that he believed she didn't know. And now he wanted her to get pregnant.

If he had been in any way understanding about her reluctance, if he had acknowledged how painful it must have been, growing up with a mother like Marianne, she would have agreed to go along with his plans. But he broke the silence.

"You're lucky you had a mother at all."

He didn't bother to take the toothpick from his mouth when he spoke. At that moment, Gillian knew it was over between her and Jeremiah.

It took another year filled with fights and make-up sex before the official end arrived. In June of 1959, Gillian began feeling sick and cranky. She'd taken up smoking since she married Jeremiah, having discovered another vice besides her husband, but even the smell of her beloved cigarettes sickened her. When she went to the doctor, he told her to expect an addition to the family by February.

Gillian did not know what to do. She'd heard of a doctor who took care of problems like these for women like Gillian, women who didn't want a baby. Or she could give Jeremiah what he wanted, a child. A son. After weeks of consideration, she wasn't sure whether she wanted the baby, but she was surer than ever that she did not want Jeremiah. One night in June, before Jeremiah suspected anything was amiss, Gillian pretended to have just found a love note in a woman's handwriting in the pocket of one of Jeremiah's sport jackets. In fact, it was one of many notes she collected from his laundry. She saved them all, not knowing why until that night, but this one number was interesting in that that woman had signed her full name, and she shared a last name with a prominent city councilman. A prominent *white* city councilman.

Gillian yelled at Jeremiah, called him a cheating dog, and ordered him out of the house. Before he left, she mentioned the councilman's name and told Jeremiah that unless he wanted that powerful man to find out what Jeremiah was up to with his wife, he should send Gillian enough money each month to keep her comfortable. She left the amount up to him, knowing that Jeremiah would send more than enough cash because he loved his business, and himself.

She never spoke to Jeremiah again.

She decided to keep the baby.

CHAPTER 24

"You're not my type"

I was riveted, but Aunt Gillian's voice trailed off. She was tired and wanted to go to bed. It was already dusk, and we had been sitting outside for hours, me listening while she told me more about her and our family than I'd ever known. I helped her inside and got her settled. I went into the kitchen and poured a glass of wine. Then I called the phone number Marvin had given me. He didn't answer, and I was relieved.

"Marvin, it's Tina. I'm afraid I need to cancel dinner tonight. Something came up, a family thing. Aunt Gillian is fine, but, well, this is something I need to take care of."

The doorbell rang. I looked down at myself, then at my watch. Marvin was early, and I was a mess in torn jeans and a sweatshirt. I considered pretending I wasn't home, but then I figured I'd let Marvin see me and scare him off.

He smiled wide when I opened the door, then handed me a bunch of calla lilies.

"You look great. A little underdressed for what I had in mind, but still lovely."

I sighed and ushered him into the living room. I sat across from him.

"I can't go."

He raised his eyebrows. "Oh, come on. Why not?"

I thought about Aunt Gillian's story, about all that I'd learned, all the questions I still had. I had no intention of explaining it all to Marvin.

"I've got some things I have to deal with." I knew it was vague, but it was the best I could come up with on the spot.

Marvin pasted a hangdog look on his face, one that I was certain was only semisincere. "If you don't want to date me, just let me know. I'm a big boy. I can take it."

The look worked, even though I didn't think Marvin would be devastated if we didn't go out. He seemed like a man who was used to getting his way, especially with women, and I suspected that he would fight long and hard to get me to go out with him, not because he liked me that much, but because a rejection would mean a blow to his ego.

But then I second-guessed myself. Maybe he really did like me. And it was rude of me to cancel a date just as he arrived at my door.

"It's not that. I just . . . hell, let's just go. The other thing can wait—it has this long."

"What thing?" He looked confused.

My family history. My entire life, and what felt like my future as well. How could you explain that to a virtual stranger?

"Never mind." I stood up and handed the flowers to Marvin. "Go put these in water while I change. There are vases in the cabinet next to the sink."

Sampson's was a small Italian restaurant a few blocks away from the ocean on Palm Beach. The door was unmarked, and the uninitiated could spend hours trying to find it. But Sampson's didn't thrive on walk-in business; it was a cozy place that catered to a small group of regulars who loved simple pastas and fresh seafood without all the bustle of the city's trendier eateries.

The décor was elegant and straightforward. The owners had shunned the traditional reds for a palette of dark blues and grays, lending a sophisticated feel to the room. The tables were set with heavy linens and real silver. Candles in crystal chandeliers were the only source of light.

Marvin was a gentleman, opening doors for me and complimenting me on the simple black sheath I'd worn. It was demure enough so he wouldn't make any assumptions about dessert, but it showed off my new figure. Throughout dinner, I alternated between liking Marvin and loathing him. I liked that he ordered veal on my suggestion, that he listened to my opinion. I loathed the fact that he related every conversational thread back to his practice. Marvin could be funny and charming, laughing at my stories about teaching and staring into my eyes while I talked, making me feel as if I were the only other person in the room. But I caught him smoothing down his tie and adjusting his shirt while we ate, which meant that he was as vain as his appearance would suggest.

Marvin was the kind of guy I had avoided in high school. They were handsome and cruel, never wavering in their sense of entitlement. I guess that was the type of confidence that came with growing up good-looking. I knew from being on the other side that people treated you differently when you were fat or ugly. The beautiful people got a pass that let them skate past many of life's roadblocks, while those same obstacles seemed as if they were put in place to stop the rest of us from finding happiness.

Actually, Marvin not only reminded me of the popular boys in high school, he also reminded me of Francisco Alexander, the bad poet and cheating boyfriend from Georgetown. Marvin had the same mild arrogance. I prayed he didn't write poetry.

Between bites, we played more of the get-to-know-you game. After our plates were taken away, we sat back in our seats. Marvin looked at me, his smile secretive.

"What are you grinning about?"

"Was I grinning?"

"Definitely."

"I was just thinking that you're a lot more interesting than I thought you'd be."

"Why do your compliments always sound like insults?"

He shrugged. "I call it like I see it."

No, I thought. Jack does that. You just say whatever you want because you can get away with it, and because you think you're funny.

We looked at each other for a moment.

"You know, you're sexy when you're mad," he said, leaning close enough so I could smell his expensive cologne.

I smiled. "That's better, I suppose, but still a kind of backhanded compliment."

He asked if I wanted dessert, but I declined.

"I really need to get home to my aunt." I didn't. Elaine was there. But I did want to go home.

Soon we were sitting in front of my house in Marvin's Jaguar. I gathered my purse.

"Tonight was nice." I meant it. In a way, it had been nice to be with someone who didn't know my history, who was different and separate from my life.

He laughed. "You sound surprised. I'll have you know that most women enjoy my company immensely."

I couldn't tell whether he was joking. "You're not my type."

He leaned back in his seat. "No? What's your type? More literary? Certainly not someone who does boob jobs."

I nodded. "And you're too pretty."

"Is that supposed to be a compliment?" he said, his expression sly.

I held up a finger. "You're also arrogant."

Marvin shrugged. "Guilty as charged." He paused. "So. Can I come in? Or, we could go to my place. I don't live far."

His smile was so hopeful that I couldn't help but laugh. "You're arrogant and presumptuous."

"So is that a yes?"

I looked up at my darkened house. I thought about how long it had been since I slept next to a man and about the musky scent of Marvin's cologne. I turned to look into his green eyes, and I knew I could never date him. I would never trust his attraction, never believe that he wasn't looking over my shoulder for something better.

When he leaned over to kiss me, I pulled away.

"Thanks for dinner." I slammed the door and ran up to my door before he could try to convince me otherwise.

Inside, I wasn't sure what I planned to do. I peeked in at Aunt Gillian, and then plopped down on the sofa and turned the television on so low I couldn't hear it. Then I picked up the telephone.

"Hi, Jack. It's me." There was a long pause.

"Hi." He didn't sound angry, just awkward. He sounded how I felt. I tried not to think about what Monica had said about him being in love with me. I didn't believe it. I was scared to believe it. I wanted to believe it.

"How was Phoenix?"

"Warm. Dry. Dull. My father somehow turned into an old man. It was the longest three days of my life."

I smiled. "Your father *is* an old man."

"Maybe so. But nobody told him to start wearing argyle sweaters in eighty-degree heat and talking with a Yiddish accent."

We laughed, and just like that, everything was back to normal.

"I need to talk to you," I told him.

Jack sighed. "If it's about the whole Dr. Marvin thing, forget it. I was out of line. You can date whomever you choose—it's none of my business."

Disappointment flooded through me. I admitted to myself that I wanted my love life to be Jack's business. But I knew I was right, and Monica had it all wrong. He wasn't in love with me. We were just friends.

"You don't have to apologize. It's not going to work out with him. And that's not what I wanted to talk to you about. It's about Aunt Gillian. And Lily."

I rushed my words together, partly because of my urgent need to talk to him about the story my aunt had told, partly because I realized that the entire time I was with Marvin I was comparing him to Jack.

Jack understood. "I'll be right over."

By the time he arrived, I'd opened a bottle of the cabernet I knew he liked. We sat down on the sofa and I folded my legs underneath me, preparing to tell him the Story of Gillian. He listened and refilled our glasses. It was close to midnight when I finished.

The house was quiet. Aunt Gillian was sleeping, the sound of her regular breathing whispering through the monitor. The only lights in the house were the small lamp and the reflection from my neighbors' Christmas display. They always put up their decorations right after Thanksgiving, sometimes that very night. I disapproved of the gaudy display of inflatable Santas and moving, lighted reindeer for aesthetic reasons, but I couldn't help liking the spirit it brought to the block.

"Wow." Jack shook his head.

"I know. I found out so much, and I have more questions than ever."

"Like, where's Lily?"

I nodded. "And my parents. I still don't know much about my parents."

Jack looked thoughtful. "Whatever happened with that trunk you told me about last summer? Did you ever look inside?"

I shook my head and smiled. "Can you pick a lock?"

Good engineers, I've learned from Jack, always have tools with them. No matter what, they have a love of seeing how things work.

"So you carry this toolbox in your car just in case of an engineering emergency?" I teased as I watched him insert a narrow pick into the lock of the metal box inside the battered trunk.

The lock made a tiny click and popped open. "Smart-ass, would you like to see what's inside or not?" He handed the box to me.

I tried to smile, but my hand shook as I took the box. I took a deep breath and opened it. The first thing I saw was a sheaf of papers, folded and stuck together. I opened it. Jeremiah's name was at the top of the page, and the text had been typed on an ancient typewriter by someone who either never made mistakes or had fixed them all. It was a short story about a little girl.

"He only talked about writing stories for other people. He never talked about his own writing."

"Let's read it."

I held the papers and he read over my shoulder.

Grace
By Jeremiah Jackson

On the first day of kindergarten, Grace woke up an hour before her mother could come and gently shake her awake, before her father could promise his famous whole-wheat pancakes for breakfast.

Tiptoeing through the house that was just big enough for the three of them, she thought about her new role as one of the big kids. She would ride the yellow bus. She would carry a lunchbox. And she would wear leather shoes with hard soles. She begged her mother to let her wear the red velvet dress usually reserved for church. It was not velvet weather. The August heat created a haze along the Milwaukee streets, but her mother agreed that Grace could wear red velvet on her first day of school. Her mother even attached her favorite pin—a white bunny with pinkish ears and a wide grin—to the straps of the jumper, just above the button on the left side, just as she liked it.

During the back-to-school shopping trip, Grace had begged for black patent-leather shoes—with heels. But her mother stood firm in the belief that a four-year-old girl had little use for heels. The compromise was plain black Mary Janes—no heel. That wasn't too disappointing, since she got to wear her hair down instead of braided. Braids were for babies.

She felt an inch taller and a year more mature every time her mother slipped the hard-bristled brush through her hair. And when she looked in the mirror, Grace fell in love. Her hair waved around her face like folds of black silk, touching her shoulders before whispering across her back. It was the first time Grace understood why people said she looked just like her mother. She understood why men stopped to stare at her mother in the A & P. Her skin was several shades darker than her mother's, more like caramel. Her hair curled tightly, not hanging straight to the small of her back like her mother's. But seeing herself in that mirror, on the first day of school, she felt a bit of the magic her soft-spoken mother held in her dusky brown eyes.

"Where's Grace?" her father had joked at the breakfast table. "Annie, what happened to our little girl?" He looked at his wife with mock concern.

"Daddy!" she giggled, accidentally spitting pancake crumbs onto the table. "I'm right here!"

Her father glanced at her in confusion. "Last night I put my little girl to bed. She had braids and wore Wonder Woman pajamas. I don't know who you are, ma'am, but you're a grown-up lady. My Grace is a little girl."

She grabbed her daddy's hand and shook her head, excited. "No, Daddy, look, it's me! Even though I'm a big girl now, I'm still Grace!"

Earl peered over his wire-rimmed glasses. "Well, I didn't even recognize you!" He laughed and hugged Grace. "You look lovely, pumpkin. You are going to be the smartest, most beautiful big girl in kindergarten, right Annie?"

Her mother smiled gently and brushed up the pancake crumbs.

"You better believe it!"

She beamed at her parents and ran to grab her lunchbox off the counter.

During the drive to Holy Angels Catholic School, she sat with her nose pressed against the window of her mother's red Thunderbird. The air-conditioning coursing through the car allowed Grace to blow steam on the window. She tried to draw shapes on the window before her breath faded away. She wished the drive to kindergarten wasn't so long.

In front of the school, she wiggled out of her mother's grasp and bounced out of the car with her new backpack. She skipped into the school yard, swinging her head from side to side so she could feel her hair swish and rustle around her ears, singing:

Miss Mary Mack, Mack, Mack
All dressed in black, black, black
With silver buttons, buttons, buttons
All down her back, back, back

But her throat dried up like a piece of stale toast as she looked around the vast yard. There were kids everywhere. Hundreds, maybe thousands of kids. Big kids. Much bigger than Grace. They sat underneath tall oak trees. They trampled the soft grass in the field. They crowded along the stairs to the school.

None of them witnessed her loose, flowing hair. No one said anything about her red velvet dress. No one even noticed her as they continued with their games of tag and kickball, hopscotch and marbles.

She stood there for a moment looking for any friendly face. Finally, in the corner of the yard next to a patch of drooping tulips, Grace spotted a group of four brown girls and she walked over. She reasoned they would welcome a new friend, especially one with red velvet and swirling hair. Why wouldn't they? Grace was always looking for new friends.

"Hi, I'm Grace. Today's my first day in kindergarten," she announced. Three of the girls just looked at her and smirked. The tallest one stared down at Grace without smiling at all. She wore brown khaki shorts with big flowers on the pockets, a white eyelet shirt with a Peter Pan collar, and brown sandals. No heels. Her skin was dark brown and ashy, as if she had been rubbing dried mud on herself. Her hair was short and messy, twisted into tiny braids that circled her head haphazardly.

"We're in first grade," the tall girl sniffed, turning back to their game. They were taking turns grabbing each other's hands and scratching. She watched silently.

"Wanna play?" the tall girl asked, her lips curled up at the ends. Grace nodded.

"Hold out your hand." She hesitated briefly before reaching out to the girl. As the tall girl held their hands together for a moment, Grace noticed how small and yellowish her hand looked next to the other girl's mahogany fingers. Just as she relaxed her palms and smiled, the tall girl made deep, moon-shaped dents on Grace's knuckles that bled immediately. She couldn't remember anything hurting as much as this. She felt like throwing up as the tall girl wiped Grace's blood on her dingy shorts and gave the other girls high fives. Grace pulled away from the tall girl, stumbled and landed butt-first on the damp grass, leaving grass stains that could never be removed from the red velvet. In tears, she groped her way off the ground and ran into the school, leaving their laughter behind her.

"I thought you said you wanted to play!" the tall girl cackled.

Grace couldn't wait to get home and be comforted. Her father offered to go down and warn those little girls and their parents about hurting his little girl. Her mother baked her chocolate-chip cookies and told her that everything was going to be all right. She also retold the story over and over, to family, friends, and when Grace was older she suspected her mother told the story to complete strangers as well. Her mother believed this story taught a lesson. Grace later thought that her mom just couldn't decide on what that lesson was.

"Grace, she was much smaller than these girls, just a baby really—she had no idea how things worked, so she chose some friends. Unfortunately, they were the wrong kinds of girls, you know what I mean, so they hurt this tiny child who never did anything to them," her mother recounted at Grace's eighth birthday party.

"The girls, they came up to my Grace and scratched her for no reason, but my Grace, she held her own, marched right into that school and didn't worry about those ragamuffins," she gushed at Aunt Lacey's Christmas dinner the year Grace turned twelve.

"When those nasty girls—they were in what, the fourth or fifth grade, right Grace?—scratched my baby, you know what she did? She scratched right back," her mother crowed at Grace's high school graduation.

But Grace's mother was wrong. It wasn't a story about a helpless girl. It wasn't a story about a determined girl. And it wasn't the story of a tough girl. It's just the story of Grace, who still thinks twice before she reaches out to strangers.

"I like it," Jack said when we finished reading. "That little girl sounds tough, like you and Gillian."

I frowned. "Aunt Gillian and I aren't anything alike. Anyway, I wonder why Aunt Gillian kept this story all this time. She made me think she hated Jeremiah."

"Well, at some point she must have loved him. That doesn't just go away."

I nodded. We looked inside the metal box again and we found a smaller black velvet case. I thought of Russian stacking dolls as I showed it to Jack.

"What do you think it is?"

He raised his hands in the air, palms upward. "I'm an engineer, not a magician."

I laughed and shoved it into his hands. "I'm scared to open it."

Jack opened the box. It contained a ring with a single tear-drop diamond.

"A ring," I said, snatching the box from Jack and looking for a note, or anything that could explain it.

"An *engagement* ring," Jack noted.

"From Jeremiah again?"

Jack shook his head. "Who knows?"

I looked outside at the blinking Christmas decorations for a long while. Jack put his arm around me and we sat watching the inflatable snowman bob in the mild wind and trying to come up with an explanation for the ring and the story. I woke up the next morning to the sounds of Elaine's key at the door. Jack was asleep next to me, his head on my shoulder, his arm still around my waist.

CHAPTER 25

"Are you a quitter?"

Aunt Gillian fell and broke her hip on Christmas Eve. Elaine was spending the holiday week with us, sleeping in the guest room, and helping me bake cookies in an effort to make this Christmas seem like the ones I'd always craved. Christmas had always been the time when I most missed having parents. I'd watch other kids shopping with their mothers, ice skating with their fathers, and I missed what I never had. I watched *Miracle on 34th Street* every year and believed that was how real families celebrated the holidays. I listened to the Jackson 5 Christmas album and wished I had so many brothers and sisters, who would share the joy of the season with me, sing carols, leave cookies for Santa Claus, who we would believe was real.

Aunt Gillian always did her best to make the holiday festive, inviting over neighbors and acquaintances for tea on Christmas Eve, urging me to invite friends over every year. But I never had many friends, and the people from the neighborhood always seemed a bit startled to be invited to the home of a woman who, for the most part, refused all but the most superficial interaction with them. I always believed she was doing it for my benefit, to make up for the family I didn't have, to make up for the social life that eluded me because of my weight. Christmas Eve also happened to be my birthday, so the yearly tea doubled as a birthday celebration that only Aunt Gillian and I knew about, since I forbade her from announcing it to our guests.

After hearing Aunt Gillian's story, it occurred to me that those Christmas Eve celebrations were also for her, to fill the gap left by her own family. I still had no idea what happened to her father, Franklin, and I had no idea how my mother came to be in the Midwest with my father when, as far as I knew, she had grown up in Baltimore. But what I did know about my aunt was that her family had not been what she wanted, or needed. We had that in common.

So I baked cookies, bought red and green sweaters for Jack and Elaine to wear (Elaine loved hers; Jack claimed not to look good in hunter green but wore his anyway), played Christmas carols, and tried to create the perfect Christmas. I was doing it for myself, but I was also doing it for Aunt Gillian, although I wasn't sure she would know what was happening. Over the last month, her moments of lucidity decreased, to the point where she spent most of her days in the amiable state of passivity that made me long for the old Gillian. Between Thanksgiving and Christmas, I spent my days preparing for finals and the end of the semester, and my evenings trying to talk to Aunt Gillian, to coax her into telling me more about herself, about Lily, about my parents. Some nights, she looked at me with no recognition at all, as if

I were a stranger who was making unreasonable demands on her time. Other nights, she knew me but refused to talk.

"Ernestine, what have I always told you about living in the past?" she asked me one evening after I asked about Lily. "What's done is done."

The comment had finality to it, barring further questioning. I decided on a different approach another night. We were in Aunt Gillian's bedroom, and I was helping her into her pajamas and tying her hair into a scarf to prepare her for bedtime. This was one of the nights when I was familiar to her, and I could feel her shoulders relax under my touch.

"Whose engagement ring is that in the box?" I thought that if I asked her in a way that suggested the continuation of a previous conversation, it might jog her memory. My aunt looked at me and smiled.

"It's mine. Ernest gave it to me."

She began humming that same Billie Holiday tune that she had sung when she first moved in with me, her face set in a distant smile that suggested memories that pleased her. I frowned. She was confused again. Why would my father give Aunt Gillian an engagement ring? I wondered as I helped her to her bed. I feared that her disease had given me a gift in the story she had already told me. But it might also have robbed me of what I truly wanted: to know who I was.

Christmas Eve morning, Aunt Gillian was watching television on the sofa, and Elaine and I were quiet as we worked in the kitchen. This was one of the many things

I liked about her. She was great to talk to, but neither of us felt an obligation to fill the silence when we were together. The only sounds in the house were the chattering and giggles of the hosts of *The View*, which Aunt Gillian liked to watch every day. Before Alzheimer's, I was certain that she would have hated Star Jones and the rest, but now, their cackling voices soothed her in some mysterious way.

As Elaine removed the first batch of cookies from the oven, I went to the living room to check on my aunt. Jack burst into the foyer and into the living room, holding an enormous bouquet of flowers and a giant balloon with the number "35" written in festive lettering. He began singing before I could yell at him for reminding me of how old I was getting. My mouth fell open as Monica followed him through the door, adding her voice to an off-key rendition of the birthday song. Elaine, who had walked up behind me, began clapping and laughing along with Jack and Monica at the surprised expression on my face.

"You know what my mother used to say: Close your mouth before you to let in the flies," Elaine cackled in her Haitian accent.

I smiled. "What are you guys doing?"

"Surprise," Jack and Monica yelled, coming closer to hug me.

I glanced over at Aunt Gillian to see how she was reacting to all the confusion. She looked a bit confused but happy. Her gaze was fixed on the swaying balloon, which she watched with a childlike pleasure. Then she stood up and moved faster than I had seen her move in years, heading toward Jack and the balloon. Time seemed to both speed up and slow down as she fell in the middle of the room. She tripped, or her legs gave way. Aunt Gillian lay in a heap, moaning in pain as we all rushed be the first to help her.

We spent the perfect Christmas alternating shifts at the hospital. At first, Aunt Gillian's fall seemed straight-forward. A broken hip: bad, but manageable. Then, her doctors told us that hers was a bad fracture, and she might not be able to walk without help after hip-replacement surgery. Aunt Gillian got her new hip on December 31, her seventieth birthday. She was not awake to appreciate the flowers Monica had brought, the soothing words Jack spoke, the way I paced her room, unable to sit still for fear I would break into pieces.

Jack and I were alone in the room with Aunt Gillian. He watched me pace for a long while.

"Why don't you sit, Tina? Relax a little." He smiled at me across the room.

"I can't. It's just too much," I said. I felt as if I wasn't making any sense, but Jack nodded.

"The fall. Gill's story."

"It's just that, she has this daughter, Lily, and I don't know where she is, what she's doing, why she's not here instead of me." I stopped my pacing next to Jack's chair. He pulled the other chair in the room close to his and patted it. I took a chance and perched on the edge of the chair, ready to get up again at the first sign of panic.

I felt the tears welling up in my eyes, and I commanded them to go away. "Knowing a little makes me want to know it all even more. And now . . ."

Jack grabbed my hand. The warmth from his skin made me blush. I looked around the white walls of my aunt's private room, out of the window at the view of the Intracoastal, down at the tiled floor.

"Don't think like that. This is just a setback. Gill's going to be okay."

I could no longer stop the tears from falling. "But what if she's not?" I whispered. "Old people don't always recover from something like this. They get infections, bad ones. And pneumonia. What if we spent all our lives arguing and being mad at each other, and this is how it ends? What if she . . . is not here, and I don't have anyone? What if I never find out about my parents, about Lily?"

My voice rose until I was sobbing out the words. Jack stood up and pulled me to my feet. He held me tight, his arms squeezing me with just enough pressure to help me calm down. When I regained control, he pulled back to look into my eyes. I tried to look away but he watched me until I had no choice but to return his gaze.

"Are you a quitter?"

I shrugged.

He shook me a little. "Are you?"

I closed my eyes for a long moment and opened them again.

"No."

"Then don't quit now. Your aunt needs you. Forget about all that stuff in the past. Focus on now, and tomorrow, and the next day."

I couldn't help smiling. "Now you sound like Aunt Gillian."

He gave a soft laugh. "She's a smart lady. A tough lady. Like someone else I know."

We looked at each other, still embracing, and my muscles felt as if they were melting into his. We might have kissed, but just then a nurse walked in to check on Aunt Gillian.

It was clear and sunny the day Aunt Gillian came home. There was just a bit of January bite in the air, and I wore a sweater for the first time in months. I came alone to the hospital, leaving Jack and Elaine to wait at home. While she was in the hospital, I'd given serious thought to what it would be like if Aunt Gillian was gone, and I wanted to spend as much time with her as possible. The doctors said she was fine, aside from needing physical therapy for her leg, so there was no imminent danger. There was just my own realization that Aunt Gillian wouldn't be here forever.

She left the hospital on a Tuesday in mid-January. Classes would be starting soon, but I didn't feel the anticipation I associated with the start of a new semester. I was too busy thinking about endings to enjoy the beginnings.

My aunt was confined to a wheelchair while she recovered from her surgery. Although she didn't say much about it when her doctors explained it, I could tell by the way she looked at the chair that she was depressed about not being able to get around on her own. Elaine would live with us full-time now, since my aunt would need round-the-clock care that I was not equipped to provide, and the doorways in the house would need to be retrofitted to allow her wheelchair to pass through. Each day took away more and more of the old Aunt Gillian, and on rare lucid days, she realized it. It was difficult for me to see her becoming more dependent. It must have been excruciating for her.

Aunt Gillian was quiet as we prepared to leave the hospital. She made a joke about her "new wheels," and she smiled when I cautioned her about driving like Dale Earnhardt Jr. She was quiet on the way home until we neared the house.

"Could we go to the beach?"

I glanced over at her. Not once had she wanted to go to the beach since she had lived in Florida. When she first arrived, it had been too hot, she claimed, and by the time it cooled off, I didn't think she remembered that she lived near the ocean.

"The beach?" I didn't want to go. I wanted to get home, get into a routine, see Jack. But I thought about endings again, and decided that my aunt should not be denied this simple request.

"You'll need to put on a sweater and a hat," I told her. She beamed at me and nodded.

I turned the car around and we drove south to Delray Beach, where I knew there were restaurants that wouldn't be too crowded on a Tuesday morning. We found seats across the street from the beach, allowing us to look out at the water while eating a light brunch. Aunt Gillian's mood seemed to grow darker as we sat, and I ordered for both of us after she claimed she didn't care what she ate. I felt a tinge of irritation but I reminded myself that she had every right to be moody. We were quiet, enjoying the view, until the food came. I was about to bite into my omelet when Aunt Gillian spoke.

"Tina, I'm not sure how much longer I'm going to be around."

I paused, fork on the way to mouth. She had never called me Tina.

"Please don't talk like that."

She grabbed my arm, sending the fork clattering to the table. She didn't seem to notice the noise. Her fingers felt bony and frail.

"You have to face reality. I've always thought of myself as someone who doesn't run from problems, who faces life as it comes."

She looked out the window, but I knew she wasn't seeing the palm trees or the calm blue water. Then she looked back at me.

"But it's not true. I've been running for as long as I can remember."

I shook my head, confused. I opened my mouth to speak, to tell her that she would live for many more years, to tell her that she was the strongest person I'd ever known. But she waved her hand at me.

"Just let me tell it to you. Let me tell you about Lily, about your parents, about you. Then you'll know."

For the first time in my entire life, I was doubtful about wanting to know. At that moment, I knew that the truth would not be easy, that what had been easy was not knowing, imagining, making up my own history to fit the person I wanted to be. Once I knew the truth, all other possibilities would disappear, replaced by facts shaped long before I was born.

I wanted to stop Aunt Gillian, but it was too late. She was already telling her story.

CHAPTER 26

"She was not alone"

Gillian hadn't seen or spoken to Brenda in seventeen years, not since her sister was three years old. They were strangers more than sisters. So when the young woman showed up at her door in Cleveland on a warm summer evening, Gillian didn't recognize her. Nor did she recognize the chocolate-skinned young man standing next to her.

"Can I help you?"

Gillian was polite but distant, thinking the young people, dressed in neat, conservative clothing, were Jehovah's Witnesses selling pamphlets and salvation. Gillian wasn't interested in either. She had just arrived home after a long shift on the neonatal-care floor at the hospital, and she needed peace and quiet after listening to tiny babies crying all day long.

"I think so. I'm Brenda."

Later, Gillian remembered her sister's nervous smile at that first meeting, and the way she had clutched the young man's hand, as if she feared one of them might run if they weren't attached.

Gillian offered a small smile, her patience running thin. It seemed that the Witnesses weren't teaching their converts to get to the point. She waited for the girl to say more, and when she didn't, Gillian took a closer look. The girl was wearing a neat skirt, the kind a secretary might wear, and a white oxford blouse buttoned up to the top. Her hair was pulled back into a severe bun, and she wore no makeup. Gillian glanced at the boy. He looked uncomfortable but handsome in his blue suit and shiny black shoes. He wouldn't meet Gillian's eyes. She looked back at the girl, sensing that *she* was the reason they were here.

Although the girl looked serious and scared, there was something familiar about the shape of her lips, the spacing of her eyes. The silence threatened to become excruciating, with Gillian watching the girl, thinking about whom she resembled. Then, the name clicked.

"Brenda?"

The girl nodded.

Gillian took a deep breath and leaned against the doorjamb. "Brenda Jones."

A wide smile spread across the girl's face, and Gillian now knew whom the girl reminded her of. Her mother. Their mother.

"I'm Brenda McElroy now, actually," she said, holding up her left hand, the one that was not clutching the young man's hand. She wore a tear-shaped diamond set in a plain gold band on her third finger. "I'm your sister."

Gillian had spent many years avoiding the past. She hadn't given much thought to the family she had left behind in Baltimore. She hadn't allowed herself to entertain nostalgia, to worry about how her baby sister was doing, to wonder if her father was still alive. She didn't have the luxury of such thought. Gillian was a survivor. She survived her marriage to Jeremiah. She survived the birth of her daughter, Lily. She survived life. She still worked as a nurse, still cashed Jeremiah's checks every month, and still held her head up high every day. Survival took up all of her attention. It was all she had.

Now, here was baby Brenda, no longer a baby, no longer a Jones. She invited them inside and poured glasses of iced tea before addressing the white elephant in the room.

"Brenda." Gillian looked over at the young man, not wanting to exclude him. "And Ernest."

She stopped there, unsure what to say or ask first. She didn't know what to feel about her sister's arrival. On the one hand, it would bring complications into her life, because that is what family members did, whether they meant to or not. Gillian prided herself on the simplicity of her life. She worked. She had casual friends with whom she had shared cocktails and dinner from time to time. She owned her home, which she still loved even though it was a remnant of her failed marriage to Jeremiah. She did what she wanted, when she wanted, and was beholden to no one.

On the other hand, Gillian felt an unfamiliar stirring in her chest as she watched her sister sitting in the formal parlor of her home. She wasn't sure, but she thought the feeling was joy.

In the end, her words to her sister were simple.

"I'm so glad you're here."

Brenda beamed, first at Gillian, then at Ernest. "Me, too."

Besides the news of her own recent marriage to Ernest, Brenda brought bad news as well. Their father had died just a month ago. He'd died doing what he loved, cutting hair in his shop. The customers said that one minute he was talking politics and complaining about the assassination of Martin Luther King Jr., and the next minute he was lying on the floor dead of a heart attack at sixty.

"It took Mom this long to go through Daddy's things, or else I would have told you sooner. I was going to call, but well, I thought it would be better to talk to you in person."

Gillian shifted in her seat and digested this. She felt a twinge at the thought of her father's death. As far as she was concerned, he had abandoned her long before she left home, and at thirty-five years old, she had put her years as Daddy's girl behind her. She couldn't miss him, but it made her feel sad that he had known where she was all these years but had never contacted her. It seemed that she and her father were more alike than she had ever realized.

The other thing that gave Gillian pause was the word "Mom." It took just a moment of confusion before she realized that Brenda was referring not to their own biological mother, but to Eloise, the woman Franklin had married when Gillian was in college. She was surprised to still feel a germ of resentment toward the woman, but she knew that it made sense that Brenda would think of her as her mother. Brenda was a baby when Eloise married their father, and she had never even known their real mother, Marianne. Gillian wondered how much Franklin and Eloise had told Brenda about Marianne, whether she knew anything about the manic depression, the hospital, the suicide.

She shook her head as if to clear away those thoughts. It didn't matter. Not now.

"How is your mother?" Gillian asked out of a sense of decorum.

Brenda didn't reply right away. Instead, she shared a long look with Ernest before turning back to Gillian with an insincere smile on her face.

"She's good. Fine."

Gillian took another look at Ernest. He was perhaps the same age as Brenda—eighteen—which she could see in the tautness of his smooth dark skin. But his eyes seemed older, more knowing, than those of her sister. She wondered what had gone on between Brenda, Eloise, and Ernest, and she made a mental note to ask Brenda about it sometime when they were alone. She had a feeling that there was more to this visit than telling Gillian about their father's death, but she didn't want to scare her away with too many questions.

"Are you hungry? I was just going to cook dinner." Gillian could see relief in Brenda's eyes. Either she was very hungry, or she didn't want to talk about her step-mother.

"Follow me to the kitchen and we can catch up while I cook."

Gillian insisted that Brenda and Ernest stay with her—where else did they have to go? She learned more about her sister over the few days that turned into weeks, then months. Brenda and Ernest had eloped. Eloise and Franklin had not approved of Ernest, who, although he had been a top student in his high school, had no desire or plans to attend college. Instead, he wanted to be a poet, and he spent his days writing in wire-bound note-books and his nights working as a fry cook at a local diner. This was not the future the Joneses had envisioned for Brenda, and they'd told her so.

"Ever since I was a little girl, I did everything they told me to do," Brenda explained to Gillian one morning. Gillian was preparing for work and Ernest was still sleeping, having stayed up late writing, according to Brenda. Gillian knew better, because the heating vents carried sound, and she did not believe the sounds she had heard coming from the guest room involved any writing at all. But she could not begrudge the young couple their pleasures, not even when their joy in each other reminded her of the early days with Jeremiah.

"But I couldn't lose Ernest. I wouldn't." Brenda still had the facial expressions and mannerisms of a child. Gillian could imagine her sister stomping her foot in frustration when she was forbidden to see Ernest. She considered telling Brenda about her own elopement, but the words wouldn't come.

From the start, Gillian enjoyed her role as big sister, as a member of a true family for the first time in many years. But she noticed things about Brenda, things that made her feel small and petty. Sometimes she couldn't decide whether her sister was petulant and demanding, always wanting her choice of food for dinner, the lights set just so, the plumpest pillow; or was Gillian's long-dormant resentment of Brenda coming through, clouding her view of her sister until truth and lies were indistinguishable?

As the weeks turned into months, Gillian wondered what her sister's plans were. Ernest had gone out and found a job at a deli much like the one he had left back in Baltimore, saying that he wanted to pay rent that Gillian refused to accept. He worked days now, leaving Brenda alone in the house for hours. Gillian wondered what her sister did during those hours. She offered to help Brenda enroll in a local college, but her sister pouted at the idea of going to college in Cleveland.

"I always planned to go to Georgetown, or at least Howard, if nothing else." Brenda said this in a snobbish tone, and Gillian couldn't help resenting the implication that Howard was an inferior choice. It had been good enough for her, but it seemed that Franklin and Eloise had demanded better for Baby Brenda.

So Brenda spent her days ignoring the lists of activities and errands Gillian suggested, doing little of apparent value, waiting for Gillian and Ernest to come home. Over time, Gillian came to understand why Brenda found Ernest so irresistible. He was quiet, and polite, and he spoke only when spoken to. His silence was in no way rude or disrespectful. He valued words and used them with care. And he adored Brenda. He doted on her, fulfilling her every wish, sometimes before she uttered them aloud. He never seemed to be frustrated by Brenda's petulant moods, giving her the same slow smile whether she was in one of her bright, talkative moods or in a pout. He treated Brenda like the princess Brenda believed herself to be.

Gillian had to admit that she also catered to her sister. There was something about Brenda that made her feel protective. That childlike quality that often annoyed Gillian was also vulnerability. When Brenda talked about their father, her grief was so naked that Gillian wanted to hold her sister in her arms and shield her from the world. Sometimes she did just that, thinking about the fact that the two of them were all that was left of their immediate family. They had found their way back to each other, and Gillian did not want to go back to being alone, to surviving instead of living. She even found a way to let go of some of her secrets, to let her sister in.

"Why didn't you ever have kids?" Brenda asked her over dinner one day. "Ernest and I want lots and lots of kids."

They were sitting in the kitchen, eating the lasagna that Brenda had requested for dinner. It was a warm spring night. Brenda and Ernest had been in Cleveland almost a year. The white curtains fluttered in the breeze from the open windows, and the night felt moist, although it had been dry the past few days. Brenda smiled at Gillian when she asked the question, but Gillian's stomach dropped and her appetite fled. She considered a lie, something innocuous and light, something that would help her forget the truth. But the truth found its way out of her mouth before she could stop it.

"I had a baby." Gillian looked down at her plate. When she looked up, Brenda was beaming, not comprehending the tone in Gillian's voice.

"That's great! So I'm an aunt. I always wanted to be an aunt."

Gillian couldn't bear her sister's excitement, so she looked at Ernest. He'd stopped eating and was watching her, his eyes soft and sad. He knew. He understood.

"She died when she was just five days old," Gillian whispered. "Her name was Lily."

Things were different in the house after that night, although Gillian couldn't have said why. Brenda agreed to enroll in summer classes at Case Western, but she signed up for night classes, leaving Ernest and Gillian to eat dinner and spend their evenings alone together. They were good companions, talking for hours about politics and poetry. Ernest showed Gillian his poems, and she played him the old Billie Holiday records that her father had forbidden so long ago. She hadn't listened to them in years, not since she had married Jeremiah, not since she had been surviving. For the first time in her life, she had a true friend. She told him all about Jeremiah, and he laughed at the ironic justice of her ex-husband's monthly payments. She told him about her childhood, about her father, about her and Brenda's real mother. He listened, and they laughed together. Each summer night was a joy for Gillian.

Brenda always returned home late, bearing outrageous stories about the classes she was taking, stories that Gillian never doubted until the night she smelled liquor on her sister's breath. She knew Ernest smelled it, too, but neither of them commented on it, and they soon went to their respective rooms. Gillian waited to hear the sounds of muffled arguing through the vents, but their silence serenaded her to sleep.

The next night Ernest explained why he wasn't angry with Brenda.

"She can't have children. The doctors, they told her she can't have children."

Gillian felt an ache spread through her chest. She knew how it felt to be a mother. She knew what it was like to have that taken away. After Lily, she had just assumed that she would never have another chance to be a mother. She reached out and took Ernest's hand.

"I'm sorry."

He nodded. "She's just struggling right now. I need to let her do it in her own way." His smile was melancholy. That was the moment when she fell in love.

Those summer nights were the best times of Gillian's life. The later Brenda stayed out, not even bothering to make up stories about class anymore, the more Gillian wanted to protect Ernest, to shield him the way she had once wanted to shield her sister. She told herself that he was like a brother to her, but this was a lie. Ernest was everything she had ever wanted in a man, and it didn't matter that she he was sixteen years younger. It didn't matter that he was her sister's husband. It didn't matter, and Gillian was ashamed. She knew the pain Brenda must have been feeling, but she resented the way her sister dealt with it. She should stay close to the people who loved her, not push them away. She should thank God for the man she did have instead of the babies she could never bear.

The night in June when Brenda stayed out all night, Gillian did hold Ernest in her arms. And they kissed. They woke up in her bed, their clothes strewn around the room, to the sound of Brenda's key fumbling in the lock.

Ernestine Jones was born in December 1970. She came early, and they weren't sure she would live. But she did. Gillian took nine months off, then worked nights so she could care for the baby during the day while a sitter stayed nights. Every time she looked at Ernestine, she felt a little of her sadness over Lily slip away.

Brenda knew the baby was Ernest's. When she found out, she ran off. Gillian never knew where she went. She took all her clothing and left behind her diamond wedding ring. Through her shame Gillian began to hope that Ernest would stay with her and forget about Brenda. They would be a family. She would have a real family.

Instead, he quit his job and spent his days looking for Brenda. Sometimes he found her and begged her to come back to him. She always refused, and on those days he trudged back to Gillian's house.

"I love her," he said.

It was that simple. He loved Brenda, not Gillian. She understood. Love was the reason she let him keep coming back.

Six months after Ernestine was born, Brenda and Ernest reconciled. He packed his bags and said his final good-byes to Gillian. She mourned him even before he died, before he was found in a Milwaukee hotel room shot dead by Brenda, who'd then turned the gun on herself.

If she had had nothing to live for, the guilt and sadness would have been crippling. But Gillian had the baby, the daughter Brenda could never have. Ernest's daughter. Gillian made a vow to put the past behind her, to love this baby, to make a life for the two of them.

She was not alone.

She stopped speaking then and just looked at me. I felt dizzy. Everything I knew about myself—everything I *thought* I knew about myself—changed in that instant.

"Ernestine, I am your mother."

CHAPTER 27
"You are still you"

After I got Gillian settled back at home, I went to my desk. On top sat the envelope from the State of Ohio. My birth certificate. I ripped it open, and there, right in official ink, was verification. The one I had seen must have been changed, a fake created to convince me my parents were Brenda and Ernest. This document, straight from the government, told the truth. Gillian was my mother.

I went for a walk. It was early evening, and I wandered around until I came to a baseball field filled with prepubescent boys wearing shorts and uniform tops. There were four lighted fields, and in each of them a little league game was underway. I stopped to watch and listen, grateful for the distraction.

"Choke up on the bat, Patrick."

"Patrick, choke up on the bat!"

Patrick looked over in confusion. He took another fruitless swing, dragging the bat in the dirt on the way through.

"Choke up on the bat, honey! Oh, wait, that's the wrong bat. You need a lighter bat, Patrick!"

Patrick frowned. I imagined what he was thinking. This bat, the one with the green handle, was the one he wanted. A lighter bat? Who cared? This one was green.

Another swing, another miss. Patrick's mom came out onto the field, to his eight-year-old horror, and handed him another bat.

"That's better. See, it's red white and blue," she said. Patrick looked it over, then used it to strike out.

Blam! Patrick whipped the red white and blue bat into the fence, threw his helmet down and stomped the dirt.

"It's okay, Patrick, you'll have time to hit again," she cooed.

Patrick grabbed the fence and shook it, giving another good kick before he walked to the dugout with the other members of the team.

I watched as the crowd of parents tried to suppress their smiles.

"Boy, he sure does get excited, doesn't he," another mom said as she watched her son, the consummate professional at eight years old, pick up the red white and blue bat and drag it to the dugout.

"You what? Can't you do anything right when I'm not there?" One of the dads was holding a marathon cellphone conversation near the bleachers. The other parents were so used to it none of them even looked up. Occasionally, he would yell out some encouragement to one of the smaller kids on the team, but the phone remained glued to his ear.

"Hey Jesse, pick up a glove and catch some balls," Jesse's dad yelled. Jesse stood daydreaming.

"Jesse, grab a glove, catch some balls," he yelled louder. No response.

"JESSE—"

"Will you shut up?" a woman who must have been Jesse's mom hissed. Jesse's dad shut up, and Jesse finally grabbed a glove and went out to catch some balls. A few minutes of silence passed.

"Corrine. Corrine. Corrine." Apparently, Jesse's dad had a way of calling your name until you couldn't ignore him, so Jesse's mom turned around before he started yelling again.

"What?"

"Corrine, I'm sorry, I just wanted him to grab a glove and catch some balls," he explained.

The mom waved her acceptance of the apology and turned back toward the field. The rival team took the field.

"Oh, look, most of them are small."

"Are you crazy? Look at that kid. And that one. They're supposed to be seven and eight years old, right? They're huge!"

Mikey's mom sighed. "It makes me glad Mikey doesn't really know the score of these games."

"Yeah, Kevin asked me who won the practice game last week, and I said, 'oh, they did,'" Kevin's mom said. "He goes, 'By how much?' And I said, 'Oh, a couple.' It was really 10-2, but he scored a run, so who cares."

The moms laughed and Jesse's dad frowned in disapproval. Kevin's dad opened his cell phone to make another call, and the batter stepped up to the plate.

It was listening to aliens speak a strange language. The casual exchanges of normality came so easily to them. Family units were assumed. These mothers watched their sons play baseball. They would always be there. Their lives were open. There were no devastating secrets, no deceptions so great they lasted for thirty-five years. They never questioned who they were or where they fit. They just fit.

I watched another inning, hoping no one could see the tears wetting my cheeks. I wanted to run. I wanted to leave Florida, my job, Jack, Gillian. I wanted her words to be lies. I wanted to go back to a time when I didn't ask too many questions, when I didn't feel I needed to know the truth. I wanted the truth to be something else, something nice, something good.

I went home, looked in on Gillian and then headed to my desk. I looked up a travel web site and booked a trip to the first place that came to mind. I had never been to Barbados, but I believed it was far enough away for me to escape. I imagined myself sitting on the beach at the luxury hotel I'd booked, sipping a drink made of local mangoes, feeling the Caribbean waters splash over my feet, warming my face in the sun. Barbados, I told myself in those moments, would be the place I could become someone new, someone whose mother wasn't a liar, whose family wasn't damaged, whose life wasn't fractured. I would walk slowly and eat well. I would be happy.

I don't know how long I sat there lost in my Caribbean fantasy. It was dark by the time Jack found me. He didn't ask me what I was doing. He glanced at the computer screen, which still showed my reservation to Barbados. He looked at me for a long time.

"Tell me," he said.

I was silent for a long time. How do you tell someone this kind of thing? How could you not tell?

"My aunt isn't my aunt."

I'd had hours to try to digest this, but it still seemed incomprehensible as I said the words aloud.

"What?" I looked at his confused face and burst into tears.

"Gillian is my *mother*." Jack took me into his arms and held me while I sobbed. He waited for me to speak again, and when I could, I told him her story, my story. When I finished, he still didn't say a word.

"So you see? Everything I thought was true wasn't. I thought I was someone I'm not. Why would she lie?" I knew I was babbling and in danger of breaking down again. Jack held my fingers between his.

"Let's go for a drive."

I looked at the computer screen for a long moment. Finally, I pressed cancel on my reservation and followed Jack.

We rode north along I-95 for hours until we reached Cocoa Beach. It was just miles from Cape Canaveral, and there was a space shuttle launch scheduled for the next day. The town was crowded with onlookers trying to catch a glimpse of a spaceship, and the sounds of car horns and booming music added to the old Florida feel of the town. There were strip malls filled with stores selling five-dollar t-shirts and cheap nylon bathing suits. There were surf shops and ice cream parlors, and restaurants boasting the freshest seafood dotted the beachside roads. The air smelled more like the sea here, fishy, a little musky. South Florida was organized, civilized to the point of repression. Cocoa Beach seemed more authentically Florida.

We kept driving, crawling behind lines of cars with no destination in mind. We talked about things that didn't matter: classes, politics, gossip. Jack told me stories about college, about his sister Maggie. He saw her once or twice a year, but never in St. Louis. She was older when their mother left, and she understood more about how things had been between their parents. She left for college just as the whole thing with the other man developed, and Jack never blamed her for not wanting to come back. She hated their father, never talked to him. She told Jack that she would rather be alone in the world than put up with James Kingston and his annoying wife.

I knew what he was telling me. No family is perfect. Parents do bad things, not because they want to hurt you, but because they don't know any better. He told me how Maggie was a successful television writer. He took my hand and I squeezed. I wasn't sure I believed him, but I loved him for trying.

As the sun set, I dozed off while Jack drove. It felt good to stop thinking for a few hours, to let everything go and just rest.

When I woke up, it was dark. I was in my bed and only a small lamp was lit. Jack sat in a chair by the window, reading. I looked at the title of book. It was one of my childhood favorites by Rosa Guy. *The Friends*. It was about pride, about a fractured family, about a girl who was trying to figure out who she was, who she wanted to be. I must have read that book five times when I was a kid.

Jack looked up and closed the worn cover.

"Are you okay?"

I sat up and nodded. Then I shook my head no.

Jack came to sit next to me on the bed. He smelled of lemons.

"Tina. You are still you."

I shook my head. "I'm not. I'm nobody. I'm not even good enough for her to acknowledge me as her daughter."

He cut me off. "Did she say that? Did she say why she didn't tell you?"

I shrugged. He nodded. "So you don't know everything. You might never know everything. So what? That doesn't change who you are. You're Tina Jones. Smart, funny, gorgeous, interesting, infuriating, nosy, and sensitive."

I studied his eyes for signs of deceit, for a signal that he was just trying to make me feel better. I saw only love.

He squeezed my hand tighter. "Marry me."

My mouth dropped open. How could he ask me this now, when I had just gotten the worst and best news of my life? I had found my mother, and she had been right there all along. How could he want me? I wanted to yell at him, pound on his chest, make him hurt.

Instead, I kissed him, a long, seeking kiss. I lost track of time, of the air around us, of everything except the feel of our lips against each other. And when it ended, I spoke.

"I want to. But I need more time."

He took a deep breath. "You can take as much time as you need."

"I love you."

"I love you, too."

CHAPTER 28

"Hollywood romance is overrated"

The day I put my mother in the nursing home was one of the worst days of my life. I was more miserable than the day I found her in Cleveland, on the floor and helpless. I grieved more than I did when she was diagnosed with Alzheimer's disease. I was more on edge than the day, just about a year ago, that I found out she was my mother. I couldn't imagine the day she died being worse than this one.

I felt like a failure for not being able to handle her anymore. There was no number of nurses that could adequately care for her at home; besides, we didn't have the money for that. She was too far gone for assisted living, or what was called a Special Care Unit. The ones in our area only accepted people in the early stages of the disease, and in the year since Gillian told me her story, the disease had progressed quickly. The day she wandered off and we found her sitting on the wall separating Flagler from the Intracoastal Waterway, wearing only a bra, jogging pants, and bedroom slippers, I knew that I had to make a change. But I changed the locks on the doors and waited, still hoping there was some other solution besides the nursing home.

The last time she was coherent was soon after she told me that she was my mother. She looked up at me at breakfast one morning and repeated what she had been telling me all my life.

"You can't change what already is."

She went back to eating her oatmeal, spilling more than what reached her mouth. Elaine cleaned her up, and I looked down at my plate, no longer hungry.

For a long time, I was angry and confused. I had so many more questions that, as Gillian's health deteriorated, she was both unwilling and unable to answer. Jack humored me, but he agreed with her that I had to let it go. I knew it was true, but months went by and I was still consumed with the lies that had shaped my life and made me a stranger to myself.

And then she fell again. This time, she did not break any bones but caught pneumonia while in the hospital. Her body healed but her mind did not, could not, and I spent the end of the spring semester visiting nursing homes in between grading papers.

I was astounded at how much her care would cost, and it seemed she would get so little in return. Certainly, for nearly $3,000 a month she would receive the best medical care, and in general, she would be comfortable. But as nice as the best places looked, they were still institutional, and placing the word "home" after "nursing" was more of a euphemism than an accurate depiction of the facility.

But I knew we were fortunate that her insurance would pay for part of the cost, and her savings would finance the rest. In late May, Gillian moved out of our home and into Palm Shores, a place that looked and sounded like a resort but smelled like old age underneath the disinfectant and potpourri.

She had a single room that was the size of a walk-in closet. There was a small, flat-screened television and a private bathroom decorated with a flowered shower curtain that the old Gillian would have despised. She would have deemed it tacky and demanded that I take it down before she set foot into the room. Now she barely glanced at her surroundings as we unpacked her belongings.

I was reminded of that day, just two years ago, when she had moved to Florida complaining of the heat and my driving. She was so different now. I never thought I would miss the old Gillian, but I did.

That first day, I stayed until it was dark, and when visiting time was over, I left a long list of Gillian's likes and dislikes with her nurse. She hates tomato soup, I wrote. She likes Jack.

I wished he were there with us, but he had scheduled a conference for that week, and I wouldn't let him cancel. I couldn't go through life letting the prince save me time and again. He was still waiting for my response to his marriage proposal. I had asked that we keep our friendship as is until I sorted things out in my head. He was great at pretending nothing had changed between us, and he never put pressure on me. I think he understood that Gillian had to be my priority. I loved him for his patience.

Gillian was sleeping when I said good-bye. I kissed her on the forehead and her brow furrowed. I smiled. She still had some of her old spirit left.

When I got home, I collapsed on the couch and cried. I cried for Gillian, and I cried for myself. Her health wasn't in any imminent danger, but putting her in a nursing home felt like an ending. When the phone rang, I had managed to stop sobbing but my face and collar were still wet.

"How did it go?" Jack asked.

I sighed. "It was horrible. I mean, she was fine, but I'm a wreck."

"I wish I was there with you right now."

"Me, too." I took a deep breath. The house was quiet but not lonely. I looked around, and for the first time in a month, everything seemed clear.

"Does your offer still stand?"

He was silent for a moment. "My offer still stands. Are you saying—?"

"I'm saying yes."

He burst into laughter, and it was infectious. I didn't realize until that moment how long it had been since I laughed.

"It's not the most romantic thing, getting engaged over the telephone. In the movies, this would never happen."

I was still giggling. "Hollywood romance is overrated. This is the most romantic moment of my life, actually."

We laughed together for a long time, and when we finally hung up, I was peaceful.

CHAPTER 29

"There is only today"

My wedding was nothing like the affair I imagined when I fell for Will Brandiman all those years ago. Then, I saw myself as the fairy-tale bride who had found her prince, the woman for whom love was the answer to everything. I used to believe in the fairy tale even though my real life was far from perfect. I used to believe in the idea of a Prince Charming who would sweep me off my feet. I was the Cinderella, a fat girl who would be saved from misery by the man with the glass slipper.

But now I know better. I found love with Jack, but it didn't solve everything. I still had so many questions about Aunt Gillian's story, about myself. I couldn't believe that I would never know more about my parents, that I came from a family with so many damaged people. Then again, I was damaged, too. Ever since I met Jack I had relied on him, maybe too much. But this wasn't something he could fix. I had to figure how to live with my history and myself, all on my own.

It's now August again, and we're getting married on the anniversary of our trip to Niagara Falls. Am I fixed? I have decided I don't really know what that means. But

I'm okay with myself, and I've decided to stop looking for answers to questions that maybe I wasn't meant to ask. I've got tenure now at the university, and I'm not using food to escape anymore. I've even started reworking my book about little Brianna. Maybe I'll finish it, use those drawings Jack made me, and stop being afraid of other people's judgments.

No, I'm not fixed. Maybe I was never broken in the first place.

My wedding will be small and quiet. We picked a Methodist church in Coral Gables, even though neither of us is very religious. I just fell in love with the look of the place, with its floor-to-ceiling windows behind the altar, facing out into a tropical garden and pond that reminded me of holding Jack's hand in the botanical gardens during our trip to Canada. A family of pure white ducks lived in the pond. I saw them and knew this was the place.

Monica and Elaine are wearing simple black strapless dresses as my bridesmaids, and I am wearing white only because they talked me into it. It's not a real wedding gown, but a simple sleeveless summer dress made of Japanese silk seersucker. One of the things I learned over the past year is that simplicity is important to me. I've spent my whole life creating complications for myself, and dealing with those created by others. I've vowed not to do it any more.

So I fought Monica when she wanted to arrange for an elaborate celebration.

"What about the floral arrangements? I was thinking something like this."

She showed me a photo, ripped from a magazine, of enormous bunches of calla lilies overtaking what seemed like hundreds of tables draped in white linen.

"You can't even see over those arrangements—no one could talk to people across the table," I pointed out.

She didn't give up. "You're planning to have a band, right? DJs are so cheesy."

A band sounded too fancy to me. "Maybe just a piano player for the ceremony and reception."

We sat on my back porch. Monica flipped through bridal magazines that she subscribed to after I refused to.

"Look at this cake," she gushed. "Ten tiers!"

I made a face. She sighed. "At least go somewhere exciting for the honeymoon. Paris? Italy?" Her face was hopeful.

We will honeymoon in Barbados.

I will change my last name, and people will call me Mrs. Jack Kingston. My life will change in ways that I can and cannot anticipate.

Jeremiah is here. When I called to invite him, he was hesitant, wondering if Gillian would be upset that he was there.

I took a breath. "I'm not sure she remembers much about what happened between you. And if she does, I'm not sure it matters."

There was silence before he spoke.

"When you came to see me, you seemed to think it did matter. What changed?"

"She told me her story. About her parents. About you. About Brenda and Ernest."

I knew I could ask him to tell me more, to fill in the gaps. But I also knew that hearing more would only raise more questions, ones that could never be answered fully enough to satisfy that need to know my family.

"So I guess you know the most important thing, now."

I didn't speak.

"Now you know that who you are isn't just about who your family is. When you're a child, you don't have a choice. I didn't have a choice to be an orphan. Sometimes I think I didn't even have a choice about falling in love with Gillian. But once I did, I made my choices, good and bad. That's who I am. And that's who you are."

I could feel the tears wetting my cheeks, the collar of my shirt.

"Thanks, Jeremiah."

"Now, you stop all that crying. This is a happy occasion, right? You're getting married. So when I come down there, we're not going to talk about all this sad stuff. We're going to talk about the future. Your future."

I smiled through my tears. "Can I ask you one more thing? It's not about the past, I promise."

He laughed. "Ask."

"Will you give me away?"

There was another long silence, and I was afraid he would say no.

"I never liked the idea of someone giving away a woman at her wedding. You give away possessions, not people. So no, I won't give you away because you're not mine to give. But I will stand next to you and walk you down that aisle."

He paused. "We're family. After all this time, it's nice to have a family again."

Jack's sister was invited, but she was in the middle of filming a movie and couldn't get away. I tried to get him to invite his father and stepmother, but he didn't want to, and I didn't want to push. We both had family things to contend with, and I was in no position to tell him how to deal with his.

Gillian isn't here. She is in a nursing home now, and she is sometimes angry, sometimes scared and always worried when I go see her. She's worried about money, about who I am, about why I'm in her room, about how she can get out. I have tried to talk to her, but she is fading. This makes my struggle to think of her as Mother even more difficult.

I have created a number of theories to fill in the gaps. Maybe Gillian told me Brenda was my mother out of guilt. Maybe giving her sister a daughter was a final, futile way to repent for the damage she had done. Maybe my father was not a cheater, but simply a boy torn apart by emotions he couldn't control. Maybe Brenda was driven by mental illness inherited from Marianne. Maybe Gillian had kept all of it from me out of love.

Or maybe none of it was true. Maybe Gillian's story was the rambling of an old woman with a failing mind. I will never get more answers. I will never know the truth. This, I have to live with.

I am nervous, more nervous than I've ever been in my life. In an hour, I will be married. I like to think that I am going into this next phase of my life wiser than before. Over the last year, I have learned that knowing is not always better than wondering. I have learned that love is complex and confusing and defies simple explanation.

I have learned that Gillian—my mother—was right. I cannot live in the past, and I cannot change it. There is only today, and, if I'm lucky, tomorrow.

The End

ABOUT THE AUTHOR

Africa Fine has published two other novels, *Katrina* (2001) and *Becoming Maren* (2003), along with short stories and essays in print and online journals. She holds a bachelor's degree in public policy and African-American studies from Duke University and a master's degree in English literature from Florida Atlantic University. She is an English professor in South Florida.

2008 Reprint Mass Market Titles

January

Cautious Heart
Cheris F. Hodges
ISBN-13: 978-1-58571-301-1
ISBN-10: 1-58571-301-5
$6.99

Suddenly You
Crystal Hubbard
ISBN-13: 978-1-58571-302-8
ISBN-10: 1-58571-302-3
$6.99

February

Passion
T. T. Henderson
ISBN-13: 978-1-58571-303-5
ISBN-10: 1-58571-303-1
$6.99

Whispers in the Sand
LaFlorya Gauthier
ISBN-13: 978-1-58571-304-2
ISBN-10: 1-58571-304-x
$6.99

March

Life Is Never As It Seems
J. J. Michael
ISBN-13: 978-1-58571-305-9
ISBN-10: 1-58571-305-8
$6.99

Beyond the Rapture
Beverly Clark
ISBN-13: 978-1-58571-306-6
ISBN-10: 1-58571-306-6
$6.99

April

A Heart's Awakening
Veronica Parker
ISBN-13: 978-1-58571-307-3
ISBN-10: 1-58571-307-4
$6.99

Breeze
Robin Lynette Hampton
ISBN-13: 978-1-58571-308-0
ISBN-10: 1-58571-308-2
$6.99

May

I'll Be Your Shelter
Giselle Carmichael
ISBN-13: 978-1-58571-309-7
ISBN-10: 1-58571-309-0
$6.99

Careless Whispers
Rochelle Alers
ISBN-13: 978-1-58571-310-3
ISBN-10: 1-58571-310-4
$6.99

June

Sin
Crystal Rhodes
ISBN-13: 978-1-58571-311-0
ISBN-10: 1-58571-311-2
$6.99

Dark Storm Rising
Chinelu Moore
ISBN-13: 978-1-58571-312-7
ISBN-10: 1-58571-312-0
$6.99

2008 Reprint Mass Market Titles (continued)

July

Object of His Desire
A.C. Arthur
ISBN-13: 978-1-58571-313-4
ISBN-10: 1-58571-313-9
$6.99

Angel's Paradise
Janice Angelique
ISBN-13: 978-1-58571-314-1
ISBN-10: 1-58571-314-7
$6.99

August

Unbreak My Heart
Dar Tomlinson
ISBN-13: 978-1-58571-315-8
ISBN-10: 1-58571-315-5
$6.99

All I Ask
Barbara Keaton
ISBN-13: 978-1-58571-316-5
ISBN-10: 1-58571-316-3
$6.99

September

Icie
Pamela Leigh Starr
ISBN-13: 978-1-58571-275-5
ISBN-10: 1-58571-275-2
$6.99

At Last
Lisa Riley
ISBN-13: 978-1-58571-276-2
ISBN-10: 1-58571-276-0
$6.99

October

Everlastin' Love
Gay G. Gunn
ISBN-13: 978-1-58571-277-9
ISBN-10: 1-58571-277-9
$6.99

Three Wishes
Seressia Glass
ISBN-13: 978-1-58571-278-6
ISBN-10: 1-58571-278-7
$6.99

November

Yesterday Is Gone
Beverly Clark
ISBN-13: 978-1-58571-279-3
ISBN-10: 1-58571-279-5
$6.99

Again My Love
Kayla Perrin
ISBN-13: 978-1-58571-280-9
ISBN-10: 1-58571-280-9
$6.99

December

Office Policy
A.C. Arthur
ISBN-13: 978-1-58571-281-6
ISBN-10: 1-58571-281-7
$6.99

Rendezvous With Fate
Jeanne Sumerix
ISBN-13: 978-1-58571-283-3
ISBN-10: 1-58571-283-3
$6.99

2008 New Mass Market Titles

January

Where I Want To Be
Maryam Diaab
ISBN-13: 978-1-58571-268-7
ISBN-10: 1-58571-268-X
$6.99

Never Say Never
Michele Cameron
ISBN-13: 978-1-58571-269-4
ISBN-10: 1-58571-269-8
$6.99

February

Stolen Memories
Michele Sudler
ISBN-13: 978-1-58571-270-0
ISBN-10: 1-58571-270-1
$6.99

Dawn's Harbor
Kymberly Hunt
ISBN-13: 978-1-58571-271-7
ISBN-10: 1-58571-271-X
$6.99

March

Undying Love
Renee Alexis
ISBN-13: 978-1-58571-272-4
ISBN-10: 1-58571-272-8
$6.99

Blame It On Paradise
Crystal Hubbard
ISBN-13: 978-1-58571-273-1
ISBN-10: 1-58571-273-6
$6.99

April

When A Man Loves A Woman
La Connie Taylor-Jones
ISBN-13: 978-1-58571-274-8
ISBN-10: 1-58571-274-4
$6.99

Choices
Tammy Williams
ISBN-13: 978-1-58571-300-4
ISBN-10: 1-58571-300-7
$6.99

May

Dream Runner
Gail McFarland
ISBN-13: 978-1-58571-317-2
ISBN-10: 1-58571-317-1
$6.99

Southern Fried Standards
S.R. Maddox
ISBN-13: 978-1-58571-318-9
ISBN-10: 1-58571-318-X
$6.99

June

Looking for Lily
Africa Fine
ISBN-13: 978-1-58571-319-6
ISBN-10: 1-58571-319-8
$6.99

Bliss, Inc.
Chamein Canton
ISBN-13: 978-1-58571-325-7
ISBN-10: 1-58571-325-2
$6.99

2008 New Mass Market Titles (continued)

July

Love's Secrets
Yolanda McVey
ISBN-13: 978-1-58571-321-9
ISBN-10: 1-58571-321-X
$6.99

Things Forbidden
Maryam Diaab
ISBN-13: 978-1-58571-327-1
ISBN-10: 1-58571-327-9
$6.99

August

Storm
Pamela Leigh Starr
ISBN-13: 978-1-58571-323-3
ISBN-10: 1-58571-323-6
$6.99

Passion's Furies
AlTonya Washington
ISBN-13: 978-1-58571-324-0
ISBN-10: 1-58571-324-4
$6.99

September

Three Doors Down
Michele Sudler
ISBN-13: 978-1-58571-332-5
ISBN-10: 1-58571-332-5
$6.99

Mr Fix-It
Crystal Hubbard
ISBN-13: 978-1-58571-326-4
ISBN-10: 1-58571-326-0
$6.99

October

Moments of Clarity
Michele Cameron
ISBN-13: 978-1-58571-330-1
ISBN-10: 1-58571-330-9
$6.99

Lady Preacher
K.T. Richey
ISBN-13: 978-1-58571-333-2
ISBN-10: 1-58571-333-3
$6.99

November

This Life Isn't Perfect Holla
Sandra Foy
ISBN: 978-1-58571-331-8
ISBN-10: 1-58571-331-7
$6.99

Promises Made
Bernice Layton
ISBN-13: 978-1-58571-334-9
ISBN-10: 1-58571-334-1
$6.99

December

A Voice Behind Thunder
Carrie Elizabeth Greene
ISBN-13: 978-1-58571-329-5
ISBN-10: 1-58571-329-5
$6.99

The More Things Change
Chamein Canton
ISBN-13: 978-1-58571-328-8
ISBN-10: 1-58571-328-7
$6.99

Other Genesis Press, Inc. Titles

A Dangerous Deception	J.M. Jeffries	$8.95
A Dangerous Love	J.M. Jeffries	$8.95
A Dangerous Obsession	J.M. Jeffries	$8.95
A Drummer's Beat to Mend	Kei Swanson	$9.95
A Happy Life	Charlotte Harris	$9.95
A Heart's Awakening	Veronica Parker	$9.95
A Lark on the Wing	Phyliss Hamilton	$9.95
A Love of Her Own	Cheris F. Hodges	$9.95
A Love to Cherish	Beverly Clark	$8.95
A Risk of Rain	Dar Tomlinson	$8.95
A Taste of Temptation	Reneé Alexis	$9.95
A Twist of Fate	Beverly Clark	$8.95
A Will to Love	Angie Daniels	$9.95
Acquisitions	Kimberley White	$8.95
Across	Carol Payne	$12.95
After the Vows	Leslie Esdaile	$10.95
(Summer Anthology)	T.T. Henderson	
	Jacqueline Thomas	
Again My Love	Kayla Perrin	$10.95
Against the Wind	Gwynne Forster	$8.95
All I Ask	Barbara Keaton	$8.95
Always You	Crystal Hubbard	$6.99
Ambrosia	T.T. Henderson	$8.95
An Unfinished Love Affair	Barbara Keaton	$8.95
And Then Came You	Dorothy Elizabeth Love	$8.95
Angel's Paradise	Janice Angelique	$9.95
At Last	Lisa G. Riley	$8.95
Best of Friends	Natalie Dunbar	$8.95
Beyond the Rapture	Beverly Clark	$9.95

Other Genesis Press, Inc. Titles (continued)

Blaze	Barbara Keaton	$9.95
Blood Lust	J. M. Jeffries	$9.95
Blood Seduction	J.M. Jeffries	$9.95
Bodyguard	Andrea Jackson	$9.95
Boss of Me	Diana Nyad	$8.95
Bound by Love	Beverly Clark	$8.95
Breeze	Robin Hampton Allen	$10.95
Broken	Dar Tomlinson	$24.95
By Design	Barbara Keaton	$8.95
Cajun Heat	Charlene Berry	$8.95
Careless Whispers	Rochelle Alers	$8.95
Cats & Other Tales	Marilyn Wagner	$8.95
Caught in a Trap	Andre Michelle	$8.95
Caught Up In the Rapture	Lisa G. Riley	$9.95
Cautious Heart	Cheris F Hodges	$8.95
Chances	Pamela Leigh Starr	$8.95
Cherish the Flame	Beverly Clark	$8.95
Class Reunion	Irma Jenkins/ John Brown	$12.95
Code Name: Diva	J.M. Jeffries	$9.95
Conquering Dr. Wexler's Heart	Kimberley White	$9.95
Corporate Seduction	A.C. Arthur	$9.95
Crossing Paths, Tempting Memories	Dorothy Elizabeth Love	$9.95
Crush	Crystal Hubbard	$9.95
Cypress Whisperings	Phyllis Hamilton	$8.95
Dark Embrace	Crystal Wilson Harris	$8.95
Dark Storm Rising	Chinelu Moore	$10.95

Other Genesis Press, Inc. Titles (continued)

Other Genesis Press, Inc. Titles (continued)

Hard to Love	Kimberley White	$9.95
Hart & Soul	Angie Daniels	$8.95
Heart of the Phoenix	A.C. Arthur	$9.95
Heartbeat	Stephanie Bedwell-Grime	$8.95
Hearts Remember	M. Loui Quezada	$8.95
Hidden Memories	Robin Allen	$10.95
Higher Ground	Leah Latimer	$19.95
Hitler, the War, and the Pope	Ronald Rychlak	$26.95
How to Write a Romance	Kathryn Falk	$18.95
I Married a Reclining Chair	Lisa M. Fuhs	$8.95
I'll Be Your Shelter	Giselle Carmichael	$8.95
I'll Paint a Sun	A.J. Garrotto	$9.95
Icie	Pamela Leigh Starr	$8.95
Illusions	Pamela Leigh Starr	$8.95
Indigo After Dark Vol. I	Nia Dixon/Angelique	$10.95
Indigo After Dark Vol. II	Dolores Bundy/ Cole Riley	$10.95
Indigo After Dark Vol. III	Montana Blue/ Coco Morena	$10.95
Indigo After Dark Vol. IV	Cassandra Colt/	$14.95
Indigo After Dark Vol. V	Delilah Dawson	$14.95
Indiscretions	Donna Hill	$8.95
Intentional Mistakes	Michele Sudler	$9.95
Interlude	Donna Hill	$8.95
Intimate Intentions	Angie Daniels	$8.95
It's Not Over Yet	J.J. Michael	$9.95
Jolie's Surrender	Edwina Martin-Arnold	$8.95
Kiss or Keep	Debra Phillips	$8.95
Lace	Giselle Carmichael	$9.95

Other Genesis Press, Inc. Titles (continued)

Last Train to Memphis	Elsa Cook	$12.95
Lasting Valor	Ken Olsen	$24.95
Let Us Prey	Hunter Lundy	$25.95
Lies Too Long	Pamela Ridley	$13.95
Life Is Never As It Seems	J.J. Michael	$12.95
Lighter Shade of Brown	Vicki Andrews	$8.95
Love Always	Mildred E. Riley	$10.95
Love Doesn't Come Easy	Charlyne Dickerson	$8.95
Love Unveiled	Gloria Greene	$10.95
Love's Deception	Charlene Berry	$10.95
Love's Destiny	M. Loui Quezada	$8.95
Mae's Promise	Melody Walcott	$8.95
Magnolia Sunset	Giselle Carmichael	$8.95
Many Shades of Gray	Dyanne Davis	$6.99
Matters of Life and Death	Lesego Malepe, Ph.D.	$15.95
Meant to Be	Jeanne Sumerix	$8.95
Midnight Clear	Leslie Esdaile	$10.95
(Anthology)	Gwynne Forster	
	Carmen Green	
	Monica Jackson	
Midnight Magic	Gwynne Forster	$8.95
Midnight Peril	Vicki Andrews	$10.95
Misconceptions	Pamela Leigh Starr	$9.95
Montgomery's Children	Richard Perry	$14.95
My Buffalo Soldier	Barbara B. K. Reeves	$8.95
Naked Soul	Gwynne Forster	$8.95
Next to Last Chance	Louisa Dixon	$24.95
No Apologies	Seressia Glass	$8.95
No Commitment Required	Seressia Glass	$8.95

Other Genesis Press, Inc. Titles (continued)

No Regrets	Mildred E. Riley	$8.95
Not His Type	Chamein Canton	$6.99
Nowhere to Run	Gay G. Gunn	$10.95
O Bed! O Breakfast!	Rob Kuehnle	$14.95
Object of His Desire	A. C. Arthur	$8.95
Office Policy	A. C. Arthur	$9.95
Once in a Blue Moon	Dorianne Cole	$9.95
One Day at a Time	Bella McFarland	$8.95
One in A Million	Barbara Keaton	$6.99
One of These Days	Michele Sudler	$9.95
Outside Chance	Louisa Dixon	$24.95
Passion	T.T. Henderson	$10.95
Passion's Blood	Cherif Fortin	$22.95
Passion's Journey	Wanda Y. Thomas	$8.95
Past Promises	Jahmel West	$8.95
Path of Fire	T.T. Henderson	$8.95
Path of Thorns	Annetta P. Lee	$9.95
Peace Be Still	Colette Haywood	$12.95
Picture Perfect	Reon Carter	$8.95
Playing for Keeps	Stephanie Salinas	$8.95
Pride & Joi	Gay G. Gunn	$15.95
Pride & Joi	Gay G. Gunn	$8.95
Promises to Keep	Alicia Wiggins	$8.95
Quiet Storm	Donna Hill	$10.95
Reckless Surrender	Rochelle Alers	$6.95
Red Polka Dot in a World of Plaid	Varian Johnson	$12.95
Reluctant Captive	Joyce Jackson	$8.95
Rendezvous with Fate	Jeanne Sumerix	$8.95

Other Genesis Press, Inc. Titles (continued)

Revelations	Cheris F. Hodges	$8.95
Rivers of the Soul	Leslie Esdaile	$8.95
Rocky Mountain Romance	Kathleen Suzanne	$8.95
Rooms of the Heart	Donna Hill	$8.95
Rough on Rats and Tough on Cats	Chris Parker	$12.95
Secret Library Vol. 1	Nina Sheridan	$18.95
Secret Library Vol. 2	Cassandra Colt	$8.95
Secret Thunder	Annetta P. Lee	$9.95
Shades of Brown	Denise Becker	$8.95
Shades of Desire	Monica White	$8.95
Shadows in the Moonlight	Jeanne Sumerix	$8.95
Sin	Crystal Rhodes	$8.95
Small Whispers	Annetta P. Lee	$6.99
So Amazing	Sinclair LeBeau	$8.95
Somebody's Someone	Sinclair LeBeau	$8.95
Someone to Love	Alicia Wiggins	$8.95
Song in the Park	Martin Brant	$15.95
Soul Eyes	Wayne L. Wilson	$12.95
Soul to Soul	Donna Hill	$8.95
Southern Comfort	J.M. Jeffries	$8.95
Still the Storm	Sharon Robinson	$8.95
Still Waters Run Deep	Leslie Esdaile	$8.95
Stolen Kisses	Dominiqua Douglas	$9.95
Stories to Excite You	Anna Forrest/Divine	$14.95
Subtle Secrets	Wanda Y. Thomas	$8.95
Suddenly You	Crystal Hubbard	$9.95
Sweet Repercussions	Kimberley White	$9.95
Sweet Sensations	Gwendolyn Bolton	$9.95

Other Genesis Press, Inc. Titles (continued)

Other Genesis Press, Inc. Titles (continued)

Uncommon Prayer	Kenneth Swanson	$9.95
Unconditional Love	Alicia Wiggins	$8.95
Unconditional	A.C. Arthur	$9.95
Until Death Do Us Part	Susan Paul	$8.95
Vows of Passion	Bella McFarland	$9.95
Wedding Gown	Dyanne Davis	$8.95
What's Under Benjamin's Bed	Sandra Schaffer	$8.95
When Dreams Float	Dorothy Elizabeth Love	$8.95
When I'm With You	LaConnie Taylor-Jones	$6.99
Whispers in the Night	Dorothy Elizabeth Love	$8.95
Whispers in the Sand	LaFlorya Gauthier	$10.95
Who's That Lady?	Andrea Jackson	$9.95
Wild Ravens	Altonya Washington	$9.95
Yesterday Is Gone	Beverly Clark	$10.95
Yesterday's Dreams, Tomorrow's Promises	Reon Laudat	$8.95
Your Precious Love	Sinclair LeBeau	$8.95

Order Form

Mail to: Genesis Press, Inc.
P.O. Box 101
Columbus, MS 39703

Name _____
Address _____
City/State _____ Zip _____
Telephone _____

Ship to (if different from above)
Name _____
Address _____
City/State _____ Zip _____
Telephone _____

Credit Card Information
Credit Card # _____ ☐ Visa ☐ Mastercard
Expiration Date (mm/yy) _____ ☐ AmEx ☐ Discover

Qty.	Author	Title	Price	Total

Use this order form, or call 1-888-INDIGO-1

Total for books	_____
Shipping and handling: $5 first two books, $1 each additional book	_____
Total S & H	_____
Total amount enclosed	_____

Mississippi residents add 7% sales tax